W9-AFA-204

DEATH IN

STILL WATERS

DEATH IN

STILL WATERS

A Chesapeake Bay Mystery

Barbara Lee

St. Martin's Press
New York

Design by Junie Lee

ISBN 0-312-13048-1

First edition: May 1995
10 9 8 7 6 5 4 3 2 1

Although Anne Arundel County, Maryland, is real, Pines on Magothy, its inhabitants, and their adventures are completely fictitious. They exist solely in the author's imagination for the purpose of this story.

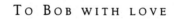

TO BOB WITH LOVE

DEATH IN

STILL WATERS

CHAPTER
ONE

You can tell a lot about a place by how fast it clears its dead off the road. Mexico, for example, lets things lie. Once, a long time ago, I counted the bodies of two horses, seven dogs, and a flock of chickens beside the road from Cuernavaca to Mexico City. And I've heard that in Brazil when someone dies on the road, people light candles at the head and the feet of the body before it's carried away. I don't know if it's true.

Having left the interstate for local roads, I was counting the dead. I couldn't help it. There were so many. A brown and white collie swam stiffly heavenward, the damage invisible beneath its silky coat. Yards away in high grass lay a tattered gray cat, its legs thin and extended, its face melting in the afternoon sun. A mile or two along, a possum lay curled in the dirt, evil and pale. I didn't want to think of all the other nameless flattened and bloody messes in the middle of the road. But this wasn't Mexico. It was Anne Arundel County, Maryland. And it wasn't doing a very good job of collecting its dead.

The drive from New York had taken longer than I expected, with traffic moving in fits and starts as motorists cast anxious eyes at half-hidden police cars. I was anxious to see Lillian Weber, my father's only sister. Her call yesterday had been unexpected and puzzling. In fact, for one reason or another, I hadn't seen her since my uncle Max's funeral a year ago. That day, like this one, had also been scorching.

The local road was empty of cars now, shimmering, with tall, dense trees on either side of the pavement standing motionless in the heat. It was hard to believe that the Chesapeake Bay lay all around me, its inlets and coves cluttered with tiny old waterfront communities. To the south was Annapolis, with its billion-dollar harbor and stiff uniformed cadets and Georgian architecture. Baltimore lay behind me to the north.

Checking my directions, I turned left at a stop light and found myself driving along a strip of small local businesses: a temporary pit beef shack, a convenience store, a sewer and septic tank company, a couple of Snow-Ball stands doing a brisk trade, and, on the right, a sign that read WEBER REALTY. I pulled the BMW into one of the angled parking spots, next to a blue Chevy with a red stripe. A wall of heat hit me as I got out of the car. In the garage next door, I could see two figures hunched and sweating over a running engine.

Shirley Bodine, my aunt's secretary, was talking on the phone and didn't look up when I entered the real estate office. I watched her, aware of the air conditioner working hard overhead. Her shoulder-length hair was full and curly and only a little gray. One strand was slightly tangled in a long silver earring shaped like a cross. She was somewhere in her forties, I guessed. She put the phone down and smiled at me.

"Eve, I'm sorry, Hon. These people can talk. I hope you had a good trip. Lillian had to show a property, then visit another listing. That might take awhile, so she thought you could join her there. She wanted to be here when you arrived, but you know how this business is."

"Sure. Just give me directions." The phone rang.

I glanced around the pink-and–forest green office, its walls hung with black-and-white photographs of Maryland, mostly scenes of the Chesapeake. Behind the secretary's desk were three empty desks, each, like Shirley's, furnished with a computer and telephones. Beyond those were a couple of enclosed cubicles and, to the right, in the back, a glass-paneled conference room with a round table. A year ago, Max, Lillian, and several other agents manned the desks. Now it must be just Lillian, I thought. Shirley pointed me to an upholstered wing chair in the waiting area.

I stood instead, looking outside. A teenage boy, oversize, maybe fifteen or so, was bent down and peering through the windows of the BMW. Ben's BMW to be exact, my husband—correction, my almost ex-husband, owner of the expensive car I hadn't wanted. But Ben had wanted it, and what Ben Elliott wanted, he generally got, including the young woman who typed his research notes.

The kid was slowly walking around the car now, trying each door. A lifetime in New York had trained me well—I had locked them all. Shirley put the phone down with a bang, took one look through the window, and raced out the door.

"Gilbert Bodine, what in hell are you doin'? Get away from there. I'll get you money for a soda." She was a foot shorter than he was, but she grabbed his shoulders and turned him in the direction of the garage next door, pointing to a sweating red metal box, as if it was possible he didn't understand the meaning of soda, despite the pictures of frosty bottles. I studied his face. Maybe he didn't. "I'm sorry, Eve. Just a sec. Let me get him some money." She went in.

The phone was ringing again. "Weber Realty, hold please." She pushed a button without waiting for a response. Grabbing a handful of change from her top drawer, she handed it to the boy. He had followed us in and was standing silently, staring at me with no emotion, his eyes empty, waiting. The heat poured through the open door when he left. I closed it quietly. The light flashed on the phone. Shirley handed me a sketchy map and some directions to Weller's Creek Road. With a wave, I left. She was still talking on the phone.

———

3

Gilbert was standing by the BMW, the can of soda in his hand. He tried the front passenger door one more time, unconcerned that I was watching, backing away only when I got in and started the engine. The air conditioning felt wonderfully cool. I tipped the vents in the direction of my face and wrists and turned onto the two-lane road.

A lot can happen in twenty-four hours. Yesterday this time, I had been at my desk in the General Motors Building at Fifty-ninth Street and Fifth Avenue. Thirty-eight stories below were Central Park and the Plaza Hotel. In front of me, studying my framed awards, was my boss and mentor, Joe Lister, partner in Lister, Klein, and Andronucci and grand old man of advertising. He moved restlessly to the window, looking down at Olmstead's swirling paths. They curved inward so when you walked in Central Park, you could almost forget that midtown Manhattan was just a block or two away. He turned back to me. In his hand was a storyboard.

"So what's the deal with this?"

"I'm sorry," I said, "but I'm having trouble pitching a cigarette account."

"It shows." He put the mechanical down. "You seem to have forgotten that the purpose of advertising is to sell the product."

"So teenagers can think smoking is cool and get hooked?"

"So that adults who already smoke will change brands." I stared at him. He couldn't really believe that. There was a long silence. "Okay, so I don't believe that. Let me say for the record, in the privacy of this office, that I don't like cigarettes any better than you do. But this agency wouldn't have survived if we'd passed judgment on every account that came down the pike."

He perched briefly on a table across the room. It was my turn to look out the window, to see the same view that I'd seen since I had started here right out of college, an energetic and very assistant copywriter.

4

"Joe, let someone else head up this campaign." Preferably someone who smokes, I thought.

Joe Lister said nothing. His mouth twitched momentarily, he got up and moved to the door. "I'm sorry, but I don't have someone else. And make no mistake about it, without this cigarette account, the agency is in trouble. If you won't head the creative team, I'll have to hire someone else."

"Yes, I guess you will."

"Look, Eve. I know you're going through hard times right now, what with your separation from Ben. Take a couple of weeks. We have a little time on this campaign. Go somewhere. Think it over. Then talk to me. Don't throw everything away." He walked out without looking back, my boss and friend of almost twenty years.

I opened my desk, pulled out a bottle, and dumped a Valium into my palm. Breaking the pill in half, I swallowed one half without water, putting the other half back in the bottle. The phone rang.

"Eve," said a recognizable voice. "Eve, this is Lillian."

"Lillian." She had never called me at the office before. Usually, we talk every week or so, early in the morning, before our workdays begin. And Lillian is a talker, full of news of real estate deals mostly. My uncle Max's death hadn't stopped her for long.

"Well, you must wonder why I'm calling you at the office. Other than to wish you a happy birthday, of course." Without waiting for an answer, she continued. "Eve, remember how we talked at Max's funeral about you and Ben buying some waterfront property in Maryland—as an investment, of course, but as an escape from New York, too, and a place for Ben's sailboat." She hesitated just slightly—"What with the recession down here, waterfront property is more affordable than I've seen it in years. I think you both should come down as soon as possible and see what's on the market."

"Lillian, Ben and I are separating. I didn't want to tell you until we'd actually signed the papers."

"Oh . . . I'm sorry, Eve. But I can't say I'm surprised. To tell you the truth, I wondered about the two of you when you were here for Max's funeral. You seemed so . . . so distant. I know it's none of my business. . . ." She hesitated again, then her voice strengthened. "Well then, you probably need to get away. Why don't you come down and stay with me for a while. We'll look at properties only if you're interested." Behind the assured voice was a hint of something else.

"Well, maybe. . . . When?"

"Tomorrow. Do you good, Eve." That something else in her voice was there again, a kind of pleading for me to understand. I'd heard it from clients who were moving their accounts to other agencies. I'd heard it from Ben, the night he moved out, as he packed a couple of suitcases to take to his assistant's studio apartment. Maybe there was something more in Maryland than cheap waterfront properties. It didn't matter. I hardly needed an excuse.

"Okay, Lillian. That sounds great. Just what I need." We made arrangements.

I put the phone down and dropped the bottle of tranquilizers in my handbag. Calm soaked through me. I looked around my desk. It was covered with cards and expensive flowers from agency people, friends, clients, from people wanting jobs with Lister, Klein, and Andronucci. There was nothing from Ben. Sitting there, I realized that I'd always assumed, maybe still assumed, that we'd celebrate my fortieth birthday together. How could we not after twenty-one years of marriage? Sadness washed through me. It had been coming more frequently the last couple of days. Half a pill suddenly wasn't enough. I reached for the bottle and swallowed the second half.

CHAPTER

TWO

Pines on Magothy was a mixture of village streets and wooded tracts. The houses were small mostly: ramblers and enlarged bungalows, all different, most lovingly maintained. Boats that hadn't seen water in years stood rusting on their trailers, parked next to vans advertising quick copy businesses or plumbing contractors. An occasional eyesore—with a dog predictably chained under the porch and a rusted kitchen stove in the front yard—was the work of renters, the blight of beachfront communities, my uncle Max once told me. An Anne Arundel County police cruiser stood in front of a white bungalow with jalousie windows and a huge tree-filled yard.

Lido Beach Road ran the length of a spit of land that led to Lido Beach, a belt of dirty sand somewhat less imposing than its namesake. The beach was adjacent to the long, low bridge to Arundel Island and its exclusive private estates. On my right was the vast Magothy River—an estuary, really—which opened into the Chesapeake. To the left was Weller's Creek, narrower, but deep and full of sheltered wooded coves.

For maybe ten blocks, the streets radiated from Lido Beach Road to the waterfront on either side. I drove past the Lido Beach

Inn on my right. A new one-story cinder-block Pines on Magothy Community Center was across the street. There was a brick church with a steeple.

Then the houses stopped suddenly and the spit of land widened. I found myself driving through a couple of miles of dense, lonely woods, the trees closing in on the road. I turned left down Weller's Creek Road and drove another mile or so, then left again into a rough, unpaved drive, past a shabby bungalow, and closer to the water. A small two-story house with a large screened porch lay in the clearing of pines trees on my right. The house was covered with the original brown wooden shakes. It wasn't much, but the surrounding woods were. There were no cars in the clearing. Lillian was late. But then, Lillian was always late.

Getting out, I smelled the pines for the first time. Cicadas wheezed from high in the trees. A dog barked incessantly from the direction of the creek. The sounds of hammering and sawing came from beyond the woods, nearer to Lido Beach and the Arundel Island Bridge. A heavy truck lumbered up Weller's Creek Road in the near distance. I locked the BMW and headed down the wide dirt road to the water.

Suddenly, fifty yards away, the sliver of water opened to a perfect cove, its half-moon beach surrounded by heavy trees and sheltered from sight of the mainland across the creek, its old dock stretching into deep water. The tide was high, lapping. A large black dog, some sort of Labrador mix maybe, stood barking at the water's edge. Nearby, a Chesapeake Bay retriever swam close to an old man who was half in and half out of the water. The man was frantically clutching a limp white dog and struggling to hold on to an ancient sycamore whose roots had found the river bottom. The dog was dead.

The man labored to pull himself and the dog up and out, then fell to the beach, holding the dog with both arms, his face hidden in its short, wet fur.

"What happened? Can I help?" The Chesapeake Bay retriever stood waiting beside the man, then began shaking, the drops flying off its reddish coat. The black dog, however, ran in my direction, stopping short but growling a little as I moved closer. When the old man shifted, I could see the white dog's pink muzzle and bulging eyes, the yellow plastic rope around its neck. It had been strangled. The man looked up at me, bewildered, still holding the dog, shaking his head. I heard a car drive up and cut its engine.

"Someone killed her," said the old man. He looked directly at me, his body soaked and resting next to the dog, his thin gray hair plastered to his head. "She's dead. . . . I can't bear this, too." His head fell down again.

"Eve . . . Ray, oh my God . . . Oh, Ray." Lillian Weber was behind me, picking her way to the cove, when she saw the old man. The black dog let her through. Dressed in a pink linen suit, her high heels forgotten, she stumbled past me to the old man. "Oh, Ray, it's Will's old dog. Where is he?" Sinking beside him, she put her arms around the old man and the dead dog, holding and rocking them both, her body absorbing the shaking. "Oh, Ray, who could have done this?"

Slowly, she helped him up, her arms around his shoulders. The dog lay lifeless at their feet. Looking up, she seemed to look beyond me. I turned to see a dark-haired young man plunging down the path to the cove, his eyes full of fear at what they saw. The Labrador let him pass. Rushing to the dead white dog, he stood transfixed for one instant, taking it in, then fell on his knees and buried his head in the white fur, his shoulders alive with emotion. Slowly, his head came up, and as we watched, he carefully removed the plastic rope, then cradled the dog again. As his sobs cut through the scream of the cicadas and the lapping water of high tide, the Chesapeake Bay retriever moved closer to him, licking his face, whining.

My mouth tasted of salt and my shirt was as wet as if I had fallen in the creek. In the distance, the rhythmic hammering played accompaniment to the cicadas. I took a step toward the sycamore tree. The black dog moved again, not growling now, but holding me off, standing guard over a scene I had no right to see.

———

By early evening, the heat and humidity had grown worse. The skies were alive with lightning and thunder, the oncoming storm still a distance away but announcing its certainty and strength. Lillian and I were sitting on the deck of her house overlooking the Magothy River, choosing the oppressive evening air over the sterile air-conditioned comfort inside. Lights in neighboring houses were bright; no one was outside. The wind was coming up, blowing trees so that the undersides of leaves shone white in the fading day. Lillian rose to answer the phone. Rifle shots echoed in the distance.

I remembered again the gathering here after Max's funeral. What a party that had been, maybe two hundred people milling around Lillian's huge waterfront lawn. They had chatted in small groups on the flagstone walk to the water's edge and on the large partially covered dock with its Adirondack chairs and colored lights. Women wearing white uniforms had provided cold beer and hot crab cakes. Uncle Max, I had no doubt, would have loved it. Tonight, though, it was not the same place.

Lillian returned to the deck. She was dressed in white slacks and a matching embroidered top, her feet in sandals. The filthy pink linen suit hung near the front door, waiting to be taken to the cleaners. Her bleached hair was thinner than it had been last year—I could see through the careful teasing to her scalp. Maybe she was thinner, too. I was very happy to see her.

"That was Shirley. She is still at the office, but she's going to try to get home before the rain." Lillian sat down again. "I'm sorry, Eve, that you had to see that awful scene this afternoon."

"Why didn't you call the police?"

Lillian shook her head. "The young man who owns the dog—his name is Will St. Claire—didn't want to. He wanted to grieve and bury his dog. I have to respect that," she said.

"But this is a small place; the police could find out who did it." Could I be saying this, a New Yorker who knew most small crimes go unreported because the police are largely helpless? Still, the scene by the water was vivid and, oddly enough, more appalling than anything I'd ever witnessed in New York.

"Try to put it out of your mind, Eve. It's over. Instead, tell me what finally happened with you and Ben. I was sorry to hear you were separating. Though, God knows, marriage can be tough sometimes."

I told her, this aunt I adored and hardly ever saw. It just poured out: how two successful careers had increasingly taken over our lives; how Ben and I had spent less and less time together these last couple of years; how, without my noticing, the constant separation had somehow turned poisonous; and how we had each looked elsewhere for comfort and love. All my anger flared up again, and, much more perplexing and difficult, my sorrow. Without thinking, I touched the pocket of my shorts. The bottle of Valium was safely there.

Lillian was silent, breathing, drinking her tea. The skies rumbled and lit with jagged streaks. My clothes felt dirty, stuck to my body. Sitting across from me, my aunt looked frail and all of her seventy-one years.

"I miss Max, Eve, on nights like this. We were almost never apart, not more than twice in forty-three years. We didn't talk much the last few years, didn't have to, I guess." She seemed then to realize what she was saying. "I'm sorry, Eve. I didn't mean to go on like that. It was insensitive of me."

I shrugged. "Why did you ask me to come to Maryland, Lillian? Was it really to see waterfront property?"

She hesitated slightly, then sat forward. "Things aren't going so well here, Eve. I guess you noticed that there's only Shirley and me left at Weber Realty. Oh, Ginger Clancy works part-time, but it's not enough. All the other agents are gone now, retired to Florida, or on their own, or with bigger brokers now that Max is gone. Shirley promises to get her license, but with Gilbert, who knows. I guess I could recruit new agents to bring in sales and inventory, but you know . . ." The thought seemed to exhaust her. "I'm a little overworked. And sales have been terrible this past year or so. In fact, just this morning the buyer for Ray Tilghman's property on Weller's Creek Road backed out. I couldn't bring myself to tell Ray earlier. Now I'll have to do it tomorrow." She sipped the iced tea. I waited.

"Oh hell, what this all really means is that if things don't pick up, I'm going to have to sell Weber Realty. This recession has nearly killed me. Everybody says it's going to turn around, but I can't wait much longer." Her voice was gathering energy. "The buzzards are circling, Eve. Well, one really, a charming buzzard named Mitch Gaylin. He's determined to do more waterfront business in north Anne Arundel County. Shirley just told me he wants to meet tomorrow." She sat back. A couple of big drops of rain splattered on the deck. "I guess I needed some moral support."

We both breathed deeply, uncertain of each other, not knowing what to say in comfort, so we said nothing.

"Lillian, I can stay for a while to help out at the office or do whatever you need me to. Although I don't know anything about real estate."

"Thanks, it would help enormously if you could. But what about your work? Can you take some vacation time?"

I laughed and told her about the cigarette account. "Joe practically insisted that I get away and think things over. My heart's not really in it anymore, Lillian, selling junk that no one needs. And I'm too good for cigarettes. I'd probably sell zillions to young people who will get lung cancer. I'm not sure I can do it. Maybe Joe will hire someone who isn't as good as I am."

Lillian smiled, nodded, then stood up. She hesitated for a moment, looking at me, then put a manicured hand on my shoulder and squeezed it.

"Thank you, Eve, for coming down. I'm awfully glad you're here. Now, I know it's only eight, but I get so tired that I go to bed early these days. Don't get wet." She pointed to the darkening sky. "I hope Shirley got ahead of the storm." She stepped inside the sliding glass doors, closing them behind her.

We deserved each other, I thought, both of us too tough, not wanting to ask for help, afraid of too much emotion. Maybe that's why she had called me, not someone who was here in Maryland. With me, she knew, there would be no clinging, no histrionics, no hidden meaning awarded her problems.

As I moved my chair back under the covered part of the deck to avoid the rain, I suddenly felt the anxiety inside of me swim to the surface. It had kept its distance for most of today. The dead dog's white-and-pink face floated above me. Shaking, I swallowed a pill, hoping one was enough.

The storm was suddenly there, the dirty ozone smell coming up from the ground as the rain streamed down, the thunder and lightning close over the water. The wind whipped the sailboats moored off the docks along the Magothy. The leaves of the trees shuddered and plunged. Sitting there in the near darkness, in the noise and wet, I could see Ben's once-dear and still-familiar face, his beard neatly trimmed, his eyes full of mischief. Grief surged and spilled over in me. Something had died between us, and even if we tried, we both knew it was no good. We couldn't bring love back. For the first time, I knew it for sure.

I don't know how long I sat, or dreamed, or hallucinated, hours maybe, since the sky had become completely black again, the trees quiet. I stood up and walked to the railing.

Although the storm had passed over, the heat and humidity lingered. In the distance, I saw a dark figure walk down the far side of Lillian's lawn to the water. It was Will St. Claire. He walked to the end of Lillian's dock and sat down to watch the river. Maybe it soothed him. The clock in Lillian's kitchen said twenty-five after ten. I reached for another Valium and went inside to try to sleep.

CHAPTER

THREE

Lillian was gone when I awoke, and the Magothy seemed peaceful, the lawn and trees fresh in the morning sun. It was almost ten o'clock. I made instant coffee and took it out on the deck. Surprisingly, the heat and humidity remained intense, not blown away by last night's storm. Small branches littered neighboring yards and the radio said thousands of people in southern Maryland were only now getting their power back.

I reread the note Lillian had left me. She'd gone into the office and would meet me at eleven at the Lido Beach Inn for an early lunch. Although she had an appointment at one o'clock, she thought that maybe I'd like to go with her to see Ray Tilghman at Weller's Creek Road afterward.

Remembering yesterday, I wasn't sure I was ready. Calm was upon me for the moment, my anxiety, like last night's storm, distant and incomprehensible. I looked out to the water, thinking about Lillian's problems, about Max, about Ben. What was I doing here in Maryland, other than feeling unfocused and indecisive? Shaking off my thoughts, I quickly showered and dressed. Studying my face in the mirror, I saw no hint of any demons staring out of my eyes this August morning. I put the bottle of Valium in my bag just in case.

The Lido Beach Inn was about half a mile inland. I entered a large room in which day and night were all the same. An air conditioner over the door worked furiously, dripping a light spot on the wooden floorboards. I sat down at one end of the three-sided center bar and looked around. There were a few wooden booths along one side of the room, two pool tables, bowling and softball trophies in a dusty glass case, and the usual neon beer and booze signs. In front of me, in the central display of liquors, was a bottle of pure grain alcohol, 190 proof, suitable only for getting drunk.

"You must be Eve." The speaker was maybe forty-five, heavy, with short gray hair freshly trimmed. She'd gotten her money's worth. The hairdresser had even shaved her neck. "I'm Marian Beall. I own the joint. Lillian called to say to treat you right. She's going to be a little late." From her squat body came a deep laugh. I shook the hand she offered. "What can I get you? Lunch is ham and cheese sandwiches or ham sandwiches or cheese sandwiches." Without being asked, she had poured me a mug of coffee, putting it in front of me with a spoon and a sugar bowl and a carton of milk. I poured in the milk and stirred.

"Don't wait for Lillian, Hon. She's always late and she never eats much of anything these days anyway. Better have what you're gonna have."

"Okay, a cheese sandwich will be fine," I said.

She reached under the counter for a six-inch pile of yellow slices, pulled a few off, and put them between two slices of square white bread. "Lettuce and tomato?" I nodded. She put the sandwich down in front of me.

"Glad you're here, Eve. Though I'm sure sorry you had to see that dead dog business. No way to welcome someone."

"Marian, that dog was purposely killed." The scene rose again in my mind: the dark-haired young man cradling the white dog in his arms, his grief seeping through the hidden cove. "Who would do something like that?"

"I dunno," she said. "Small place like the Pines. We'll find out. If not now, later." She shrugged, as if to shake away bleak thoughts. "In the meantime, I'm glad you're here to help Lillian. Things aren't the same at Weber Realty without Max. Of course, if you sell, you'll have to get your license, but that shouldn't be too hard. I've even thought of takin' the course myself, but I never get around to it."

"Lillian told you I was going to become a real estate agent?" I studied Marian, dumpy in long red cotton shorts and a red sleeveless blouse. Was I hearing right?

"Oh, no. Just wishful thinking on my part, I guess. I'm worried about your aunt. Everybody is. She's got a lot on her plate right now." Marian refilled my mug.

There was a noise behind me and a good-looking, slightly overblown young man, maybe in his mid-twenties and wearing faded jeans and a T-shirt, struggled to open and close the door while propping two cases of beer on his hip. He managed it and stood grinning at us, pleased with himself.

"Two cases, Marian. You gonna need more?"

"Couple more, Russ. Put them around in back here," said Marian. She motioned to a refrigerator behind the bar. "Also, that second keg is low, the light stuff. If you'd go back down and tap another before lunch, I'd appreciate it."

"Light stuff," he repeated. "Sure thing, Marian."

"Before you go, meet Eve Elliott, Lillian's niece."

He finished loading bottles into the refrigerator, then stood up, taking his time and wiping his hands on his pants, looking at me with frank male interest. I doubted whether he even knew how rude he was being.

"Hi. You here on vacation?" he asked.

Good question, I thought. Marian answered for me. "She's gonna to help Lil out for a bit."

He nodded, sticking his fingertips back in shallow front

jeans pockets. "I better go do that keg." In a couple of minutes, we could hear him going through an outdoor hatch into the basement.

"Russ is Hank Crouse's son. Hank's been with the Anne Arundel County Police for maybe twenty-five years." She was energetically wiping off the bar. "Russ helps me out part-time. Been out of work since he dropped out of the community college last semester. Had to move in with his father again, which, I'm tellin' you, is hard on him. I try to use him when I can." She threw the dishrag at the sink and missed. "Can't pay him much, but he makes it up in beer. Certainly did last night, though you can't tell, can you? Damn hardhead can drink anything and not show it. Youth."

Marian looked up when Lillian entered. My aunt was dressed in a pale blue summer suit with a long pleated skirt, her hair perfect, her nails polished bright pink. Lillian was warding off her demons with good grooming, I thought.

"There you both are. Hi, Marian. You sleep, Eve?"

"For a very long time." Lillian perched on a bar stool, shaking her head when Marian pointed at the coffeepot.

"Storm knocked down a bunch of power lines," said Marian. "They're just getting juice again down in South County. Much worse down there. Shirley come in?" Lillian shook her head slightly. "So what's the problem today?" she asked my aunt.

"A possum got in the house last night and apparently Gilbert, who was home alone, took a stick to it. By the time Shirl got home, he had bludgeoned it half to death. She had to call Bob Fletcher to come over and finish it off. All this was during the storm. Apparently Gilbert was so upset and the place was such a mess that they went and spent the night with Valerie." Lillian turned to me. "That's Shirl's daughter. Well, anyway, she's home cleaning up the mess so I can show the place. Gilbert is still very upset."

"Gilbert," Marian said to me, "is always upset. That's one troubled kid. Does some pretty strange things."

"I met him yesterday. What's the matter with him?" I asked. Marian tapped her temple with her forefinger and rolled her eyes.

"Shirl's had her hands full with those two kids," said Lillian. "Though Valerie has straightened up, I hear. Got an apartment over in Asbury Bay and a job selling cosmetics at the mall."

"That girl must have had a couple of abortions in high school, to say nothing of the drugs and booze," said Marian, shaking her head. "I don't know how Shirl handled it." Did Marian and Lillian know the details of everybody's business? It certainly seemed that way. "Speaking of Shirl, you get any offers for her house yet, Lil?"

"One, and it's a little low. Mitch Gaylin's client. I can't present it until my seller comes back from vacation—which is probably just as well, since God knows what damage there is now to the kitchen." She sighed, then turned to me. "You remember I told you about the broker who is trying to buy me out? That's Mitch Gaylin."

I was having trouble following all of this and said so.

"Shirley rents the house on the waterfront property two over from Ray Tilghman on Weller's Creek Road," explained Lillian. "It's in pretty bad condition, but it's a cheap rental and it's on the water. When I sell it, she'll have to move. And no landlord is exactly going to welcome Gilbert. Of course, they aren't supposed to discriminate, but somehow people get around the rules. We'll find her something, I guess."

"Where's Shirley's husband?"

Marian looked at Lillian, then shrugged. "The lockup at Jessup. With luck, for a good long time. Armed robbery. For about the fourteenth time."

Shirley Bodine did seem to have her hands full. Having seen her handling things at Lillian's office yesterday, I thought she was bearing up remarkably well and said so.

Lillian nodded, collecting her handbag and portfolio and sliding off her stool. "You have to give her credit. And we all try to help."

Lillian held the door to the bar as Russell Crouse returned with a couple more cases of beer.

"Shirley was real grateful to you, Russ, for taking Gilbert crabbing the other day." Lillian patted his shoulder and turned back to me. "Gotta go. See you later at Weller's Creek Road." She glanced at her watch. "Maybe three."

"Okay, that's fine, but are you sure Mr. Tilghman will be comfortable with me there while you talk business, Lillian?"

"He's an old friend. Marian will fill you in about him. I have to go." She grabbed her handbag and portfolio and left.

"She didn't eat again," said Marian. "But there's no makin' her. Believe me, I've tried."

The bar was beginning to fill up. Russell Crouse had disappeared back downstairs and Marian went to wait on a uniformed gray-haired cop who had taken a seat at the other side of the bar. His expression was sober, made more so by a nose that looked as if it might have been broken a long time ago. Marian filled his mug with coffee and offered him a couple of sandwiches, which he polished off in about six bites. He stood up a few minutes later. Marian made introductions but I already knew he must be Hank Crouse, Russell's father.

"Russ been in today?" he asked Marian.

"He's downstairs tappin' a keg or maybe drinkin' it," she said.

Hank Crouse's features formed themselves into a half smile, half scowl. "He hadn't better be. You tell him I said that. And tell him to see what he can do about borrowing an electric saw. That old silver maple in the yard came down in the storm last night and the handsaw was too damned small and dull. I nearly cut off my fingers." He held up a freshly bandaged hand and grinned sheepishly at me. Then, carefully putting on his hat, he left.

Marian was soon busy drawing beer, making sandwiches and change. She was surprisingly quick on her feet, joking with her customers. Russell Crouse came back after a few minutes and relieved her at the tap. "Beats teachin' fifth graders," she said as she

19

sped by me to the refrigerator. We were the only two women in the dark bar. The men, I noticed, weren't particularly shy about looking me over. When the rush was over, Marian came around and pulled up a stool beside me.

"So what's your situation?" she asked, lighting up a cigarette.

"Getting divorced and maybe out of a job." She nodded, as if that was perfectly normal.

"You really should think about staying and helping Lil out, then. I know she feels better already just to know that you're here, though don't tell her I told you so."

"Marian, what did Lillian mean that you'd fill me in about Ray Tilghman? Is it something to do with that strangled dog?"

She inhaled deeply, looking unhappy. "Nah, I don't think so. I don't know what that was about. Lil has been trying to sell Ray's place for some time. She thought she finally had a buyer, but the deal fell through yesterday. Ray is going to take it hard."

"And that's why she wants me there?"

"Yeah. You see, Ray has bad heart disease and he needs to sell soon. But he's stubborn and there's a condition on the sale."

"Which is?" I felt like I was playing twenty questions.

"Ray has two big dogs he adores. You saw them. Convalescent homes don't allow dogs, so as a condition of the sale, Ray insists the buyer has to take care of them on the property until they die. In return, he's selling dirt cheap. And it's the best property around here."

"Why did the buyer back out?"

"Cold feet, I guess," said Marion. "Lil said he didn't like the idea of having the lawyer check up on the dogs regularly to make sure that they were cared for."

"And that was part of the agreement?"

"Yup."

"So now what happens?"

Marian stubbed her cigarette out and then cleaned out the ashtray with a paper towel. "I guess Lillian keeps trying to sell."

CHAPTER

FOUR

I decided to head over to Weller's Creek Road a little early and let Marian get on with her lunch cleanup instead of having to entertain me. As I neared the water, the air became as oppressive as it had been yesterday. Overhead, cicadas exploded into long crescendos, then fell suddenly silent to wait for the next impulse.

There was a small, old pickup in the drive next to the bungalow at the entrance to Weller's Creek Road. Fifteen years ago, it had probably been red. Lillian had told me that Will St. Claire, Ray Tilghman's tenant, lived in the bungalow. Now, easing the BMW past the bungalow and down the long drive to Ray's house, I tried to put the scene at the cove yesterday from my mind. It was impossible. I kept remembering the young man gently cradling his lifeless dog in his arms, then later last night, his walk alone by the water after the storm. From down the road came the sounds of the house next door being built—sawing and hammering, a cement mixer painfully grinding. A couple of motorboats purred from the direction of Lido Beach.

As it had yesterday, Ray Tilghman's place appeared deserted. I walked to the brown-shingled cottage, the scent of the pines all around me. Fierce barking came from the interior of the house.

The screen door on the porch was slightly open and from behind the heavy front door there was a crash as a dog threw himself at it. My presence only infuriated it more.

"Mr. Tilghman?" From inside the porch, I moved a few feet to a window and, cupping my hands, tried to see into the darkness. It was completely black inside. The furious barking was louder and more insistent now, both dogs enraged. I rapped once again, this time a little harder. "Mr. Tilghman?" To my dismay, the door swung open under my knock and both the Chesapeake Bay retriever and the Labrador rushed out, ignoring me and heading off the screened porch and into the nearby bushes.

"Mr. Tilghman? Hello?" The inside of the house was dark, almost cool. I stepped inside a couple of feet and at once backed away from the powerful smell of urine and feces. The dogs had been in here a long time and the living room reeked. There were no sounds, but the odor was overwhelming. Instinctively, I backed out. The screen door on the porch slammed behind me. The dogs were gone. I could hear them crashing toward the beach, barking intermittently until they hit the water. There was loud splashing.

Half-running now, I headed down the wide path to the little cove, driven by some unnamed fear. The scene opened suddenly in front of me. And in the distance, near the sycamore, I saw the Chesapeake Bay retriever push someone out of the still, shallow water and onto the sand and then lie down full length, stretched out beside the body, panting. The dog then began to lick the dirt carefully off the face and hands. On the beach, the Labrador stood dripping, quiet and watchful. In the distance came the sound of a motor and the brief passing odor of gasoline as someone unseen started a boat.

Without thinking, aware only of the unbearable sight of the old man's body gently attended by his dogs, I tore up the wide path, no longer hearing the motorboat, the hammering, the lapping water, the cicadas. I ran maybe a quarter of a mile in the soaking heat, my screams coming back at me from the tall trees.

The little bungalow came into view and Will St. Claire walked toward me, his eyes uneasy.

"There's been a terrible accident. I think Mr. Tilghman's drowned. We need an ambulance, though I think it's too late."

"Phone's inside. In the bedroom." He was running toward the water, not looking back. I stumbled through a small plant-filled kitchen and into a sort of bedroom and living room. In the corner was a single bed. Books and magazines and newspapers were everywhere. A fan hummed. The phone, its beige cord twisted and stretched, sat on a old desk among half-filled coffee cups and more magazines.

Dialing 911, I heard myself give directions in a voice that seemed not to be mine. The emergency operator asked a question, then told me to stay on the line. I obeyed, unable to do otherwise. Like last night in the storm, time got lost. Through the bedroom window, I saw a police cruiser pull up outside, then another move past the bungalow, toward the creek. Then an ambulance. I put the phone down and went outside.

It was close to seven and Lillian and I were again sitting on the deck overlooking the Magothy, this time with Weller Church, her lawyer and friend. He was named after Weller's Creek, my aunt told me, and the creek was named for his family. Dark clouds were speeding over the sun. There was thunder in the distance. The wet heat wormed its way into every pore of my body. I wanted a shower, not the cold salads and cheeses Lillian had pulled from the refrigerator and placed on the table in front of us. She and I were drinking iced tea. The lawyer, his seersucker jacket over the chair and his bow tie a bit askew, was drinking something alcoholic from a bottle he had found in the sideboard in Lillian's dining room. He waved away the food. I ate a little to keep Lillian company.

"I knew that heart condition was going to kill him," said Weller. "After Will's dog was killed, he probably went back down to the water to look around, had an attack, lost his balance, and fell in. I'll put money on it." He leaned back. "What do they call it? An accident waiting to happen."

Lillian was shoving a spoonful of potato salad around on her plate. Abruptly, she gave it up and pushed the half-full plate away. "I don't think so, Weller. I don't think this can have been an accident." We both turned to look at her.

"Lil, what are you saying?" asked the lawyer. "Of course it was an accident. He wasn't well. You know that."

"What makes you think that it wasn't an accident?" I repeated. It seemed incredible and not so incredible all at once. I was thinking of the strange words I'd heard Ray Tilghman speak yesterday: "She's dead. . . . I can't bear this, too." What else had he had to bear?

"The dogs . . ." my aunt said slowly. "He always took the dogs with him to the beach. He never left them in the house." Weller Church was sitting forward in his chair now.

"I hadn't heard that." He turned to me. "You found the dogs in the house?" I nodded. "Well, that's different. . . . That's very different." Weller looked off at the water. "It's a little like that Penny Hart business all over again," he said quietly, to himself more than to us.

Lillian shrank into her chair. It was starting to rain a little, light, hot drops staining the pale wood. We moved closer to the house, under the protection of the enclosed section of Lillian's deck. Still no one spoke. My mind returned to the events of the afternoon.

The hours after the police came had been a nightmare of their own kind—quite unlike that of finding Ray's Tilghman's body in the cove. This was all numbness and waiting. Lillian had arrived, her face and body sagging when she heard the news from Hank Crouse. The cop himself appeared depressed and dumbfounded, his earlier joviality at the Lido Beach Inn gone. The rest of the police were matter-of-fact, milling about, chatting, and laughing a little sometimes. There were no tears, just the hushed horror of a terrible death in a beautiful spot on a hot August day. Mostly we waited.

The police asked me questions for what seemed like hours. I answered them over and over, telling my story first to Hank Crouse, then to another cop who carefully took notes, then again from the beginning to a fat-faced plainclothes homicide detective who took me through it all over again, minute by horrible minute. A kind of paralysis set in and weariness like I'd never felt before.

Police cars and vans came and went. After awhile, a stretcher crew from the ambulance carried the body away. Uniformed cops had sealed the scene at the beach and at Ray's house. Someone brought me a cold drink. A local news crew showed up with its satellite truck, then taped an attractive young black reporter talking, the peaceful cove behind her making her story a little hard to believe. I could see her gestures and her mouth moving, but no words floated up to where I stood. A police spokesman near me was answering questions without really answering anything at all. Someone had rounded up the dogs—Lillian had told me their names: Lancelot, the Chesapeake Bay retriever, and Zeke, the black Labrador mix—and herded them into Will St. Claire's bungalow. We could hear them barking forlornly in the distance. Will himself sat on a stump a few yards from Ray's house, his head in his hands, his face expressionless and pale when he looked up. Lillian and I waited in her car for a time, the air conditioner running.

Now, hours later, sitting on the deck, I felt as if I hadn't slept in weeks. I hadn't, I realized, not without Valium. I watched Lillian take a sip of iced tea, unaware that I was looking at her. My aunt was made of something that didn't need pills. Then, oddly, instead of Ray Tilghman's lifeless body, the image of Will St. Claire's anguish over the loss of his beloved dog floated through my mind. It had been raw, almost indecent. Was that what the pills neutralized, loss and sadness? Touching the plastic bottle in my pocket, I knew I didn't want to depend on them anymore.

Weller Church was getting up now, putting on his wrinkled

jacket. I'd almost forgotten he was there. He looked his seventy-some years, red from the booze, tired from a dreadful afternoon. He didn't have far to go home, I knew, since he lived on the Arundel Island estate where he'd been born and grew up. The Wellers had always had money, Lillian told me earlier, and power and influence in Annapolis.

He briefly touched Lillian's shoulder. She looked up at him. The rain was ending.

"We can't jump to conclusions about Ray's death, Lil. We just don't know, so we have to leave it to the police. The autopsy should tell what happened. I'll make a couple of calls when I get home and see if they can't do it tonight or early tomorrow. Then I promise to be by here first thing tomorrow on my way to work to tell you what they find."

Lillian nodded.

"We'll also find a way for you to get out of this financial mess so you don't have to sell Weber Realty to Gaylin," he said to her. "Lend you money myself if I have to."

"You already did, in case you've forgotten," said Lillian. "No more loans, Weller, although God only knows how much I appreciate it. There has to be another way."

"We'll find it. But you need to take care of yourself, Lillian. Get some sleep. That's important."

"Thank God I'm not married to you, Weller Church, what with your nagging," she said. He made his mouth into a kind of pout, then smiled and turned to me.

"You should also get some sleep, Eve. You look all in." Real sleep, I thought.

He looked up at the sky and then turned back to Lillian. "Got to go home, Lil, and finish putting up the fence around my garden before the deer eat everything." He left the deck and walked around the house to his car.

"Can he do that? Get the autopsy done tonight?" I asked her.

Lillian nodded. "Never underestimate Weller. He's the iron

hand in the velvet glove. Some of us only see the velvet side, but there's iron there, and he's not afraid to use it."

"Lillian, who is Penny Hart?"

My aunt took a deep breath. "Penny Hart was a local young woman with a promising acting career in New York. On a visit home, she was accidentally drowned. This happened maybe twenty-five years ago. Ray Tilghman found her body in his cove."

CHAPTER
FIVE

I got up and cleared the table of our largely untouched supper. Lillian folded the antenna on the cellular phone.

"That was Shirley. She'll be in tomorrow. She just heard about Ray's death on the six o'clock news."

"Lillian, what happens now to Ray Tilghman's property?" I asked. "Did he have relatives?"

My aunt shook her head. "No relatives. I sell it, just as before, except now the money goes into a trust. He had all the details worked out with Weller. Ray was quite well off, despite the way he lived. Years ago, his back was badly hurt in an accident at work and he got a big settlement. Did Marian tell you any of this?"

"No. Just about caring for the dogs."

My aunt nodded. "Ray knew he couldn't live alone much longer, even with Will down the road to help him. In addition to his back problem, he had heart disease. We were trying to find him a retirement home while he could still walk in." She shifted slightly in her chair. "Now it doesn't matter, does it?"

My aunt disappeared into a well of memories. I sat drifting in my own thoughts, waiting for her to return.

"Selling that property is going to be even harder now, waterfront or not, great value or not," she said.

I was surprised. "Why should you have more trouble selling that beautiful piece of land than before? Won't the conditions about the dogs be the same?"

Lillian hesitated. "Well, yes, but the property may now be stigmatized by Ray's death. And Penny Hart's drowning, if anyone remembers that. People don't like living where someone has died. Too many ghosts." She sat back. "And that poor dead dog doesn't make things easier. Not when it was purposely killed. There's something . . ."

Her words trailed off. We sat thinking our own thoughts. I shook myself free first.

"Lillian, what about caring for Ray's dogs?"

She nodded. "Ray wanted his dogs cared for on the property and had the condition written into the sales contract, Eve. Conditions are normal enough, God knows. When people sell their homes, they often don't want to lose certain things, so they put conditions in the contract to keep them. This usually means special improvements like a light fixture or drapes or an appliance, but I've even had a seller put in a condition that allowed him to dig up the bones of the family cat buried in the backyard before he moved." She sat up straighter. "Ray's conditions were just a little more extreme." I waited. "He wanted the buyer to adopt his two dogs, Lancelot and Zeke. They were the main reasons he didn't want to go to a retirement community. No community would let him bring those two giants. A little dog might have been different."

"Did Ray insist on approving the buyer?"

"Absolutely. And whoever bought the property would not only have to accept the legal responsibility for his dogs until they die but also agree to have Weller, as Ray's executor, regularly check up on them to make sure the dogs are okay. It was that last that broke the contract I had." Lillian shook her head. "The wife didn't care, but the husband thought about that last and decided it was too intrusive. Which it is, I guess."

"And now you and Weller will decide who you want to sell the property to? Isn't that, ah . . . illegal?"

"Weller worked it out," she said. "I don't know the details." She sat quietly. "So who do you suppose, would want a property like that? Even at a price that hardly begins to approach its real value?"

Suddenly, she began to laugh. "In some ways, it's Ray's last attempt to keep the Yuppies out of the Pines. He was dead set against the changes he saw happening. By deliberately selling his house below value, all of the other houses will be undervalued, including that of his new neighbors, who are doing a major renovation." Lillian drank the last of her tea.

"Lillian, did you really think that Ben and I might be interested in Ray's property with these crazy conditions?"

She turned to pour another glass of tea from a nearby pitcher. "Well, no, I didn't. I just hoped you might come down to Maryland to visit." Her voice was a little tight.

"You could have just asked, you know." But I knew she couldn't, any more than I could have asked her to come to New York and stay with me while I mourned my marriage. "I might be interested in staying here for a while, Lillian. After the last twenty years of sixty- or seventy-hour workweeks, I've earned a sabbatical—from advertising and from New York. I might even be interested in Ray's property." She stared at me. "Not to buy, but maybe I could live there for a while. Rent the place. I could take care of the dogs while you look for a buyer. Is renting the house a possibility?"

"It might be. I'll ask Weller tomorrow morning." She stood up, hesitated a little, then picked up her empty glass. "You don't have to do this, Eve. Stay here with me."

"I know."

She smiled. "Thanks. I'm going to bed. You should get some sleep, too."

———

*　*　*

I was exhausted but not sleepy. Oddly, my anxieties were not on the prowl, not like a few hours ago. I decided a walk down to the water would do me good.

Heading across the lawn down to the Magothy, I wondered if Joe Lister was interviewing for my replacement yet. He had said we'd talk in two weeks when I got back, but advertising moves faster than that. Perhaps even today someone had been sitting at my desk, in my office, looking down at Central Park and dreaming of ways to sell cigarettes. I felt oddly indifferent.

I stood on the dock and looked out at the faint lights on the water. Pines on Magothy was a riparian community: landowners privately owned the land along the water's edge. Longtime neighbors felt free to crab from one another's docks using buckets of raw chicken necks for bait. Or as Will St. Claire had last night, just to sit and stare at the dark river. It was only newcomers who posted and enforced the no trespassing signs.

There was a distant rumble of thunder. I walked out along the dock and sat down, my feet hanging near the water. It was higher than usual due to the heavy rain the past few days. Although a breeze had blown up, it was still hot. Across the water came the unmistakable and familiar odor of gasoline. It reminded me of summers on Adirondack lakes in upstate New York, as a kid and later with Ben. He and I had had no need for others then, I thought, the long days of swimming and sunning and reading in each other's company were quite enough. Our old sheltie, Mac, had kept us amused with his antics. Nightfall always brought the distant sounds of children playing and music from across the lake. Then we'd slowly make love on the couch in front of the fieldstone fireplace, unable to imagine wanting anything or anybody else. But that time was gone. And Mac, his eyes blind with cataracts, had died quietly in my arms almost five years ago.

The dark Magothy lapped at my feet, bringing me back. Behind me, gravel crunched. Looking around, I saw a dumpy figure

31

walking along the gravel near the water. I got up to greet Marian Beall.

"Evening. How's Lil?"

"In bed, exhausted, I think. You heard what happened to Ray Tilghman?"

"Yes. It's very sad and strange, Eve. Like Will's dog. Not right." She pointed to a bench. In the distance came a volley of rifle shots. Marian looked up.

"What is that?" I asked. "I've been hearing shots off and on all evening."

"Someone killin' squirrels and raccoons. Not legal, but there are some who do it, anyway. Russ Crouse, for one. And who's going to stop him if his father doesn't? In case you haven't guessed, the NRA has a few supporters around here."

"Somehow I suspected."

"What happened this afternoon?" she asked. "Or are you all talked out?"

I shrugged and told my story once more, this time in abbreviated form. I had it down to a few precise sentences and paragraphs, almost as if I was writing advertising copy for a client. Focusing on the telling rather than on the story itself seemed to keep at a distance the appalling image of the dog licking the dead man's face and hands.

Marian listened intently, asked a few questions, then settled back on the wooden bench. Fishing in her pants pocket, she pulled out a pack of cigarettes and lit one. I watched as the smoke curled into her nose.

"Ray Tilghman," she said, "never went down to the water without his dogs. What happened to him was no more an accident than what happened to Will's dog."

"Lillian and Weller Church believe that, too."

"Course they do. Everybody does. Pines is a small, busybody village. Be interestin' to see what the police decide." She exhaled luxuriously. "I mean officially. Unofficially, I'm sure they believe the same's everybody else. But the county has only so many cops, so if the evidence points toward a suicide or an accident, they'll have to slam the case closed, I guess, even if the investigators personally feel somethin' doesn't add up."

Marian snubbed out the cigarette and threw the butt into the river.

"Lillian said Ray wasn't happy about outsiders," I said. "Yuppies, you know, buying property here. That true?"

"Oh, God yes. And he wasn't the only one. Most people here don't think change is so great. A D.C. couple bought the property next to Ray Tilghman last year, aimin' to tear down the old house and put up a new one. It's hard enough to jump through all the government hoops in order to build on the water. You have to get permits for this and permits for that. And the folks around here made it worse, watchin' like hawks, reportin' every move to the powers that be."

"I heard construction yesterday on Weller's Creek Road."

"They got it worked out, I guess, but it took lots of time. Kept bein' delays. There were two trees that needed to be cut down in order to build, so the county forester comes out and looks, then says no, the trees are too close to the water. So the trees stay and there's no building permit. So much for the architect's plans. They had to start all over again. Cost 'em time and money. It was their fault for not checkin' first, but I felt kinda sorry for them."

"Which side of this are you on?"

Marian laughed, stamping her feet. "Oh, I'm on both sides. This is my home and I don't want to see it filled with wealthy hotshots from D.C. Pretty soon we'll have to lock our doors if we walk to the mailbox and we'll have traffic like Annapolis." She lit another cigarette. "The other side of the coin is that our property values are expandin' wildly, and to tell you the truth, maybe we need a little change around here."

"But you don't say that too loudly, I gather."

Marian laughed. "True enough. Come to the inn some evening, when everybody's relaxed and gettin' a little tight. You'll get an earful. We are not what you'd call a politically correct community." She inhaled thoughtfully. "Lillian feels a little guilty sometimes, I think, for sellin' to outsiders. A few around here even hold her responsible for some of the changes. Of course, that's ridiculous. If she doesn't do the sellin', someone else will."

"Like Mitch Gaylin?"

"Like Mitch Gaylin. But even he isn't all bad. He sold the property next to Ray to the Blackburns rather than to a developer. Course, maybe he tried and couldn't get permits to divide the land, what with all the environmental laws and the sewer and water regs." She threw the second cigarette butt after the first. This time it made a tiny hiss.

"Marian, what about a woman named Penny Hart, the one who drowned here?"

"Oh yes, everybody's got Penny Hart on their minds and nobody's sayin' much about it. I'd forget it if I were you. It was a very long time ago."

She got up. "I better get back. I left Russ workin' the bar and he has probably bankrupted me by now, givin' away free drinks or, more likely, drinkin' them himself." She patted her pocket, checking for lighter and cigarettes, then sighed. "It's too bad about Ray. We'll know soon if he died of a heart attack or what," she said. "Just glad you're here for Lillian. Why don't you get that Realtor's license I told you about? Should be a snap for you. Think about it. Night."

"Night." I watched her disappear across the lawn, up to the street, then I walked back the length of Lillian's dock again, standing at the very end to watch the water. An invisible web was drawing around me. Hesitating only a little, I pulled the plastic bottle out of my pants pocket and opened it and tossed the pills into the Magothy. Turning, I headed across the lawn to Lillian's house. I didn't look back at the river. One shot echoed in the trees somewhere across the water.

CHAPTER
SIX

Weller Church was just leaving when I awoke. I could hear his voice mingling with my aunt's, bouncing off the twelve-foot fireplace in her vaulted living room. I had slept for nearly ten hours. For the second day in a row, I had no schedule, no plans, no need to be anywhere. I felt better this morning, though, not the same person who had stood last night at the edge of the river. I showered, then dressed in jeans and old sneakers, no makeup. Passing by the full-length hall mirror on the way downstairs, I stopped, seeing not quite myself, but someone a little different, as if some barely perceptible and slow-moving metamorphosis was stalking me.

Lillian was pouring herself a second, or maybe third, cup of coffee by the time I made it to the kitchen. She was wearing a yellow silk full-length robe. On her feet, were flat black slippers, their toes covered with gold embroidery. Her ankles looked vulnerable, bluish white and mottled.

"Morning, Eve. Coffee?"

"Sure. I'll get it." I sat down at the table after filling a large mug. In front of me were several fat red tomatoes, the tops cracked and black and smelling hot and vulgar. Weller Church must have brought them from his garden.

"That was Weller," said my aunt. "The autopsy was done early this morning and the medical examiner says that Ray drowned. There were no other marks on the body, nor any signs of a heart attack. He did not struggle with anyone. Nothing was taken from the house. No other evidence was found outside or near the cove." Lillian's voice was neutral as she reported the news.

"When do they think he died?"

"Sometime between about eight P.M. and ten Wednesday, probably closer to eight, but I don't think they really know. No one in the neighborhood saw anything or heard anything, probably because of the storm."

"So what happens now?"

"Nothing. It's been ruled an accidental death. It's all over. The police think that Ray was down at the cove, as he often was, maybe on the dock, and that he just slipped in the wet sand during the rain, fell into the water, and couldn't get up. So he drowned. End of story."

"And why would Ray go to the cove with the storm coming up?"

"I don't know, though he was often down there." She got up and pulled a poppy seed bagel from the freezer, then put it in the microwave. "Look, Eve, I don't believe Ray died accidentally, but there's no evidence. If there's another explanation, we'll probably never know what it is." She put the bagel on a plate, pulled an unopened package of cream cheese out of the refrigerator, and handed both to me, along with a heavy silver knife.

"Aren't you eating?"

"I had some toast and juice earlier. I have to get dressed now. I'm going to work here this morning, I think, since Shirley's at the office today. I also need to make funeral arrangements."

Lillian was standing by the door of the kitchen. "What do the police say about Ray's dogs being locked in his house?" Or about Will's dog, for that matter?" I asked.

"Weller brought them up," she said. "Neither is strong-enough evidence. I gather that since Ray's death has been classified as an accident, it will remain so unless someone comes forward or some very compelling evidence surfaces." Her voice grew weary. "Weller isn't happy, either, but there's really nothing more we can do."

"Just one other thing, Lillian." I swallowed a chunk of the bagel. It was dry and unpleasant and balled in my mouth, but to my surprise, I found I was very hungry. "I've been thinking about Ray's dogs. Why didn't he just arrange for Will to take care of them? He apparently loves animals and he's taking care of them now. Why not permanently?"

"Well . . . to tell you the truth, I don't know that, either. I suggested it, of course, but he said no. Maybe because he didn't know if Will would stay here in the Pines." She fiddled with the tie of her robe. "He's young and only been here about six months or so. And you didn't know Ray. He may have been sick, but once he made up his mind, it was made up. He had plenty of money and he knew what he wanted." One foot played with a black slipper, lost and then found it. "I have to get busy," she said. The phone rang and she went to pick it up in the bedroom.

I rinsed my dishes and put them in the dishwasher. From Lillian's kitchen window, the Magothy looked benign, the early-morning sun creating white glints on the still water. The wind couldn't have been much. Was I going to live here in the Pines for a while? Rent Ray Tilghman's house until my aunt could find a bona fide buyer? I decided to go have another look at 1014 Weller's Creek Road. If there were ghosts there, I wanted to know about them.

My aunt was at her desk when I stopped by her office off the living room to get the keys to Ray's house. She had changed into her work clothes: a beige silk blouse with a soft bow and a navy-and-beige-plaid pleated linen skirt. A matching short jacket hung over the back of her office chair. Waving me away, she turned back to the pile of legal papers on the desk, the phone in her hand.

The village of Pines on Magothy was tranquil this Friday morning, hot and humid, but still bearable. A few people were out clearing tree branches downed in the storm or working in their gardens before the day's full noonday heat swept through. Will St. Claire's truck was parked in the clearing near his house when I drove up. Both dogs were sleeping in the pine needles outside his cottage, lazy in the steamy morning. The Chesapeake Bay retriever, Lancelot, ran to greet me. Black Zeke wasn't so sure. He stood back, waiting, dark murmurs coming from his throat. Maybe he was remembering yesterday. I was remembering, too.

The door to the bungalow opened and Will St. Claire came out. He was dressed in jeans and sneakers, with no shirt. He waved at me, then crouched down to discuss me with the Labrador. The black dog listened carefully, tipping its head. Why indeed had Ray Tilghman not given custody of his dogs to Will? Above us, a cicada began its long song, peaked, and fell silent. The pines smelled dark and living.

"He'll accept you now, I think." I was petting Lancelot, who clearly had no fears of me. The dog's back was damp, the dark rich brown curls of fur thick and a bit greasy. "Zeke has always been a bit more reserved," Will said.

The black dog came when I called. I carefully stroked his sleek head, as solemn brown dog eyes watched me. He may have accepted me, I thought, but he wasn't liking it much. "They went swimming earlier," said Will.

"Have the police been back?" I asked, uncomfortable suddenly that I was intruding. Glancing behind him and his cottage, I could see a freshly mounded heap of dirt, a cross made of two sticks tied together with rough twine and planted in the ground. He followed my glance.

"Hank Crouse was here this morning and took down all the yellow tapes at Ray's house and down at the creek. He said Ray drowned." He waited for a moment, as if wanting confirmation. I nodded. "I don't believe it," he said. "The dogs would have been with him at the creek. Lance here would have tried to rescue him." The dog, hearing his name, ran to him and stood waiting, ready to play.

"Everybody's saying that," I said. I wondered briefly if I should ask about his dog and decided against it. "What do you think happened?"

He shrugged. "I don't know. You going down there?" He pointed at the creek.

"Yes. I'd like to see the house, too. Lillian gave me the keys." His eyes were brilliant blue, not as dark as I remembered. He was black Irish, I thought, with light skin and dark hair and those unbelievable eyes. He walked to the front of the truck and pulled an old chambray work shirt from the cab and put it on, then turned to me.

"Mind if I come with you?"

"No." I was oddly glad for his company and that of the dogs running beside us, sniffing trees and stumps along the path. The Labrador had forgotten me, more interested in the smells left by others yesterday. There were tire tracks where some vehicle had turned around, breaking bushes on both sides of the path in the process. We passed Ray's house and continued down the winding path, the narrow swatch of water widening as we neared the creek.

I thought about yesterday afternoon and the afternoon before it. Both times, the hidden cove opened suddenly, then moments later surprised me with its gruesome scene. My first view today was no different, but this time the beach was empty. Tracks and footprints were the only remains of many people looking for something. On my left, the beach narrowed to nothing but a patch of woods and overgrown bushes, the waterfront lined with large rocks jutting into the creek to form what was almost a short jetty.

We walked down to the water, silent. The dogs were already swimming in the creek. Will leaned against the deformed sycamore tree, looking out to the trees on the other side of the cove.

"You going to buy the place?" he asked.

"No, no. Rent it maybe, for a few weeks or a month. Depends on the house, I guess," I said.

"The house needs work. I'd be happy to help you fix it up. Have to earn my rent-free bungalow, you know." It was the first time I'd seen him smile. It changed his face.

I nodded. "Thanks. Will, how come Ray didn't just give you custody of the dogs?"

"I don't know," he said. "Probably because I'm not from around here, so maybe he thought that I'd be leaving sooner or later."

"Will you?"

He shrugged. "I haven't yet, but now I don't know."

I asked to see the house. He signaled the dogs, who raced out of the water, shaking big drops over both of us.

Ray's house was larger than it looked from the outside. Will took the key from his pocket before I could fish out the one Lillian had given me. Stopping for a moment to check out the broken screen, he opened the front door and motioned for me to go in. The back of the door, I noticed, was covered with scratch marks where the dogs had tried desperately to get out. The stench was incredible. No one had bothered to clean up after them. Behind me, both Lance and Zeke waited on the porch. Maybe they had bad memories of being trapped in the house.

Will quickly opened windows on all sides, then went into the kitchen, returning with a bucket of water, paper towels, and disinfectant. We both went to work.

"This place should be okay when it's aired," he said. "The dogs must have been in here for eighteen or more hours."

I wondered where he had been during those hours, but I didn't ask. Standing up, he went back into the kitchen, returning with fresh water. I took it from him.

"Thanks, Will. It's a lot better in here already. I'll finish."

"Okay. I need to go to work anyway," he said. I nodded. "I do landscaping for some people around here." I was surprised somehow, then I remembered the rakes and shovels sticking up in the back of the pickup.

"How long have you been here?"

"Only about six months. It's a pretty nice place to live, if you can bear the heat and humidity." With that, he told me to leave the dogs in the house and to leave the windows open. He'd be back for them later in the afternoon.

CHAPTER
SEVEN

The foul smell was beginning to fade. On the far end of the main room was a stone fireplace. Nearby, a battered couch with extra pillows and blankets faced a couple of overstuffed chairs. Tables of different sizes were scattered about. One held an old-fashioned fringe-shaded lamp complete with metal chain to turn it on. Next to the lamp were a pair of reading glasses and several cups, a circle of brown liquid dried and coagulated in the bottom of each. I turned the lamp on, producing a small yellow circle of light near the chair. This must have been where Ray Tilghman spent his time, reading, drinking coffee, and caring for his dogs.

I sank down on the couch. The springs creaked. Behind me there was movement. I turned to see Lancelot standing in the open front door, Zeke behind him, waiting for an invitation. I whistled and both dogs came bounding, the retriever leaping onto the couch, turning several times and letting out a long sigh as he sank into the pillows at the far end. Black Zeke stood near me, still unsure. Both dogs were nearly dry and smelled sweetly of sun and salt water. I reached out my hand to the Labrador, who backed away slightly, then, watching me with his brown eyes, changed his mind and moved closer, sinking onto the floor against my feet, his face turned upward. A golden fleck in his left eye spun and melted away in the dim light.

I don't know how long I sat there, perhaps only minutes, maybe more. The dogs slept gently, lulled by the hot, unmoving air. Neither stirred when I leaned forward to stroke damp heads. It was odd, I thought, how restful Ray Tilghman's cottage was, despite the terrible events of the last two days. Looking around, I felt a sense of calm I hadn't felt in a long while, since long before Ben and I had begun to withdraw from each other. So deep was the peace, I could have slept there on the couch. Instead, I forced myself to inspect the rest of Ray's house.

The kitchen, with white porcelain-covered appliances, must have been new in the 1950s. Black metal now showed through worn spots in the wide, flat sink and on the stove burners. The refrigerator was small, rounded. Inside was a carton of milk, now sour, some eggs, a tub of margarine, and crusted bottles of condiments, long unused. Store-bought macaroni salad spoiled in a plastic container. On top of the refrigerator were half a dozen opened bags of cookies.

Across the room were white wooden shelves, brightened by Fiesta ware, the red, blue, green, and yellow dishes the only color in the room. A worn black-and-white-checked oilcloth covered the table. There were two unmatched wooden chairs. Turning to go, I found both dogs standing in the doorway. Surely Will had fed them.

"It's a trick to get a second breakfast, isn't it?" Lance wagged his tail. Zeke waited. I filled a bowl with fresh water. They ignored it. Then I handed them each a giant dog biscuit from a bag I found on the floor. Both went to work, Zeke watching me as he ate.

The bathroom was also vintage 1950s, but in better condition, the black-and-white diamond-shaped floor and wall tiles a little moldy but unbroken. There was a footed tub and no shower. Could I live without a shower? With some difficulty, I opened the window wide. Outside stood some short variety of pine tree, its long, soft needles touching the house.

The upstairs had two bedrooms and no bathroom. The only bed looked unused. Had Ray spent his nights on the couch in the living room, not feeling well enough to climb the stairs?

The dogs followed me up and were sniffing about. The second bedroom was filled with boxes and a set of agreeable white wicker furniture. I went back downstairs, wondering why a man who had plenty of money had lived like this. As pleasant as it was, in a shabby sort of way, it was also very primitive.

A phone rang. It took a bit of looking, but I found an old black dial instrument on the rolltop desk at the far side of the living room. It was Lillian, worried that I wasn't back yet. I reassured her and then sat in the swivel chair that went with the desk and looked around Ray Tilghman's living room. Maybe with a few changes and improvements, I could live here. It was sort of like summer camp. The smell had lifted and the spirits were friendly.

The steamy air, hanging heavily among the pines, had ratcheted up a few degrees in the last hour. I wanted to see the cove one more time, this time by myself. Walking down the pine needle–covered path to the creek, the dogs running along beside me, I felt less troubled than I had earlier walking this same path with Will. Perhaps because Ray's house had welcomed me, I now expected the cove would do so, too.

Sun and shadows played with each other as the trees swayed slightly. There was a slight breeze near the water. Half-sitting, half-leaning against the sycamore, I looked out at the creek, then watched the dogs run on the beach and in the woods. I could almost forget what had happened here yesterday, and the day before. There was a stillness here, in me and around me.

Lillian was waiting impatiently when I returned, stuffing her papers into her briefcase, carefully reapplying her lipstick.

"How did the house look to you? It's pretty primitive, I know, but I don't think it would take much to fix it up," she said. "Were there any ghosts?" She was watching me closely.

"Only ones I can live with. Will was there for a while. He

offered to help me fix things up. In fact, there's something almost magic about the place." I knew suddenly what it was: not the pines or the glistening water, but the golden fleck spinning in Zeke's eye, a tiny warm spot that had wormed its way into my heart. "Can I rent the house on a month-to-month basis?"

My aunt nodded. "Weller says that would be fine, just as long as you know that if the property is sold, you'd have to leave within a certain period of time."

I nodded. "I might be there for only a few weeks, or at the most, a couple of months. You know that? I haven't decided what to do about my job or even if I want to go back to advertising. But if I do, I will have to go back to New York."

I sat down on Lillian's brocade couch and looked across the room at my aunt. Her eyes changed, I thought, when I spoke of going back to New York. She needed me here. Well, I would cross that bridge when I came to it. I looked down and studied my hands and the place where my rings used to be, thinking about the river last night, about Will St. Claire putting on his work shirt as we stood among the pine trees, about the peaceful dog smell of Ray Tilghman's worn-out couch, about the searing song of the cicadas, about the tomatoes with the black crevices.

"Okay," I said. "Go ahead and draw up the rental contract."

For maybe the first time in my adult life, Lillian hugged me. It was awkward and we were both a little sorry. The gesture sat there between us for a minute, then she cleared her throat.

"I'm going to an AA meeting. Over at the Methodist church on Mountain Road. I haven't been there in a few months, but today I need to go." She picked up the narrow briefcase she had left on the floor by the wing chair.

"AA meeting? You?"

My aunt nodded. "You didn't know I am an alcoholic?" I shook my head, stunned. What else would I learn about this surprising aunt I thought I knew so well? For the second time, Lillian sat back down.

"I stopped drinking twenty-two years ago, so I don't talk

45

much about it anymore," she said. "But don't you remember the fight between your father and me? Of course, you must have been at college by then, so maybe you weren't around when it happened. But surely you wondered about it. Why our families weren't together at holidays?"

I sat still, not knowing if I had or hadn't wondered. Overwhelmed by the events of youth, I couldn't remember thinking much about it. My father had died of a heart attack the year after I went to college and my mother had, I knew, begun to visit Max and Lillian occasionally after his death. "I thought the fight had to do with . . . I don't know what I thought. It had to do with alcohol?"

"Your father didn't want to be around me. I was in AA and Jeremy didn't want to be reminded of that, since he was drinking more and more himself," she said. She was watching me closely again. "I guess I was pretty obnoxious. Recovering alcoholics usually are. There was a very bad scene. You weren't here, and I guess your parents never told you about it."

I was astounded. How could I not have known? "You have liquor around here, Lillian. And Weller was drinking just last night. You sat with me at the bar at the Lido Beach Inn. You serve beer and wine at your parties."

This time my aunt laughed. "I've been at this recovery business a very long time. It doesn't bother me so much anymore, not like it used to the first few years. I don't talk about it. That may be why you never knew. It is true that I could drink again at any minute, but I know it won't matter if there's booze in the house or not. What will matter is what's going on inside of me." Then she laughed again. "You can come to the meeting if you like."

"My father never acknowledged he drank too much," I said, unwilling to let the subject go. Lillian shook her head. "Did my mother know?"

"She knew, but I think she never really faced up to it."

My mother had died a few years after my father. A couple of

weeks before she died, she had told me how weary she was from her life alone. Busy with my career, I hadn't known.

Lillian was looking at her watch, the briefcase in her hand. "We can talk more about this later. If I'm going to make that meeting, I need to leave now. I will draw up a month-to-month rental contract for Ray Tilghman's property this afternoon. Be back in a few hours."

CHAPTER
EIGHT

Anxiety I hadn't felt at Weller's Creek Road swept over me as soon as Lillian closed the door. I had just agreed to rent Ray Tilghman's house and care for his dogs. A house in which an old man . . . an old man what? What was I afraid of? Ray Tilghman's ghost or living away from New York? Taking a leave of absence from the agency? Maybe leaving advertising for good? I didn't even know how to begin to think about it. And now there was Lillian's alcoholism. And my father's.

I poured myself a glass of juice and headed for the deck. The Magothy was almost white in the noonday sun. I thought some more about my father. Dependency was inherited. Was I a time bomb waiting to become a substance abuser? It seemed incredible in the daylight, but last night at the river I must have thought so when I poured the pills into the water. In the distance, an outboard motor coughed to life, then another. Around the front of the house, there was the crunch of tires on gravel, then a car door slammed.

"Anybody here?" A man rounded the corner of the house and stood below the deck. "I saw your car. I guess you didn't hear my knock. Mind if I come up? I guess you are Eve." He was already on the deck, pulling off his sunglasses and shoving them into the breast pocket of a black knit short-sleeved shirt with a turned-up collar. He must have been in his mid forties, obnoxiously good-looking, dark blond hair a little gray at the temples, clipped short by someone who didn't call himself a barber. Brokerage firms everywhere were overrun with guys who looked just like him. "I'm Mitch Gaylin," he said.

Mitch Gaylin, the Realtor who wanted to buy Weber Realty. I'd forgotten to ask Lillian about her meeting with him. "My aunt isn't here," I said.

"I know. Caddy's not in the drive. I tease Lillian about driving that living room on wheels. Mind if I sit down?" I shook my head. He slouched into a deck chair. "I heard you were going to be helping Lillian out."

"You did? Where did you hear that?"

He pretended to think about it. "I don't really know. Anne Arundel County is a big place. And I talk to a lot of people."

"So I hear."

"You've been here before?"

"For a few days, now and again, over the years."

"If you like the water, you'll like it. Have you been to Annapolis yet?" he asked. I shook my head. "It's a little overrun with tourists this time of year, but I know some crab places that are off the beaten path." He had another thought. "Do you sail? We could go out some evening. Night sailing is best this time of year. You don't get fried by the sun. Not like this." He held out his forearms. They were deeply tanned and covered with blond hairs.

"I don't sail," I said. Ben had loved sailing, too. He'd even bought a small sailboat. Maybe if I had been more interested . . . My mind began to explore paths untaken when Mitch Gaylin cleared his throat, bringing me back to the present. What did this guy want? He had been here about one minute and he was asking me out. His eyes were deep brown, frank.

"Doesn't matter. I can teach you. You look like you're in good shape. Should be a breeze." He was looking me up and down but trying not to let it show. There was a short silence. "Too bad about Ray Tilghman. I heard you found the body yesterday. That's rough." He made sympathetic sounds. "I heard about the dead dog, too."

"You seem to have heard a lot." I stood up. "I think my aunt is at her office. I was just getting ready to leave." He scrambled to his feet, putting his sunglasses back on in one motion.

"Oh, sorry. The sailing offer is good anytime, by the way. As long as there's some wind. Just let me know."

I watched him disappear around the house. What had he been fishing for? And where had he heard that I was going to help Lillian at Weber Realty? The net was twisting tighter, with even her competition helping to entangle me. Maybe I should stop struggling.

After putting my glass in the sink, I changed clothes and wondered what I was going to do until Lillian returned. Maybe I could do something useful, like getting us dinner.

I headed for the car, still thinking about Mitch Gaylin. Maybe I was reading things into his visit. Maybe he was just being friendly. Maybe he wasn't fishing at all.

Fifteen minutes later, I found myself driving past an overbuilt commercial strip lined with car dealerships, shopping malls, fast-food restaurants, and discount stores. The occasional local shop looked very small and weird and out of place. Traffic was terrible, even midday. I pulled into a parking lot and got out my map. I was on something named Governor Ritchie Highway. If I was going to shop, this was apparently the place. I looked around for a super-market but didn't see one.

Pulling the car around I noticed a sign. FREE REAL ESTATE CLASSES FORMING. INQUIRE INSIDE. I pulled over again, sitting for a few seconds in the car before getting out. Maybe I should learn something about real estate if I was going to help Lillian.

The woman at the front desk was wearing a lime green two-piece outfit and what looked like an all-purpose smile. She greeted me with enthusiasm.

"You're in luck. Our intensive classes are beginning next week. Monday through Wednesday mornings for four weeks. Then you take the national licensing test." She paused dramatically, holding my eyes. "Our students have a ninety percent pass rate. Then you can affiliate with a broker and begin your new career."

My new career. From creating advertising to sell diapers for adults, greasy snack food, malt liquor, and banking services, now I was going to sell houses and trees and land? Did I really want to get mixed up in all the dirty little financial and personal secrets that plagued people when they bought a house? Part of what I had always loved about advertising was the chance it offered to stay out of messy individual lives. Advertising was interested only in making the faceless crowd buy things, something I was very good at. But could I sell real houses to real people?

"It's absolutely free," said the lime green woman behind the desk, "and there is no obligation although you might want to consider a career with us. Our Realtors do very well."

"What do I have to do?"

"Just leave me your name and phone number. Then be here Monday morning at nine. Bring a notebook and a calculator and forty dollars for the textbook." I left my name and Lillian's number and walked to the car. I realized I didn't even know the name of the place. I turned around. PACKER KING REALTORS. I had seen their black-and-purple for-sale signs stuck in lawns in front of houses.

I traced my way back in the direction of Pines on Magothy, past a bait shop, past a bungalow with a hand-lettered sign that read DEER CUT AND WRAPPED. I began to see familiar landmarks. Lyle's Market appeared on my right. Below its large sign was another: TRY OUR FAMOUS BARBECUED CHICKEN.

Lyle's sold everything, from food and drugstore items to liquor and greeting cards. Out front, there were bags of peat moss along with garden rakes and plastic-webbed lawn chairs and baskets of hanging plants looking a little wilted in the heat. Inside, the aisles were crammed. I grabbed a shopping cart.

Two elderly women with upswept bluish hair stood blocking the bread aisle with their carts. The heavy one leaned near her thinner friend. "I don't think the police are going to do anything," she said, "but for my money, Ray Tilghman didn't drown. Why else would that girl from New York have found the dogs in his house?" Why else? I thought. The other woman hauled her rebellious cart out of my way. I thanked her.

"And you remember that actress years ago?" Her friend nodded knowingly. The thin woman lowered her voice. "And did you hear about the dead dog?" she asked her friend. "Makes you wonder is all I can say. Police ought to look into it. Dollars to doughnuts . . ." Jostled by a shopper coming in the other direction, I couldn't hear the rest of the sentence.

I swept past the vegetables. How could everybody be so sure that Ray Tilghman hadn't just this once left the dogs in the house? Maybe he didn't want them to go swimming. Maybe . . . well, anything was possible. Sometimes people just do things for no reason. If almost twenty years in advertising had taught me anything, it was that people are unpredictable. But apparently people in Pines on Magothy didn't think that way. I headed toward the prepared foods.

Lyle's had the smell of a store whose standards of cleanliness were maybe just a fraction below that of all those famous national stores on Ritchie Highway. Not enough to raise the ire of the inspectors, perhaps, just enough to make my nose twitch. Nevertheless, I picked up a couple of prepared salads and the famous barbecued chicken and got in the checkout line.

In front of me was Hank Crouse, in uniform, his hat in his bandaged hand. He didn't appear to be buying anything and he didn't see me at first.

"Officer Crouse," I began. He turned around, not smiling. "I'm Eve Elliott . . . I was just—"

"Yes, Miss Elliott, I know. You were just what?"

"Wondering if you had any more information about Ray Tilghman's death."

"I would have thought you'd have heard by now. What with Weller stoppin' by this morning." He looked at me closely. "Our investigation established that the victim drowned accidentally." His face then softened somewhat, but it cost him something. "I'm sorry you had to find the body. That's tough. And I know it's hard on Lil. Is she holdin' up okay?"

"I guess so, though she's upset, naturally. Ray was her friend." He nodded. "Is the case closed, then?"

"Yes, there's nothing there."

"What about the dogs locked in his house? Everybody says that Mr. Tilghman never, ever went down to the creek without the dogs." His expression tightened. It had the effect of making his face smoother and younger under his prematurely gray hair.

"There is no evidence, Miss Elliott, that Ray Tilghman ran into any foul play. He was an old, sick man who didn't want to leave his property and go into a nursing home. He went down to the creek without his dogs, a storm came up, and he accidentally fell in and drowned. It's tragic, but that's all. People do things sometimes that we don't expect."

Exactly what I had been telling myself five minutes ago. Why did it sound so unlikely when Hank Crouse said it? The line moved up. Hank Crouse bought a roll of breath mints and while the clerk made change, he turned back to me.

"Try to put it out of your mind, Miss Elliott. Lillian could use your help right now. I know she's been swamped at work since Max died, and I know she's worried about losing Weber Realty. Everybody's glad you're here to help her." With that, he left, putting his hat on before he exited the store.

"That will be fifteen seventy-three," said the clerk. I handed him money, took my change, and, carrying my bag, went to the car. Running steps came up behind me.

"Excuse me." I turned, to find a blond woman in her late

thirties, dressed in a gray linen suit and lizard pumps. "I'm sorry, but I couldn't help overhearing your conversation with Hank Crouse. Did something happen to Mr. Tilghman?"

"He drowned two nights ago in the creek, down by his cove." I stopped, waiting.

"I'm sorry," she said again, this time holding out her hand. "You don't know me. I'm Lindsay Blackburn. My husband, Hal, and I own the property next to him. We are here for the weekend and this is the first we heard. Everybody in Lyle's is talking about it. What happened?"

I explained about Ray, about who I was, and then answered a few questions. She shifted her bag of groceries from hip to hip, shaking her head at the story.

"It sounds like a dreadful death." She glanced over her shoulder at a man carrying a case of imported beer, which he deposited in the trunk of a dark green Saab 900.

"Hal?" A man who could have been a high school coach in a business suit walked toward us. "Hal, this is Eve Elliott. She's Lillian Weber's niece and she found Ray Tilghman's body in the cove."

"I heard inside that the old boy drowned. Maybe we can get our house and dock done now."

"Hal . . . he was just an old man who was trying to protect his way of life. . . ."

"He was an old man who made our life a living hell since Mitch sold us the property eleven months ago. Have you forgotten the time and money he cost us, to say nothing of the dead squirrels?" He looked at me directly. "For the first six months, every weekend we'd come here, we'd find a dead squirrel or something, in various stages of decay, on the front step. My wife seems to have forgotten this."

"You think Ray Tilghman put dead squirrels on your front step?" I asked.

"No, not personally, but I think he or some other Neanderthal in Pines on Magothy put that weasel of a kid up to it. Have you met Gilbert yet? He's a real piece of work."

"Hal . . . he's retarded; he can't help it." I had a feeling a lot of conversations between them went this way.

"Of course, they don't discriminate among outsiders here," Hal said. "There are a couple of other new property owners in the Pines, and I've heard they had their share of dead squirrels."

"But why dead squirrels?"

"The ultimate redneck form of communication. These people think that they have the right to use the water, whether or not they own the property. I don't think so." Lindsay had the good grace to look embarrassed. Hal saw the look. "Go right ahead and say I'm not being a good neighbor. You want Gilbert hanging around?"

We stood talking for a few more minutes. They looked at me with new interest when I said I was from New York and staying around for a while to help Lillian out.

"Well," said Hal, "you really ought to get a real estate license. Anne Arundel County is a great place to do business. Lots of turnover and lots of people in D.C. looking for weekend homes on the water. Old Ray have a will?" he asked.

"Hal . . ."

"Yes, he did."

Hal Blackburn laughed. "Well, someone's going to get rich. It's the best parcel of land around, larger and more private, even better than the one on the other side of us, and Mitch says that's going to go for a half mil."

With that, Hal decided he'd chatted in the parking lot long enough. Lindsay issued a blanket invitation to stop by anytime. I watched the Saab pull away.

CHAPTER
NINE

I dragged the last of the wicker furniture out of the living room and onto Ray Tilghman's front porch. In two sixteen-hour days, with the help of Will St. Claire, the house had been transformed from a dank summer camp to a livable cabin in the pines. It was still rustic, but many gallons of hot, soapy water and some fresh paint had helped. Will had even promised to build me an outdoor shower. My anxieties had gone underground, driven away by hard physical labor. A certain sadness still hung over the hidden cove, but no ghosts had spoiled my peace.

My aunt was sitting in a small rocker, sipping iced tea she'd brought in a big thermos and thumbing through a small pile of legal papers she'd pulled out of her briefcase. A ballpoint pen was stuck in the bouffant hair over her right ear. "I've gone over everything with Weller again. He plans to stop by, but it's all in order. I will need you to sign these." She dragged a small table a few inches closer.

My heart unexpectedly flew away. This was it, and all of a sudden I wasn't sure. I hadn't called Joe Lister for a formal leave of absence from the agency or even told Ben that I wouldn't be living in New York for a bit. My uncertainty about renting Ray Tilghman's place had faded over the last two days. I had enjoyed the hard work, the play with the dogs, the small talk with Will. Now suddenly, I didn't know about staying in Maryland. I hoped Lillian couldn't read my eyes. I took the pen she offered, then leaned back in my chair, stalling for time.

"Tell me about Ray's will?" I asked. "Doesn't it have to go to probate?"

"I don't know, actually. But it doesn't matter. The money from the sale of his property, which he held free and clear of encumbrances, will go into a trust," she said. "I do know you can do anything you want with a will and trust and a good lawyer. And Weller's a very good lawyer."

"Who or what is his money in trust for? Since Ray had no heirs, who gets the money?"

"In twelve years, from the day of his death, the trust will distribute the money to his beneficiaries, a foundation to save the Chesapeake Bay, I think, and a local animal shelter."

"Why twelve years?"

My aunt looked down at the dogs sleeping at our feet. Zeke opened one eye. "Because by then, Zeke and Lancelot will no longer be alive." I didn't understand. "That's in case whoever buys the property doesn't take proper care of them or has to sell the property back to the trust. That's provided for in the sales contract." With a long red-polished nail, she carefully scratched her scalp through the teased pouf of hair. "Of course, that probably won't happen, but Ray was a careful man."

"This is bizarre, you know." Lillian nodded. "Just how much money are we talking about in Ray's estate?" I asked.

"About a million or a little better, I should think. As you well know, he didn't spend much." She leaned down to stroke Lancelot, who yawned and stretched and went back to sleep. "Ray was eccentric. And eccentric people who have money can do what they choose."

"And yet he chose to live like this." I pointed to a huge heap of musty overstuffed furniture and dozens of boxes of clothes and magazines and household goods waiting at one end of the porch to be hauled away. The man hadn't bought anything new in years. "What was he like, Lillian?"

"I would want to know the answer to that, too, given the fact that you are going to live here." She sat back in her chair. "He, not Max, was the person who helped me get sober. He was my AA sponsor, helping me through that terrible first year when I wasn't drinking and crazy as a loon. I can't tell you, Eve, how many times I've sat on this porch talking half the night as Ray listened." She sipped iced tea.

"Marian said he wasn't very neighborly to outsiders." I tipped my head in the direction of the house down the road. There hadn't been any hammering over the weekend.

"Ray didn't like change much. And he usually didn't like people on his property. And he didn't like a whole bunch of other things. But he was my friend and I'm going to miss him."

"Is the property posted?" I asked.

"Yes, of course, but even though it's private property, most people here are more neighborly about their land than Ray was. He hated it when people went down to his cove." She paused, thinking. "I wonder if it wasn't because the beach was often a sort of lovers' lane, with high school kids sneaking down there at night. Nobody could see them from the water or the other side, of course, but Ray would hear them and chase them off sometimes."

"What about Gilbert?" I asked.

"Oh, Gilbert, that was a constant battle. Ray didn't like him and was forever chasing him off."

"And he was within his rights to do so?"

"Yes."

I was getting a picture of a crotchety old man, unhappy with most people, fighting change with everything he had.

"As he got older and sicker, he became more of a recluse, only going to AA meetings, and not even many of those in recent years," said Lillian. "I've always thought that something about that accident all those years ago must have affected him deeply. He never was physically the same, certainly. A crane hit him in the back. It caused him great pain, but he wouldn't take medication because he was afraid of getting addicted to the narcotics."

"Which happened first," I asked, "the accident or AA?"

"The accident. I think it got him to AA. It was back in 1969, and he had been sober since then."

"Was he sober when he found Penny Hart's body?" I asked.

Lillian looked at me for a moment, her expression unreadable. "Yes, yes, he was. He had just returned from an AA meeting, in fact."

Weller Church's old Lincoln pulled into the clearing. We watched as the lawyer got out and stood looking for a moment in the direction of the slice of creek visible from the clearing, the creek that was named for his mother's family. He turned and strode toward the cottage. A squirrel scampered in front of him.

The lawyer sat down in the chair next to Lillian, a little wearily, I thought, his color high. "The old place looks quite fine. You have obviously been busy."

"There's still a lot to do. Will helped a lot."

He nodded. Lancelot was standing by his chair and he vigorously scratched the dog's ears. Zeke sat down again by my legs, leaning heavily. I had learned that Zeke didn't sit much on his own accord, finding it easier to lean on whatever or whoever was next to him. "The dogs seem to have taken to you," he said. "And Ezekiel there is not always easily won over."

"And I've taken to them," I said. "Why is his name Ezekiel?"

"When he was a puppy, he chased cars. Ezekiel and the wheel," said Lillian. She turned to Weller. "You look all in."

"I am, you know," he said. "Deer problem again. They are completely out of control. And getting rid of them is such an emotional issue." He turned to me. "We have to cull the population on Arundel Island some years. We do it humanely with professional marksmen, but it raises a hue and cry in the community. I just came from a meeting. The board has decided not to announce it in advance this year, except to the few of us who live on the island.

I'm not sure this is democracy in action, but they think it will make things easier. I think it's bound to leak out, and then I don't want to see the newspaper headlines."

The lawyer pulled out a fresh handkerchief, carefully unfolded it, and wiped his face, then, folding it back, tucked it away. His bow tie had gone askew in the process.

Lillian pointed in the direction of the lease and the pen I was still holding. "Well, at least we can get this lease done so you can go home." I glanced at my watch. It was almost 8:30. The sun was nearly gone, the day's heat subsiding. I might not even need the large window fan Lillian had brought me to use until I could get an air conditioner.

In a few minutes, we were done. Weller had explained my responsibilities again about vacating Ray's house if a buyer was found. I didn't have any questions. The dogs were now my temporary charges. I had agreed to rent the property for what by New York standards seemed almost a joke, less than it cost Ben to garage the BMW on West Eighty-third Street. I wrote Lillian a check for the first month's rent, plus my security deposit.

What was left was to tie up all the many loose ends of my life in New York. I'd had a talk with my lawyer last night. Now I needed to talk with Ben and to Joe Lister, two conversations I wasn't exactly looking forward to.

"Don't be surprised if your moving in here raises some eyebrows in the community," Weller said to me. "People around here are suspicious about outsiders. But since you're Lil's niece, I doubt if anyone will say anything to you."

"Don't worry about it, Eve," said my aunt. "People know that the dogs need care and that I've had Ray's property listed for almost five months now. I've had a million calls about it, but the buyer who backed out a few days ago was the only serious offer I'd had. The condition about the dogs just puts people off." Zeke turned over in his sleep, grunting wearily. "Selling this place isn't going to get any easier, I don't suppose," she said to no one in particular.

When they left, I tried to feel as if I had just done something good for myself, as Weller remarked I should. I was not only going to help Lillian but at the same time get away from the pressures of New York and give myself time to think and make some decisions. I sat on the porch, listening to the birds singing in the dark, half-way between numb with relief and paralyzed with misgivings.

What about the co-op apartment in New York? It was on Central Park West, near the Museum of Natural History. In winter, when the trees were bare, you could look out the eleventh-story window and see people in the park below. How many evenings had Ben and I stood there, tired from the day's work and relaxing with glasses of wine, watching the lights. It had been grand, but those evenings were gone now. I reminded myself that whether or not I stayed in New York, they were gone. There might be another man, I thought, and we might stand at the window, but that man would not be Ben. The sorrow that I had been drowning with Valium washed over me.

When the night dropped down and surrounded the house, the dogs went for a last run and then joined me again on the porch, Zeke leaning against my legs and Lancelot sleeping heavily a few feet away. I sat for a few minutes longer, thinking about nothing, then went inside. Things were certainly going to be different now.

CHAPTER
TEN

I knew I couldn't put off phoning Ben any longer. Sitting in Ray's swivel chair, I dialed. His voice greeted me again on the answering machine, telling me to call another number. This time he picked up on the first ring. In a few words, I explained I was staying in Maryland for a while longer.

"What about the car?" he asked.

"The car? I have the car."

"We didn't talk about it, Eve. We were supposed to talk about it first—before you just took it. What am I supposed to use?"

"You could rent a car, Ben, like everyone else in New York." He made a strangled noise I hadn't heard before. I made a quick decision. "Actually, I plan to buy a car, so you can have it back. Which brings me to why I called."

I could hear a muffled discussion at the other end. He wasn't listening. Ben rarely paid full attention on the phone, as he was usually busy talking to someone in the room at the same time. For too many years that person in the room had been me. It drove me crazy. Now I sat holding the heavy old rotary phone receiver, realizing it no longer mattered.

"I'm back," he said.

"I called because I am going to try to get back to New York at the end of this week—to get my clothes and make a few arrangements. Thursday, probably. We need to meet. At Peter's office. Are you—"

He had disappeared again, talking to someone in the room. I thought instead about Peter. Peter Fox. He was my lawyer and my friend of many years. I had called him last night to tell him that I might be in Maryland for a while and to talk over finances and legalities. Poor Peter. He had been surprised at first, then reminded me to consider carefully how this would affect my career. He didn't think money would be a problem. Over the years, Ben and I had amassed more money than we needed, what with his media-consultant work for ABC News and my rising star in advertising. We'd work out the specifics of our financial life when I got back to New York to sign the separation papers.

"Am I what?" Ben asked.

"It would be nice if you could just this once manage to listen to one complete sentence. Is that possible?" All the anger I thought I had dealt with surfaced. And the sadness and longing I'd felt about him and our marriage just a few minutes ago had fled. We needed to be apart.

"I am coming up to New York on Thursday." One sentence and he was still listening. I tried another. "I need to get my clothes, talk to Joe Lister, and make arrangements to get my mail and pay my bills." Two sentences. "Will you meet me in Peter's office on Thursday afternoon to sign the papers and tie up a few more details?"

"Sure." I was surprised. It must have been the car. I decided to wait and tell him that I had signed a lease to rent the Weller's Creek Road cottage. I didn't know if I would tell him about Ray Tilghman and how he died. I hung up before he could, still feeling angry. Was it going to be possible to ever be friends again?

Feeling restless, I decided to see the cove at night, to clear the conversation with Ben from my head and heart. Would Ray's ghost be waiting for me at the sycamore tree? It wasn't. Instead, there was a partial moon and the water lapped lightly at the beach. The air was cooler and less humid than it had been since I arrived. The dogs ran in circles.

I walked to the end of the dock and sat down, a dog on either side. Lancelot looked longingly at the water. I shook my head. Suddenly, in the direction of the Blackburns' house, came the sounds of a piano sonata, Schubert maybe, very faint, aching and slow. It was a relief from the country and rock music that permeated northern Anne Arundel County and it made me feel more sympathetic to my weekend neighbors from D.C. When the piece ended, I sat in the silence for a few seconds, hoping that something else equally wonderful would drift across the trees. Nothing did and I walked back up to the house, more tired than I realized. My first real estate class was tomorrow morning. I wondered why I hadn't told Lillian about it.

It was only just after ten. I took my first bath in the footed tub, leaning back in the soapy water, listening to the pine needles scrape across the window as the breeze off the water came up. The dogs sat side by side in the door, watching. Things were okay, I told myself, just different.

I sank into Ray Tilghman's double bed, dogs sprawled alongside on the floor. Zeke then changed his mind and launched himself up next to me. I lay quiet for a while, drifting near sleep, my thoughts jumping randomly from the old man who had drowned in the storm, to Lillian's business deals and Weller Church's bow tie, to the strangled white dog, and then back to Ben's bad habits and Will's penetrating blue eyes, to piano sonatas and lapping water.

There was a noise from downstairs. Zeke growled low in his throat. Lancelot struggled to his feet and shook himself awake. The clock said just after eleven. I had been asleep less than an hour. Another noise came again from below, outside, in the front of the house.

I threw on my shirt and shorts, then realized my sneakers

were in the bathroom. Zeke whined loudly. The Chesapeake Bay retriever was already down the stairs. I looked around for something to grab. In the upstairs hall was an old lamp without a shade. Clutching it, the cord and plug dragging behind me, I inched down to the first floor and through the darkened living room. No lights showed outside. Lance was at the front door, sniffing. Zeke held back, pushing against my legs, blocking my way.

I stopped and listened. No sounds came from the yard or porch. Through the windows I could see the outlines of the wicker furniture I'd found in Ray's upstairs storeroom. If there was anything in the front yard, I thought, it was probably just a wild animal. Will St. Claire had warned me about raccoons shaking the lids off garbage cans, rabid raccoons sometimes. The dogs, he had assured me, were vaccinated. Another tiny noise came from the clearing. The dogs bristled, on full alert.

"It's nothing," I said. This was ridiculous. "Look, I'll show you." Pushing the dogs behind me, I unlocked the front door that led to the screened porch and stepped out. Under my foot was something cold and wet and dead. There was a faint smell of flesh beginning to spoil. In front of me, the screen door was swinging open on its hinges. A scream filled my ears, my own scream. I felt the lamp slip out of my hand and break as it hit the floor. Slamming the door shut, I ran to turn on the light by Ray's desk. My toes were covered with blood. I had made wet prints on the wood floor. Lancelot stood at the door whining. Zeke barked once.

I picked up Ray's heavy black phone and dialed 911, giving my address and name to the operator and then hanging up. I could think of only one thing. Half-running and limping toward the bathroom, I stuck my foot in the tub and turned on the hot water. Zeke watched as I scrubbed, first frantically with my hands and then with a sponge and soap. Slowly, my revulsion quieted. Drying off and putting on my sneakers, I sat down on the edge of the tub to wait. Both dogs watched me anxiously. What had someone put on my porch?

Bright lights swept into the clearing within minutes. I got up and looked out. A cop I hadn't seen before got out of his cruiser, his flashlight in his hand, and, looking around, headed for the house.

"Hello. . . . Oh God . . ." The rest of his sentence as he walked onto the porch was lost to the dogs barking.

Putting them behind me, I commanded that they sit and stay. To my surprise, they did. I opened the door, to find a young blond cop staring at a bloody rat, thick and squat and bludgeoned so badly that its insides had spilled onto Ray's hemp welcome mat. The blood trailed in an arc on the floor from the broken screen door to where the thing had landed.

"I'll be right back," the cop commanded. "You stay in there." I closed the door. Someone had thrown a bloody rat on my porch. I sat down again. The dogs whined desperately, searching my face for an explanation. The cop came back, carefully opening the door and closing it behind him.

"What happened?" I asked him, keeping the dogs beside me. He was very young and serious, with a blond crew cut. "This is Ray Tilghman's place, isn't it?" He made some notes in a little note-book. "There's nobody out there now. I'm afraid, Miss"—he checked his notebook—"Elliott, I don't really know what else I can do."

"Get rid of the rat, maybe?"

"Okay, yes, I can do that." He put his notebook away and gingerly opened the door again. I wondered if Hank Crouse would have been so kind. The young cop was gone a few long minutes.

"I had to throw away the mat," he said. "And I checked down at the cove, too. Nothing there."

"Thank you." I could still see the tracks my bloody toes had left on the worn wood floor. His eyes followed mine.

"Will you be okay?" he asked. "I don't want to scare you, but there's been a problem with this kind of thing before. Though we haven't seen it in awhile."

"Dead squirrels at the Blackburns' house? Gilbert Bodine's work?"

He looked surprised, then shook his head up and down. "Well, yes, though I don't actually know if there's proof it was Gilbert. It's pretty hard to find out. Sort of hit-and-run."

"And Will St. Claire's dog?" I asked. "Do the police think that was Gilbert, too?"

"The police weren't called about that," he said, "but I hear people around here have been wondering."

I tried another question. "Only newcomers find dead animals on their front doorsteps, right?"

He studied me, slowly agreeing. "Are you here by yourself?" I nodded. A look of something crossed his face. "Well, you've got the dogs. But if I were you, I'd . . ." He stopped, considering. "I mean, if you were my sister or something, I'd . . ."

"What? Get a gun?"

"Well . . . yes. You have to protect yourself."

"I think I'll rely on the dogs," I said.

"Suit yourself." He nodded and left. I heard the cruiser's engine turn over, then die. As I watched, he got back out of the car and returned to the house. I opened the door.

He glanced around the room, his eyes lighting on the old phone. "You could at least put in an extension upstairs, if you need it. And get yourself a better lock on the door tomorrow."

"That's a good idea. I will. Thank you."

I felt better, more, I thought, because of the young cop than his suggestions. I went to work cleaning up the blood and broken glass, thinking that the streets of New York were downright safe and welcoming compared with this.

CHAPTER
ELEVEN

I threw the sponge back in the pail of soapy water and stood up to study the wet boards on the porch. Will St. Claire's truck slowly made its way into the clearing, its headlights shining through the porch screens, distorting my shadow against the dark walls in a wavering circular motion as he turned around and parked. Looking thin in his jeans and white T-shirt, his hair damp, Will walked toward the house in long strides. The dogs whined to be let out, greeting him joyfully and running in rings around his legs.

"I saw the police cruiser. Something happen?" He looked around the porch, seeing my pail and sponge.

"Someone threw a dead rat on the porch. So I'm back to cleaning," I said. "Did you hear anybody or see any cars go by?"

He shook his head. "I was reading. I only saw the lights as the cop went past the house and down the road here. What happened?" he asked again.

I repeated the story. He was standing on the steps leading up to the front porch, holding the broken screen open as we talked. The dogs danced in front of him and bugs streamed to the yellow porch light attached overhead. There was a rifle shot from somewhere, hard to tell if it was near or far. He seemed not to notice.

"This isn't the first time this has happened, is it?" I asked. I could feel anger rising, replacing fear. "Throwing dead animals in front of someone's house. I know that the Blackburns found dead squirrels when they first moved next door. And other people did, too. Why is Gilbert doing this?" He batted at the mist of bugs above him and stepped onto the porch, closing the screen door behind him as best he could. "Just to get us to leave? Is he doing it of his own accord?"

He stood in silence, hands at his sides, his face expressionless, a trace of dark beard visible. Then he shrugged. "I'm sorry that it happened," he said.

"I'd also like to know why so many bad things are happening around here," I said. "Like Ray drowning. Like your dog being killed."

His face remained calm but the blue eyes clouded. He sat down wearily on the edge of a wicker couch, the dogs near him. Zeke leaned against his legs.

"Will, are these events related? Nobody is saying anything, not even my aunt."

He sat still, studying the wet floor where the bloody rat had been. "Don't you even want to know why Ray drowned?" I asked. "I know everybody around here thinks that it wasn't an accident. Because the dogs were still in the house. Only the police have no other proof and so nobody is going to try to find anything out."

I couldn't see his face anymore. He was looking straight down, head in his hands, curls of dark hair spurting through the fingers wound tightly at the back of his neck.

"And what about your dog?" I asked, too exasperated now with his silence to care if it pained him. "I saw the rope around her neck, Will. She was strangled. Does someone want you to leave, too?" His shoulders were quiet, tense. "Are you just going to let it go?"

He finally looked at me, his face empty but his eyes full of some emotion I couldn't begin to describe. He stood up, disturbing Zeke, who jumped back, uncertain of what he had done.

"Yes. And so should you," he said. He walked to the screen door, running his hand over the broken hinge. "I'll fix this tomorrow." He turned back to me. "Will you be okay tonight?"

"Yes, I'll be okay." What would he have done if I'd said no? He turned then and walked to the clearing. The breeze was strong, the trees brushing against each other. The dogs stood at the broken screen door, silent, watching him climb into the old truck.

I locked the front door and feeling uncertain and no longer sleepy, I sat in Ray Tilghman's wing chair, turning on the nearby light. Will knew something about what was going on here, something he wasn't going to tell me. And Lillian and Weller Church probably knew the same thing and they weren't telling me. But surely Lillian wouldn't have rented me the house if she knew I would be in danger.

Was I in danger? Tonight was the first time it had occurred to me. The dogs were comfortingly near, Lancelot sleeping on the slate floor in front of the fireplace, Zeke lying at my feet. Were all newcomers to Pines on Magothy in danger? My mind rejected the notion. This wasn't, after all, the rural South. Washington was only a hour away, for God's sake. No, it was something else, something specific. I leaned back in Ray Tilghman's old chair. It was comfortable. Maybe I'd keep it, have it re-covered. I got up and walked around the room, still not sleepy. I recognized the desire to get something down on paper, to write in order to discover what I thought. I wished I had a computer. Why hadn't I brought my laptop?

Sitting down at the rolltop desk, swiveling in the office chair, I studied the pigeonholes and opened the drawers, looking for a pad. Ray's desk was the one thing in the house I hadn't cleaned out. Lillian would turn his papers over to Weller, she said, although she doubted that he had kept anything of value, like stock certificates, in his house. A clock in a bell jar on the desk said quarter after twelve.

The smell of old lead pencils emanated from the large drawer on the left. It was crammed with fraying legal-size ledgers. Beneath them was a yellowed newspaper—not a clipping, but the whole paper. I sat back in the swivel chair to read.

The newspaper was called the *Magothy Leader* and the date was August 25, 1969. The scrolling and graceful headline said LOCAL GIRL DROWNS IN WELLER'S CREEK. The story was written by one Ward Justice, who reported that Penny Hart, a 1968 graduate of Magothy Bridge Road High School with a promising New York stage career, had accidentally drowned in Weller's Creek. Her body had been found by Ray Tilghman, owner of the property. He had given her permission to use his beach that Sunday afternoon. Her towel, shorts, shirt, and sandals, plus the script of a stage play and her sunglasses, were found on the beach. Since she was known to be a strong swimmer, no one knew why she had drowned. Her parents had been interviewed and they confirmed she had gone to church and eaten dinner with them before going to the Weller's Creek cove for the afternoon: to sun, swim, and memorize her part in a new Off-Broadway play.

I put the old newspaper down on the desk. I remembered my aunt's lecture on stigmatized property. Ray Tilghman had found Penny Hart's body and I'd found his. A shudder passed through me. The dogs drew closer, steady and comforting.

I wondered about Will. Did he know about Penny Hart? He was an outsider, but, like the Pines on Magothy residents who had lived here their whole lives, he became remote when I asked too many questions. I remembered his grief at the beach when he'd found his dog. That hadn't been remote. It had been excruciating and immediate. Who was Will St. Claire? I remembered he said he'd lived in the Pines less than six months.

My body sagged with exhaustion, but the events of the day would not retreat. Why, I thought, do people do what they do? I reviewed all of the motives I knew so well from my advertising days: greed, love, revenge, the desire to protect a self-image or avoid embarrassment, insecurity, curiosity, fear. Years ago, when I had been a young copywriter, Joe Lister had suggested I go down through the list whenever I was stuck for ideas. Focus on one or the other, he had said, direct every sales pitch to satisfying or defending oneself from one of these basic human motives. He had never been wrong.

Now as I sat in Ray Tilghman's chair, I thought of this advice and then of the events of the last few days, of how little I knew about what really had happened. Faces of people I had only just met drifted in front of me: Ray Tilghman, Marian Beall, Hal and Lindsay Blackburn, Weller Church, Russell and Hank Crouse, Will St. Claire, Shirley Bodine, Gilbert, Mitch Gaylin. And then there was Lillian.

I thought of love and revenge and greed. Money. Ray Tilghman's land was very valuable and whoever bought it would buy for a fraction of what it was worth in return for caring for the dogs until they died. Undoubtedly, others wanted the land—Mitch Gaylin certainly did—and he probably wasn't the only one. Had someone killed Ray for his property? My mind said no. It was too crazy, and besides, Ray dead was no better for anybody than Ray alive, if you considered the conditions.

I longed for relief from the relentless questions. I paced around the room, aware I was getting more entangled in events I didn't understand. And now I was also trapped in Ray Tilghman's house. A jolt of anger suddenly went through me. I hadn't thrown away a bottle of Valium to be held captive by anything or anybody, dead or alive.

"Come on, Lance. Zeke." I opened the door and the dogs ran into the pine-needled clearing in the trees, happy to be free and out in the night. I strode after them, heading in the direction of the cove again. The breeze was up a little, cooling my neck and face. Was it just a few hours before when I had been here?

The moon had risen higher and brighter in the sky, illuminating the water and cove. A cloud passed overhead, momentarily darkening the beach as I came out of the woods and stood looking at the scene. The dogs circled about, sniffing. I called them to me, hoping their desire to please me was stronger than their desire to swim.

On the night air came the low sound of two people talking. A woman laughed. I looked down the curving beach to my left, at the spot where it faded into dense woods and heavy rocks that jutted perilously out into the water. I could just barely see two figures holding each other. The woman was slight, with long hair streaming against the night sky. I recognized the man as Will St. Claire. The dogs whined a little, looking at me.

"Stay," I commanded. They did, moving closer to my side, unsettled and not understanding, but obedient. The couple kissed slowly, their heads and bodies swaying, leaning into each other. Zeke barked then, a short, clipped sound. The couple immediately faded back into the woods. I felt a strange involuntary twinge of envy. Will had a girlfriend.

I commanded the dogs to come. They obeyed, running in front of me on the path back to the house, checking out the bushes on either side. Suddenly, from the heavy brush came a loud sickening snap and Lance yelped a little, then crashed through the underbrush and came back to my side. I pulled him to me, Zeke hovering nearby. Crouching down, I could see in the bright moonlight where something had grazed his leg, just slightly, enough to bring up a scratch, from which a few drops of blood were beginning to ooze. The dog shivered when I touched it but remained obediently still.

Someone had laid a trap for the dogs. Someone who wanted not just to frighten me off with a dead rat but to hurt or kill them. Someone who knew the contents of Ray's will. I stood up, rejecting the logic of an hour ago. With the dogs dead, Ray's property would be sold unencumbered. The night sounds exploded around me, water slapping on sand, wild animals stirring in the darkness. Grabbing at the dogs' collars, I headed for the house, my heart racing. Lancelot ran beside me, apparently untroubled by his scratched leg.

I locked the door and stood looking at the phone. I really was a prisoner here tonight. There wasn't anyone to call. I collapsed on the musty couch, my mind awash with images, my body exhausted and reeling. The dogs lay down beside me. I watched them falling off to sleep, trusting, my responsibility. I had signed on for now. As I dozed off, I knew that if I was to live here, I needed to find some answers.

C H A P T E R

T W E L V E

I woke early, stiff and damp from the couch, my neck hurting when I turned my head. I longed for a shower to pelt away the musty smell and the pain. Instead, I gulped instant coffee, fed the dogs, and dressed in slacks and a sleeveless turtleneck shirt. Lancelot, I noticed, had licked his scratched leg clean of blood. Still, after last night, I wasn't taking any chances. I put on their leashes.

The August day was cool and fragrant, the kind of summer day that grows too hot too fast. Pine needles crunched under my feet as I tried to keep up with two dogs used to covering ground. The cove, the water glimmering, lay peacefully before us.

"Okay, you can swim." I watched them plunge into the early-morning creek. Turning back up the path, I carefully pulled apart the bushes where Lancelot had been scraped last night. A twig snapped, grazing my arm. But there was no trap. I walked back down the path to the beach, furious with myself and embarrassed for letting my imagination get the best of me last night. The dogs joined me near the sycamore, shaking water. As I snapped on their leashes, I noticed something iridescent in the sand near my feet.

Grabbing a long stick, I carefully fished a used condom out of the dirty sand. Will and the woman on the beach must have come back last night. I looked down at the pearly latex, the cold remains of their lovemaking, then at the worn sand beneath the sycamore. Distaste swept through me. Why had Will chosen this place? Where his dead dog had lain strangled, where a day later Lancelot had tried to lick life into old Ray Tilghman's dead body? Where Penny Hart had washed up twenty-four years ago? Was it to put the ghosts to rest? Lillian had, I remembered, told me Ray's cove had long been used as a lovers' lane because it was so protected. Somehow I didn't think that was the reason.

Dropping the condom in an old trash can that stood not far from the path down to the cove, I was assaulted by the putrid smell of the decaying rat. I slammed the lid back on and ran up the path, sickened and repulsed, remembering the feel of that cold and bloody mess underneath my foot last night.

A heavy woman in a pink cotton shirtwaist cheerfully greeted me at the front desk when I entered the office at Packer King Realty.

"We'll get started in a few minutes. Coffee and doughnuts in the lounge." She pointed. Nearby, a couple dozen people stood milling about, most of them clutching plastic cups of coffee. I headed right for the pastries.

"No breakfast?" A pleasant-looking man, medium height, with wavy brown hair and dressed in slacks and sport shirt, stood next to me. He picked up a plastic cup and the pot. "Coffee?"

"Thanks." I was ravenous, unable to remember the last time I had eaten. I grabbed a second doughnut. Sugar and caffeine—two of what my secretary in New York always called the four basic food groups. The other two were, I remembered, alcohol and fat.

"I'm Dave," the man said, starting to hold out his hand, then pulling it back when he realized that both my hands were full. He laughed a little, not embarrassed.

"Eve Elliott," I mumbled, my mouth as full as my hands. I

didn't know if I was ready for small talk this early, but he seemed nice enough. I gestured toward the classroom.

On the blackboard, the instructor was printing her name in block letters. Marge Henderson. I sat down and Dave sat next to me. The small double desk had not been built with two middle-aged adults in mind. I opened the textbook and found myself looking at geometry problems.

"You'll need a calculator," Marge was saying. "Now, we have a lot to do, so let's get right down to it. You will notice a packet on your desk. Please fill out the information and return it to me. I'm handing out the syllabus." A young man in jeans groaned. Someone else got up to get more coffee. Marge moved around the room with difficulty, her hips getting in her way.

"Do you live near here?" Dave asked.

"Weller's Creek Road." It must be official, I thought, if I was telling strangers that I lived there.

"Weller's Creek Road. In Pines on Magothy? Isn't that near where that man drowned a few days ago?" he asked.

"It's not just near," I said. "It's his house." I studied his face for signs of shock, but apparently he didn't subscribe to the stigmatized-property theory.

"You must know Lillian Weber, then," he said. "I knew she was listing it. She's got one of the best reputations for selling waterfront real estate in the county."

"She's my aunt."

Dave looked at me with new eyes, opening his mouth to say something when Marge threw him a withering look and called the class to order.

I looked around the room as Marge asked us to introduce ourselves. My classmates ranged in age from early twenties to late fifties, more men than women. There were those unhappy with their jobs, housewives with either toddlers or grown children, a banker, a developer, an architect, one woman who wanted to learn how to buy a house, the unemployed, and several young men in repair or construction work, and my new friend Dave. His last name turned out to be Kramer, but, like most Marylanders I'd met, he didn't bother with his last name. He told the class he was looking for a second career. It was an okay answer and I used it when it was my turn to give my name and reason for being there.

"What do you do now?" I asked.

"I used to work at NSA."

"NSA?" It wasn't his fault, I supposed, that people outside of the Washington area didn't think or talk in initials.

"National Security Agency." He grinned. "I took early retirement."

A spy. A week ago I was an advertising executive in New York. Today I was going to real estate school with a retired spy. It was my turn to look at him. He smiled blandly back, then turned to the page that Marge was demanding we look at.

Within an hour, I had new respect for Lillian and every other real estate agent in the country. To pass the national licensing exam, we were, Marge informed us, going to have to memorize enough real estate law to paralyze a dead man. Her words, not mine. Then, she said, we could happily and instantly forget 98 percent of what we'd learned, since it was largely useless in the actual practice of listing and selling houses. But not to worry. She would get us through the exam as she had many others. If we would just do what she said. I studied her sturdy pink bulk and trim gray hair. Ex-schoolteacher maybe.

By one o'clock, the first class was over. My brain was awash in law terms and contracts. The horrifying events of the last few days seemed very far away, driven out by the stupefying quantity of legal mumbo jumbo we had just endured. Dave stood up and stretched.

"That was god-awful," I said.

"Your aunt didn't tell you?" he asked.

I shook my head. Served me right for walking in off the street, not even telling Lillian what I was up to.

Dave was packing his papers and books in a frayed briefcase.

"Well, in my experience, torture can often bring people together. You don't want to have lunch, I suppose? Maybe discuss the abuse a little more?" He sounded hopeful.

"Can't, but thanks." I didn't know why I couldn't.

"How about dinner tomorrow?" With this kind of tenacity, he was going to make a great real estate agent, I thought. "I live near Annapolis. I'll give you a tour. If you are going to sell real estate in Anne Arundel County, you should know it."

"No thanks, really." He shrugged, undeterred, I was afraid.

I left the real estate office and got into the BMW. For the first time since I arrived last Wednesday, I felt free of the sickening emotion and anxiety I'd been feeling for weeks. I vowed to tell Lillian I had begun the course and encourage her to start training me about all of the practical things I needed to know to sell real estate. I felt relief that one decision, at least, was made for now.

The dogs were resting in the pine needles in front of Will's bungalow when I pulled up next to his pickup. They jumped up to greet me, damp from what must have been another swim, pleased with life. My dread and anxiety came flooding back.

"Will?" I waited, then banged on the door. "Will? Are you in there?" Zeke barked. The door opened and he stood there behind the screen, wearing the same jeans as last night, his dark hair still damp. There were ridges and shadows on his face. He'd been sleeping. I tried not to think about the middle-of-the-night tryst on the beach and the used condom. So what if he had a girlfriend and they didn't use the narrow bed I'd seen in his bungalow?

"Will, the dogs are out. Did you let them out?"

"I took them swimming." He pushed open the screen, moving into the hot sun, blinking and stretching. He looked at me. "You should go swimming. It's too hot for anything else. Can't work this time of day." I watched as he threw a couple of sticks for the dogs to fetch. "Too hot for any more, guys." The dogs slumped, panting.

"Will, don't you understand? Zeke and Lancelot may be in

danger. Someone may want them out of the way. And . . ." I stopped. He had thrown himself down on the damp pine needles and was looking up at me. I sounded ridiculously melodramatic, even to myself.

He was silent for a few seconds. "Because of the conditions of Ray's will?"

I nodded.

He picked up a handful of pine needles, letting them flutter through his fingers to the ground. His body was thin but wiry, and tanned. My eyes were drawn again to the humped dirt grave with the stick cross.

He looked up at me, his eyes steady. "Has something happened since last night? Since the rat?"

"Something else? No. But isn't it enough to worry you that your dog was killed and Ray drowned in the creek? At least I have an idea why someone threw a dead rat in front of my door." He was sifting pine needles again, watching me. "What's wrong here, Will? With this property?" I had asked this question last night and there had been no answer.

Will shrugged this time. "I think," he said slowly, "that Pines on Magothy is a hard place to be an outsider. But people will accept you after awhile, I think. They just don't want their way of life changed, you know." He shifted a little. "But it's changing and they know that ultimately they can't stop it. So there's all this rage and then you have dead squirrels and bloody rats."

"Did you have problems when you first came here?"

He laughed a little. "With Gilbert and dead animals? No, but I'm a little different from you or the Blackburns or the others from D.C. who have bought property here. I don't have any money or a New York career or influence in Washington. This is a working-class town and I'm working-class. People here just kind of accepted me."

"But you aren't much like them, are you?"

"Well, if you mean like the guys who hang out in Marian Beall's place, no." He stood up, brushing his jeans. Pine needles stuck to the bare skin on his back and shoulders, which, like the sleep marks on his face, made him seem vulnerable and at the same time provocative. He knew it, I thought, and was enjoying my discomfort.

"Why are you here, Will? Why Pines on Magothy?"

"Just one of those things, I guess. Ray Tilghman gave me a place to live in return for doing a few chores and I found it easy to get landscaping work." He suddenly smiled his ravishing smile, his eyes crinkly and deep blue. "So I stayed."

The heat was beginning to get to me. I wanted to clean up and I wanted real food, not just doughnuts. There was more to Will than anyone had cared to find out. My mind created a picture of him last night—spent from sex, the condom discarded near the water, rolling onto his back beside the girl, then standing up and brushing the sand away. Maybe he and the girl had gone for a midnight swim. Inexplicably, my throat tightened.

"Will, leave Zeke and Lance in the house when I'm out. Please. They are my responsibility now." I'd think about the dogs, I thought, but I'd be damned if I was going to think about him, too.

"Sure. I can replace your screen door now, if you like, and the lock." Will was pointing at a new door resting in the back of the red truck. I hadn't noticed it. "As soon as I get my tools." I nodded, getting into the BMW, calling for the dogs to follow me. They jumped onto the leather seats. Ben, I thought with a certain pleasure, would have a fit to know they had sullied his precious car. I must remember to tell him about it, I thought, then wondered at my rising exasperation, vaguely aware that it had more to do with Will St. Claire than Ben.

Ten minutes later, I was eating a tuna sandwich from a blue plate as cool water filled the footed tub. I would really have to get a shower. I should have reminded Will that he'd offered to build me one outside. After all, he was still living here for free and apparently nobody thought to change the arrangement he'd had with Ray.

The tub looked more inviting when I squirted in some dish detergent, the white bubbles foaming up. Sinking into the suds, I heard Will's pickup in the clearing. He was, I thought again, a strange man, a mixture of Lady Chatterley's lover and the new sensitive man. And I was sure he knew things he wasn't telling me. I would have to ask Lillian about him. I'd made plans to meet her at the Lido Beach Inn shortly. In the meantime, the cool water washed away my fatigue.

CHAPTER
THIRTEEN

The Lido Beach Inn was doing a brisk cocktail-hour business when I arrived, if half a dozen guys in dirty work clothes and various states of inebriation could be called a cocktail hour. They were pouring down drafts as fast as Marian Beall could pull them. Russell Crouse wasn't around. All heads turned in my direction as I found a stool, Zeke and Lancelot at my side. The dogs had whined so piteously as I was leaving that I relented and brought them, hoping that Marian liked dogs.

"Ray's dogs," said Marian. She came around the bar and leaned down to scratch ears. "Let's hope that the health inspector doesn't show up."

"Maybe they can lie down behind the bar, where no one will see them?" I said.

"I was just jokin'. They're welcome. In fact, I've got customers who pose more of a health threat." She nodded in the direction of the bar, where a gaunt, red-faced man wearing an Orioles baseball cap sat staring into space. He suddenly grunted, took out a cigarette, and stuck it in his mouth. A thin string of saliva dribbled down his chin as he lit a match and tried to find the end of the cigarette, the flame coming perilously close to the end of his nose. "See what I mean. By the way, Lillian's goin' to be late."

I ordered a beer, feeling the stares of Marian's other customers.

"Lillian's always late," said the man sitting two stools from me. "You her niece?" I nodded. "Name's George Mink. Own the septic business a couple of stores down from Weber Realty. Maybe you saw the sign?" He coughed then, hawking up something I didn't want to see into a cocktail napkin. It appeared to shake him a little. I nodded again.

"Hey, George, better give up them smokes," called a man down the bar. "They're killin' you."

George had gotten control of himself now and was wiping his mouth with another napkin. He turned back to me. "That's Bob Fletcher over there, the one with the mouth and the gut. Kills rabid squirrels for a livin'."

"You should be so lucky, Georgie, my pal. And it's better'n septic tanks, when you think about it. Hey, Marian, how about it?" he said, holding up his mug, then turning his bulk in my direction. "Hear you found Ray Tilghman's body? That true?"

"Yes, it's true." I leaned down to pet Zeke, who was standing silently at my side. Lancelot had taken my advice and was snoozing behind the bar.

"The Chessie back there had to drag the body out of the creek, all bloated and whatnot," Bob Fletcher said to no one in particular, pointing to the sleeping dog. Everyone at the bar nodded. "Bad scene, if you ask me. And what the hell are the police doing? Nothing," he said, answering his own question. "Not one damn thing."

"Can't do nothin', Bob," said a red-haired younger man halfway down the bar. "No hard evidence. Hank Crouse said he drowned, no marks, no nothin'." He lit a cigarette. The air was nearly blue already. I had apparently given up a smoke-free office and a cigarette account for the firsthand experience of being killed by secondhand smoke at the Lido Beach Inn.

"If you're so smart," asked Bob Fletcher, "you tell me then, wise guy, how come Ray's dogs were locked up in his house." He turned back to me. "You found 'em in the house, right?" I was doing a lot of nodding with this crowd. "See, she says she found 'em in the house. That just goes to show you. Ray Tilghman never left the house without those dogs, let me tell you. Never. Bet on it."

"Listen to the dogcatcher talkin'," said George Mink. "He's with Animal Control," he explained to me, "which makes him an authority on every damn thing." Others at the bar laughed, including Marian. Bob Fletcher looked pleased. He turned to me.

"Mark my words," he said. "Ray Tilghman was killed. Just the way Will St. Claire's old white dog was. Oh, the cops ain't gonna do nothin', but we all know. Am I right or am I right?" He looked around. There was silence. I guessed they thought he was right.

"Hey, Bob," asked George Mink, "what happened at Shirley Bodine's during that storm the other night? The wife was talkin' with her at Lyle's. Something about a possum in the house. I didn't get the gist." He turned to me. "Some storm, huh?" I nodded.

Bob Fletcher was enjoying his moment in the spotlight. "Possum got in the house. Shirley called me right in the middle of the storm and a little after nine, when I got there, there was blood and guts and mess all over the kitchen, let me tell you." He took a swig of beer. "You know Gilbert, Shirley's crazy kid? Well, he had whacked that possum good, had blood and guts all over 'em. Like a mad dog foamin' at the mouth. And ready for more. Poor Shirl, she'd just gotten home, like her dress and her hair were all soakin' wet and muddy from the storm 'cause she said she'd slipped and half-fell gettin' out of the car. Course, I was pretty soaked myself. Well, you know how little she is, and she had to pull that great big kid off so I could get the damn possum out from behind the refrigerator. Let me tell you that possum was no match for Gilbert." He chuckled and took a deep breath, then motioned Marian for another beer.

I ventured a question. "How come there are so many squirrels and possums this summer? They're all over the road."

Bob nodded seriously. "You don't even know the half of it. A couple of cases of rabies, too. Coons bite people's dogs, who then bite the people. And right in their own backyards, too. Serious stuff. Why it's best if a wild animal gets in your house, you call me. Don't try to go and kill it yourself, you hear me." I nodded.

"Deer population's outta control, too," said the redhead. "Arundel Island's gonna have to have a shoot again."

"Yeah, but first all them Bambi lovers will have to go nuts and get the media all whipped up with their protests," said Bob Fletcher.

I was trying not to look like the Bambi lover I was.

"They're eatin' everything," said the man with the Orioles cap from the end of the bar. It was the first thing he had said. Everybody at the bar turned to look at him.

"It speaks," said the redhead. The others laughed. "What else do you know, old man?"

The man with the Orioles cap turned and looked at the redhead directly. After twice clearing his throat, he said, "I think maybe the kid, he killed Ray Tilghman. Ray Tilghman used to run him off all the time. Whilst he was crabbin'. Kid's off his fuckin' rocker, beggin' your pardon for my language, miss," he said to me. "The kid got revenge." He looked around the bar at his audience. "Revenge. He's a big kid, Gilbert is; he could do it. Just push him in and hold him under. Not hard t'all."

The silence was complete. Even Marian was listening, smoking quietly, waiting to see what would happen.

"Maybe you better hold your mouth, Walt," said George. "Shirley's good folks."

"And she's had a bad time," said Bob Fletcher, "what with Ed still over in Jessup. At least Valerie's goin' straight now. After all the crap she was into."

"Why don't you just go drink somewhere else instead of here?" The redhead was growing visibly more agitated.

"Didn't mean nothin' by it," apologized the man with the Orioles cap, beginning to recognize the tension he'd caused.

Zeke stood up beside me, understanding something was about to happen. I grabbed his collar, hoping no one would notice I was still there. Marian moved toward the end of the bar. The door to the inn opened and Shirley Bodine came in.

"Hi, everybody. Marian, I need some documents notarized."

"Buy you a beer, Shirl?" asked Bob Fletcher.

"No. I'll buy you one," she said, pulling a bar stool over between him and George Mink and putting her arm around Bob's shoulders. "Bob's my hero. He saved me and Gilbert from the possum."

"You get the mess cleaned?" Bob asked. "It was a mess."

"You're telling me. Took me all of the next day. We went to Valerie's that night. Just too much." She turned to me. "I heard about the rat, Hon. I know, uh . . . Gilbert has a reputation for doing stuff like that, but he didn't do it this time."

The others at the bar perked up. This was news.

"What rat?" asked George. I explained in as uncolorful terms as I could what had happened last night.

"Just like at the Blackburns' when they first come," said Bob. He turned to Shirley. "Gilbert didn't do it?"

"No, I don't think so." She sounded as surprised as Bob Fletcher had. "But I can't watch him every second."

"Here you are, Shirl," said Marian. She handed my aunt's secretary a sheaf of legal-size papers. "You sign while I watch. Can't be too careful about these things." She laughed at her joke as Shirley signed, collected her papers, and left.

"Now that's some woman," said Bob admiringly.

"He says that 'bout every woman," the redhead said to me.

"You still pouring concrete there up at the Blackburns'?" Bob asked the redhead.

"Yeah. You know they ain't so bad," he said. "You kinda get used to 'em when you're around 'em for a while."

"They don't buy American," said Bob, "and that ain't good for the economy." I remembered the green Saab.

"The Blackburns are good for my personal economy," said the redhead. Everyone at the bar nodded at that. He turned to me. "Say, you livin' at Ray's house?"

"Yes," I said. "I'm taking care of the dogs."

"That mean you goin' to buy it and put up a big new house?" he asked.

Was he looking for work?

"Oh, no, I have no plans to buy it. I'm just here for a while to help my aunt out. I certainly have no plans to buy or build a home." His expression was noncommittal. "I'll be helping Lillian at Weber Realty," I repeated. The tension around the bar visibly cleared.

"Well good, good, glad to hear it," said George. "She's needed help since Max died last year."

Marian looked about to say something when the man with the Orioles cap spoke again, this time directly to me.

"You what they call a Yuppie?" I reassured him I was far too old. Everyone laughed at that. "What's Yuppie stand for, anyway?" he asked. "Any you people can tell me?" Someone told him. He sat and considered.

"Well, Yuppies are better than them niggers," said the redhead. "We don't need or want none of them."

Marian rolled her eyes. "Here they go," she said to me. "Their very favorite subject in the world. I'm glad Russell isn't here, or we'd never be through with it," she said.

But she was mistaken about the conversation. The man in the Orioles cap was still thinking about Yuppies. "You know a guy named Gaylin?" he asked me. "Might be a Yuppie like yourself. Anyways, he wants my land. Came right to the house the other night to see if I'd be interested in selling. Said, hell no, I wasn't selling. Especially to someone like him." He lit another cigarette with difficulty. Marian, I noticed, had stopped serving him. He looked up at me when the match was out. "Or any of them others. Hell no." I wondered what his house looked like.

The pay phone on the wall rang. Marian answered it and turned, holding it up. "George, it's Myrna. Wants to know if you plan to eat dinner tonight. If you do, now's the time." The others laughed, releasing the tension.

"Meat loaf again," said George, getting up. "Story of my life."

He greeted Hank Crouse, who had just opened the door of the bar. It was the first time I'd seen the cop in street clothes. He nodded hello and pulled up a stool on the other side of the red-head and ordered a soda.

"So, Mr. Po-lice-man," said the man with the Orioles cap, "what do you know about who killed Cock Robin? Or Penny what's-her-name? You remember her?"

Hank Crouse scowled and chose not to flatter him with an answer, choosing instead to ask the redhead about the Blackburns' construction. Bob Fletcher and Marian were both looking a little uncomfortable.

Marian leaned close to me. "Don't pay any attention to him." She pointed at the man with the Orioles cap. "He's kind of a big mouth when he's half in the bag. And nobody believes that Gilbert killed Ray. He's just rantin'."

"Why did he bring up Penny Hart?"

This time Marian looked downright troubled. "Well," she said slowly, "Penny Hart used to date Hank Crouse in high school. Along with Bob Fletcher and George Mink and everyone else in town. So everybody was pretty broken up when she died."

"I read a newspaper account of her death. What did the autopsy say?"

"That she drowned." Marian found her dishrag and was mopping the bar in front of me. It was already very clean.

"And the case was closed? Just like the case with Ray Tilghman?"

"Yes, guess so."

"Why?" I asked. "Everybody thinks there is more to Ray's story."

Marian didn't answer. She didn't need to. I suddenly knew the answer. They didn't think anyone from the outside had killed Ray Tilghman. No, they were afraid it was someone in the community. Maybe someone who sometimes sat at this bar and shot the breeze. They had closed ranks to protect that person.

CHAPTER
FOURTEEN

The Lido Beach Inn was beginning to fill up when Lillian finally arrived, briefcase in hand. She waved at everybody at the bar and motioned me to come sit with her in the last available booth. Marian brought me another beer and Lillian a long iced tea. My aunt took a drink and sat back, probably relaxing for the first time that day.

"Sorry I'm late. How was the licensing class?" she asked.

So much for surprises. I squirmed, a picture flashing through my mind of myself as a ten-year-old kid. My reaction to tense moments at meals with my parents had been to slide under the table, down to where I was only visible from the eyes up. This time I managed to stay in my seat, even laugh.

"Well, you were bound to find out, but somehow I thought I'd have a bit more time," I said. "I was going to tell you about the class, Lillian. I really was. It's just that I'm not sure if it's the right thing. Can you see me selling real estate? I'm not exactly the type."

"What's the type? You'll do just fine. And I'm pleased as pie."

"I was afraid of that. Suppose I make an ass out of myself and flunk the exam? After this morning, I think that could be a real possibility. Hell, I could flunk the quizzes."

Lillian laughed. "Stupider people than you have passed that exam."

"Exactly." Lillian laughed harder. "The problem is that the class is largely useless. I can't see that much I'm going to memorize will help me help you out in the office."

"Well, that's true enough," she said. "But I can start teaching you how to show a property or hold an open house, or how to list a house with the multiple-listing system or write ads, plus all the financial and legal stuff. It'll be a private professional-practices course."

"I don't know about this, Lillian," I said.

"We'll have a great time. You'll see. Selling real estate is fun once you get into it. I could tell you stories. Of course, you'll have to pass that licensing test before you can actually call yourself a salesperson." She leaned across the table and patted my hand enthusiastically. Then her smile died.

"I heard about the rat. We've got to get you a little more security out there until this thing blows over." She played with a name tag on her silk dress. It said Lillian H. Weber in dark green letters under the Weber Realty logo. "It will blow over, you know."

"It had better, since I don't think I care to step on another dead animal. Shirley doesn't think that this is Gilbert's work."

"Well, she doesn't want to think so, but I'm afraid that it might have been sometimes," she said. "Although maybe not always."

"If he is doing it, is someone putting him up to it? Or is he doing it on his own?"

Lillian shrugged. "Who knows? Will can put on some new locks for you and fix the windows more securely. I don't think this is serious, Eve."

Will. I pictured him lying relaxed against the pine needles, his skin glistening from sweat, his blue eyes unreadable. "Lillian, I think Will is a little strange." My aunt sat up. "What do you know about him?" I asked.

"Will's a fine young man, Eve. Keeps to himself, but solid

and trustworthy. And smart. Ray couldn't have survived without him the last few months."

"But what do you know about him?"

"He came here maybe six months ago from upstate New York. I think that's right. Marian knows more about it than I do." She waved the bar owner over.

"Marian, didn't you introduce Will St. Claire to Ray?"

"Sure did. A stroke of genius on my part, if I don't say so myself. I remember that day, rainy and cold. He said the heater didn't work in his truck. He was traveling with his dog and he needed some work and a place to stay. He brought that old dog into the bar to get her some water, I remember. That poor old dog. I bet he misses her." Marian said hello as a man in overalls passed her on the way to the door. "Worked out real well with Ray." I had a momentary flash of Will holding his dog, gently removing the yellow plastic rope that had strangled her, his shoulders hunched in pain.

"Will's the quiet type, but likable and smart," said Lillian. "He'd done landscaping, so last spring he went around to some of the estates and asked for work. Within a few weeks, he had built a reputation as talented and hardworking." She drank her tea. "Anyway, he's very well thought of around here. In fact, the rich folks on Arundel Island fight over his services."

I was thinking of all those rich women at home alone during long, hot summer afternoons, waiting for his pickup truck to park in the driveway. "Does he date?"

My aunt gave me an exasperated look. "Yes, I think he dates sometimes. I mean, he's not the type to come in here after a day's work and pound back beers with the boys, but he goes out with women. I think he reads a lot, too."

I remembered seeing bookshelves and newspapers and magazines stacked in the cottage.

"What about his family?"

"He doesn't have any, I don't think."

I sighed. What it came down to was that no one knew anything about Will St. Claire. He'd just become part of the community and everybody took him for granted.

"Why are you asking all these questions about Will?" Lillian asked. "Did he say something to you?"

"No. Not really. I just find him odd, that's all."

"Well, don't worry about him. He gets along with everybody in the Pines, and in the time he's been here, I've never heard anyone say anything bad about him." My aunt was putting on her white linen jacket. She stopped and looked at me. "What else is on your mind?"

"Penny Hart. The woman who drowned in the cove twenty-four years ago. Do people think she just drowned accidentally?"

Lillian stopped with one sleeve on and the other hanging, then finished putting the jacket on. She nodded hello to Russell Crouse, who had come in and taken his place behind the bar. She then turned back to me.

"Penny Hart accidentally drowned." My aunt studied me. "This is a place where people use the water for recreation all the time—to swim and boat and crab and all the rest. Unfortunately, we occasionally have a tragedy. It's very sad, but it happens in all waterfront communities."

"Did you know Penny Hart?"

"Yes, I knew her a little. She left for New York not long after high school to become an actress. She drowned during a visit home. She was an only child and her parents were devastated."

"Did she actually get work acting, or was she like half of the other young women in New York, waiting on tables and waiting for the phone to ring?" I asked.

"No, I think she had some success, though I can't for the life of me remember what it was." Lillian considered, then shook her head. "This was just forever ago, Eve."

"But Ray Tilghman found her at the spot where he drowned," I said.

"That's true. And now you're completely spooked?" she asked.

I nodded. "It gives me the creeps a little. I can't pretend that I can forget all the bad things that have happened in that cove. Lillian, is the real reason that the property is going to be difficult to sell not so much the dog clause but because it is stigmatized? First by Penny Hart's death? And now by Ray's?"

Lillian was shaking her head. "I hope not. And in my heart, I think that if it wasn't for the dogs, people would be falling over themselves to buy Ray's place. There might even be a bidding war, because it's the best piece of waterfront land around." She looked at me now. "Do you want out of the lease, Eve? Are you feeling nervous about living there? I can't blame you if you are."

Zeke, who had been lying beside me, chose that moment to get up and shake, then stood staring at me. The golden fleck spun round in his eye. "No. I don't think so," I said slowly. "I just have to get over this dead animal business."

"Atta girl," said Lillian. "I know that it's hard to be an outsider in the Pines, but people here aren't vicious. Once they get to know you, things will change. Ask the Blackburns. They had a time of it for a while, but it died down pretty quickly."

"You mean Gilbert backed off?"

"Whatever or whoever," she said, her voice impatient. "I just know it will stop soon." She glanced at her watch, slid out of the booth, and smoothed her dress. "Listen, Eve, I'm going to another AA meeting. Something I need to do for myself right now. You are welcome to come and see what it's all about." Reaching over for her briefcase, she turned to look at me. "In fact, I'd like it if you would come with me."

"Look at the way I'm dressed!" We both looked down at my shorts and sneakers. "What about the dogs?"

"You're fine. And Marian will keep the dogs for now. I'll go ask." I watched as my aunt approached the bar, where Marian Beall was holding court. She nodded at Lillian. I left some money under my empty glass. Nothing like going to your first AA meeting smelling of beer.

*　　*　　*

The meeting was in a church basement. About twenty-five or thirty people were sitting in folding chairs or milling about, chatting. A woman in a business suit sat at an old table at the front of the room, an empty chair beside her. In the back, a man with heavy black-frame glasses was in charge of refreshments, fussing with the coffeepot and packages of store-bought cookies. He greeted Lillian warmly.

"Oh, Lil, I'm so sorry to hear about Ray. We all feel just terrible. Who's this?"

Lillian introduced me to those she knew. Others gathered around to talk about Ray's death. I felt my aunt relax completely, as if she was home and safe. If I was feeling a little awkward and out of place, I was the only one.

Behind us, a striking young woman with long blond waves and a pouty lipsticked mouth poured coffee into a Styrofoam cup and then stirred in nondairy creamer and sugar substitute. As I watched, she took her place beside the woman at the speaker's table as the meeting was called to order. I couldn't take my eyes off her. Where did I know her from? We sat down.

"My name is Lillian and I'm an alcoholic," said my aunt.

"Hi, Lillian, welcome," intoned the group. My aunt turned to me.

"My name is Eve, and ah . . . well, I'm not actually an alcoholic. . . . I'm just here . . . uh . . ."

"Hi, Eve, welcome," said the group, not missing a beat.

"You didn't tell me about that," I hissed at Lillian. "I don't even think I should be here. I stink of beer, and these people don't want to tell their secrets in front of some outsider. . . ."

"Eve, just shut up," said Lillian. She was smiling, as were many others in the room. Great. They all thought I was an alcoholic in denial. "Just sit and listen. Nobody cares."

The woman at the front table was introducing the blonde who was going to speak to us. Qualify, she called it. The blonde took a nervous sip of coffee and stood up.

"Thank you. My name is Valerie and I'm a recovering alcoholic and drug addict. I've been clean and dry for five months now."

Valerie. This must be Shirley Bodine's daughter. How many other girls named Valerie could there be around here? Suddenly I knew. She was also the woman on the beach last night, the woman Will St. Claire had made love to. I felt a little thrill and nudged Lillian.

"She's sleeping with Will," I whispered to my aunt, who rolled her eyes and shushed me. I sat back in my chair and listened as Valerie launched into a long story of drug and alcohol abuse and casual sex and then how she came to turn her life around. In many ways, it was a story of great courage, told by a young woman who looked like one of Botticelli's graces. I found my heart was hammering a little, as if Valerie was some sort of missing link in the mysteries that had surrounded my life since last Wednesday. I had no idea why.

"So I got my GED and now I'm applying to the community college to study word processing," she said. "And with the help of my higher power, I'll stay clean and dry one day at a time." She sat down, flushing but pleased. There was a huge round of applause, even whistles and foot stamping.

The woman at the front table smiled and opened the meeting to comments. Mostly, everyone thanked Valerie for her insights and then launched into their own problems and observations, some at irritating length. Lillian said a few words about Ray and announced that his funeral would be at Miller's Funeral Home on Ritchie Highway the next afternoon at 4:30 if anyone wanted to attend. Then we all rose and joined hands for the Serenity Prayer. I had heard it somewhere before. About God granting us the serenity to accept what we couldn't change, the courage to change what we could, and the wisdom to know the difference. Sounded simple, but how on earth did anyone ever find that much wisdom?

Lillian looked renewed. As did many others. The meeting had worked a kind of magic. I felt a little sorry that my father had never gone to an AA meeting. But he hadn't and that was that.

Valerie was standing quietly, accepting congratulations from everyone. Watching her, I thought again about Will. I could see him sinking onto the pine needles, although that sensual picture didn't quite square with the long hours he unselfishly spent helping me pack Ray's belongings, wash walls and windows, and move furniture. And now there was tough, courageous, beautiful Valerie.

It was about seven. Lillian and I made tentative plans for me to go with her to show a property the following afternoon after my class. After refusing her offer to buy me dinner, I stopped to pick up the dogs at the Lido Beach Inn. I needed to study, and with luck there wouldn't be any dead rats tonight.

Will's cottage was dark and his pickup wasn't in sight when I drove by. Lancelot's cold nose snuffled my hair from the backseat of the car as I pulled to a stop in the pine-scented clearing in front of Ray's house.

CHAPTER

FIFTEEN

The new screen door closed and latched nicely from the inside. Will had done a good job. I fed the dogs and myself, though canned soup wasn't exactly my first choice for an August evening. Looking around Ray Tilghman's 1950s-era kitchen, I thought it would soon reduce me to 1950s-type food. By tomorrow, I'd be eating Spam, lima beans, and Jell-O salad for dinner. I needed a microwave. Actually, I needed a lot of things. And they weren't all in the housekeeping department.

I dragged an old floor lamp to the front porch and settled in a wicker rocker, my feet planted on the little table. Marge had promised a quiz in the morning. Picking up my textbook and thumbing through to the chapter for tomorrow, I stopped at a section on trusts. According to the author, they could be created during a property owner's lifetime and provided for a trustee to administer the trust for a beneficiary.

This was obviously what Ray Tilghman had done. Weller Church was the trustee for the beneficiaries, in this case the Chesapeake Bay environmental group and animal shelter, that would benefit from his estate in twelve years. Zeke, lying at my feet, groaned in his sleep, his eyes and legs moving as he dreamed of chasing squirrels. He and Lancelot were taken care of in the mean-time, if whoever bought Ray's property turned out to be an unsuit-able guardian.

I turned to the section on wills and probate. Lillian had been right. If you have money and a competent lawyer, whatever curi-ous wishes you might have will be carried out after your death.

I put the book down, thinking about Ray Tilghman again. Here I was, sitting in his chair on his porch, with his dogs, and I still didn't know anything more about him than the bare facts of his life and death. What had made him so reclusive? The booze and the accident that hurt his back, as Lillian thought? Or was there something else?

The night air hung hot and oppressive on the porch. The yard echoed with unfamiliar noises. In the distance, there was a splash. Unable to concentrate, I wanted to escape with the dogs down to the cove to watch the moon splattered across the water. Instead, I got myself a beer, then wandered around the living room, staring at what was left of Ray's possessions, the few I hadn't packed to give to charity. Maybe they would reveal something more of him to me.

And, I thought, maybe a cigar was just a cigar. An old man stumbled during a storm, fell into the water, and drowned. The dead rat and dead squirrels were the means by which Gilbert or some other local person expressed contempt for outsiders. Penny Hart drowned accidentally. Will's dog was killed as the result of . . . of what?

I sat down in the swivel chair at Ray's desk and thought about the way the dog had died. Clearly deliberate, it was the one thing that had no easy explanation. Nor would Lillian talk about it except to say that it was better to let Will handle his grief in his own way. A couple of rifle shots sounded from far away.

I found a yellow legal pad in the desk and made a list of everybody I had met since last Wednesday. There were several cat-egories—natives and newcomers, the living and the dead—any-body who crossed my path, however fleeting our encounter. Then

I thought about what I knew about each person: age, occupation, and possible motives for their behavior.

When I looked at my watch, the better part of an hour had passed. And I was forced to admit my theories were largely that: theories. How could I really know what motivated these people I barely knew? Still, it was a beginning. A glimmer of apprehension unfolded inside of me.

The phone rang. It was Mitch Gaylin. He asked me to dinner in Annapolis the following night. I surprised myself by agreeing, then tried to persuade myself that what I wanted was information. Maybe, being an outsider, he'd tell me things that even Lillian wouldn't. I squashed the tiny sensation that I was going to, er, consort with the enemy.

Headlights appeared suddenly in the clearing in front of the house as I put the phone down. Zeke jumped up, barking, and Lancelot ran to the screen door, his sturdy body wiggling with excitement when Will knocked. He was carrying a bag from Lyle's Market. A large bunch of zinnias and marigolds and bachelor's buttons poked out from the top.

"Mostly vegetables," he said, handing me the paper bag. "They are from an Arundel Island estate where I work."

"Thanks, they're lovely." I arranged the flowers in a yellow teapot and put the zucchini, tomatoes, corn, and some oddly scalloped-shaped whitish green disks into the refrigerator. Will had followed me into the kitchen.

"Those are pattypan squashes. They're completely tasteless, so I cook them with tomatoes and Parmesan cheese." I turned to look at him, surprised. He grinned and stretched. "I can give you the recipe if you like."

I laughed at the absurdity of the thought. "I'm not much of a cook. Mostly, I eat spaghetti and cold cereal when I'm by myself."

"Are you by yourself much?" he asked.

"Sometimes," I said.

I pulled a beer out of the refrigerator and offered it in his direction. He took it, drinking from the bottle as he wandered around the living room. My list of names fluttered to the floor, brushed off the rolltop desk by Zeke's feathery tail. As I watched from the kitchen door, Will leaned over and picked it up, glanced at it briefly, then put it back down on the desk. The real estate text lay open to the chapter on wills and probate.

"Do you always read what you find on other people's desks?" I asked. Will blushed and moved away from the desk. Zeke stood between us, looking at him and then back to me, brown eyes worried at my tone.

"Sorry," he said. "Look, it's none of my business what you do, I know, but since you are here and I'm here, I thought it was time we got a little more acquainted. I also wanted to apologize for this afternoon."

"For what?"

"For not taking your concerns about the dogs seriously enough. You have walked into more than your share of terrible events this last few days. Although I don't think the dogs are in danger, I didn't mean to dismiss your fears as trivial," he said. "I didn't want you to think that I thought you were being frivolous. Not after finding a dead man."

"I'm glad you don't think so."

He shook his head, leaning down to pat Lancelot. "No, I don't."

"Thanks. And thanks for fixing the screen door," I said. I pointed to the porch and we settled there, the dogs padding behind us, each slumping into his favorite spot. "Will, tell me about Ray. What was he like?"

Will sat facing me, slouched almost horizontally on the little wicker couch, his legs open and sneakers flat on the floor, the half-empty beer in his hand.

"Ray was difficult, although we got along okay. I made no demands on him and he made very few on me." He took a swig of beer, nearly finishing the bottle. "He was in constant pain from an old accident at the Port of Baltimore, where he used to work. That happened a long time before I got here, but I think his back was getting worse. And he had heart disease." He sat up a little. "I probably shouldn't be telling you this, but Ray was also a recovered alcoholic. But Lillian probably told you anyway, right?"

I nodded, then got up to get us a couple more beers. "What did he do all day?" I asked, handing him the cold bottle.

"He read a lot, played solitaire, and walked down to the cove several times a day to sit and watch the water. Mostly, though, he just sat with the dogs—here on the porch or on the dock or in his chair. They comforted him in some way that people didn't." I understood that. Will's eyes flickered a little as he remembered. "He was glad to see your aunt and Marian Beall, of course, but he said they were the only people who came by the last couple of years. Except for the real estate agents trying to get him to list his property."

"Mitch Gaylin?"

"Yeah, among others. But mostly him. I don't know what that guy said, but he made Ray very mad every time. And he never gave up. Have you met him? He's sort of an aging Yuppie, if you know what I mean."

"Yes. Sort of like me," I said.

Will snorted, then got up and stood at the screen door, staring out into the hot night. He stretched his right arm upward as if to relieve some ache.

"Being with Ray never made me feel very heartened about being human," he said. "His back pain was intense, I think, and he refused to take pain pills, so maybe that's the reason he was so critical of everything."

"He was afraid of drugs, Lillian said, because of his alcoholism. How come Ray had no television?"

Will shrugged. "Oh, that. He said it was ruining America or some such thing. And like everything with Ray, there was no changing his mind. He did listen to the radio, classical music and baseball and the news." Will still stood at the door, observing the moths splattering against the outdoor light.

"What about you? What do you do all day?" I asked. He

turned away from the screen and sat down again, this time in the rocker, his legs stretched out in front of him.

"You ask a lot of questions. Are you a shrink?"

I laughed. "This place makes me need one, I think. No. I work for an advertising agency in New York. Or did."

"Married?"

"Separated."

"Children?"

"No," I said. "Are you avoiding my questions, Will?" He leaned back in the chair.

"No. I'll tell you about myself if you really want to know. It's probably not all that interesting. I grew up in Westchester County in New York. My father was a gardener. He died the day before I graduated from college. Afterward, I got a job with a big landscaping firm. When my mother died after a long illness last year, I decided to take some time off. I'm an only child, so it was a pretty traumatic time. I took my dog and headed out to see the rest of the country. That was about seven months ago. I ended up here. Ray gave me a place to live, I have work that gives me a living, and I like the water, and so . . ." He shrugged.

"So you're still here. What did you study in school?"

"English."

"Married?"

"Single."

"Children?"

"No." We both laughed. "It's late and I need to get up early," he said. "Thanks for the beers. Call me if you need me to do anything around here. I'm a lot better than I used to be at home improvements."

"Thanks. I might just take you up on your offer to build an outdoor shower. The heat gets to me."

"I like the heat. It makes my muscles feel sort of flexible, not so stiff and tense," he said, standing up. "I'll get the lumber and plumbing stuff tomorrow. I think there's an outdoor faucet on the side of the house that I can use as a water source."

Lillian had been right about him, I thought. He was a nice guy, a bit mysterious, but intelligent and kind. And he was my closest neighbor. "I'll walk out with you," I said. "The dogs need to go out once more."

The dogs raced each other out the door and through the clearing, jumping and rushing at each other in some wild dog game. The heat and humidity were still intense and I could see a sheen break out on Will's skin again. As I watched, he untucked his shirt and leaned over to mop sweat from his face with his shirt-tail.

Suddenly, Lancelot plunged out of the woods at top speed, running hard to escape Zeke. I felt my legs go as one hundred pounds of Chesapeake retriever thudded into me to avoid the black dog. I stumbled helplessly into the side of the pickup, then fell hard on the ground. I felt Will clutch at my shoulders and arms, then half-lift me to my feet. We could hear the dogs around the back of the house, chasing each other into the bushes.

"You okay?" he asked. I nodded, not sure. The fall had nearly knocked the wind out of me. "I think," he said, smiling the smile that changed his face, "that the dogs may need a little more exercise."

I began brushing off the dirt and pine needles and then suddenly I was crying, for many reasons and for no reason. Will's arms wound tightly around me. The dogs raced back to the clearing, full of play, wanting to be part of the fun.

"Come on, let's go back in," he said. He pushed me toward the house, whistled for the dogs, who now lay resting in the pine needles, each on guard against the next playful attack from the other. Inside, Will latched the screen, turned off the lights, and in the darkness we went upstairs.

The sex was slow and fierce. The dogs sat in the doorway, quiet, watching, two silhouetted voyeurs. Will smelled of hard work and creek water, his body more substantial than I had imagined. His breathing became rapid and shallow. My tears were gone, replaced by uneasy pleasure.

When we were done, he silently put his clothes on, then turned to look at me, his face without expression. I couldn't see his eyes, and maybe I didn't want to.

"I'll let myself out," he said. He touched my hair, then patted the dogs. I heard the front door lock and his truck come to life in the clearing. Zeke, still damp from exercise, jumped onto the rumpled bed. I leaned against him and fell asleep, steeped in sadness and weary beyond all dreams.

CHAPTER

SIXTEEN

The real estate licensing class had thinned a bit the second day.
The woman with small children and a couple of others must have
come to their senses. I was having second thoughts myself. Marge,
dressed in a yellow cotton skirt and blouse, cheerfully reminded
us it was going to get worse. My quick flip through the textbook
last night had confirmed that she was right. There were hundreds
of pages on deeds, titles, financing, and land-use regulation. One
young man was muttering to himself as Marge went over it with
us, line by excruciating line, explaining in plain English what the
legal terms meant. Dave Kramer, sitting next to me, earnestly followed along with a yellow Hi-Liter.

Four hours of this had put me in a fiercely antagonistic
mood. I had awakened early, my head pounding. And the memory
of last night lingered, my body weary, my heart and mind used up.
Will's truck hadn't been in his yard when I drove past his bungalow.

"Well, that was pretty bad," said Dave. "Unless you happen
to be a real estate attorney. Sure you won't reconsider for dinner
tonight?"

I politely refused again, thinking about dinner with Mitch Gaylin. I had told him I'd go directly to his house after Ray Tilghman's funeral.

"We can always study if you like," he said.

I just squeaked through today's quiz on the homework assignment I hadn't done last night. I tried to smile as I shook my head a second time. It was barely afternoon and the day stretched out long and hot in front of me.

The heat and locusts were at full throttle when I reached the house on Weller's Creek Road, the creek shimmering silver in the sunlight, the pine smell potent and sensual. Suddenly I wanted very much to go swimming. I could study at the cove. Sliding into my bathing suit, I grabbed a container of yogurt and started out the door.

Halfway to the cove, I stopped, realizing I'd forgotten the loathsome real estate textbook. With the dogs perplexed and saddened at my change of heart, I trudged back to the house. The book was on the rolltop desk, next to the list I'd made the night before. Feeling a little guilty, I nevertheless grabbed both.

Zeke and Lancelot plunged into the water as soon as we reached the cove. I stood watching their play for a minute, then waded into the creek near the old dock. It was colder than I expected. Tendrils of some green fuzzy plant tangled in my legs. Kicking free, I swam out a bit to higher water, in the direction of the dogs, who were happily finishing last night's punishing attack game in the creek. A long brown shape swam off to my right and disappeared into dark water. Shivering, I turned back toward the cove and to the safety of the dilapidated dock.

The sun dried my bathing suit almost immediately, then burned my back, forcing me to move to a shady spot under the peeling sycamore. I ate the yogurt, watching Zeke and Lancelot romp in the water, my mind lazy and full of impressions that shifted as the sun moved lower, gleaming off trees and water.

The list fell out of the real estate book when I opened it. I had planned to force myself to focus on deeds and titles. Instead, in the haze of the afternoon's sun, I read over my list. Will's name jumped out at me. I thought about what I knew about him, the few facts that Lillian and Marian had revealed and what he had told me. Reading through the other names, I pondered the relationships among the people, their differences and similarities, their quirks and mannerisms.

There was one thing, I noticed. Most residents I had met during this week in Pines on Magothy fell into three distinct age groups. Lillian, Weller Church, and Ray Tilghman were all in their early seventies. Shirley Bodine, Marian Beall, Bob Fletcher, George Mink, and Hank Crouse were in their forties. Penny Hart would have been about the same were she alive. Will, Valerie Bodine, and Russell Crouse were in their mid-twenties. Gilbert didn't fit.

Leaning back, I listened to the cicadas shriek, each crescendo louder than the last, then lapse abruptly into silence. Lulled by the steamy heat and my swim, I dozed a little, unwilling to pretend any longer that I planned to study. Then I was wide awake. Will, Valerie, and Russell Crouse were all born about the time that Penny Hart drowned and her body was found by Ray Tilghman. It seemed important, but I didn't know why.

I stood up. A few yards from me was the place where I first saw Ray holding Will's old dog and, the next day, where Ray himself had bobbed in shallow water. Twenty-four years earlier, he had discovered Penny Hart in the same place. And nobody saw anything either time.

Or had they? I considered. Would it have been possible for anyone to have seen what happened to Ray from the other side of the creek? Or from the end of the beach bordering his property? Or even from a boat? It seemed unlikely. The cove was very hidden, with tree branches overhanging the water, sheltering the shallow alcove behind the dock. I could probably swim here naked. No one would see me unless they stood at the entrance of the wide pine-needled path that led to Ray's house. That's why Will and

Valerie had come back to make love two nights ago, then swim in the night water.

Will. Was I going to keep replaying the scene with him last night forever? It happened, I told myself, a chance thing when I was tired and needy. He was attractive and available. It changed nothing. And if Will and Valerie wanted to make love on the beach and go for a swim afterward, that was fine with me. They could do it again. With my blessing. It was no big deal. I stopped short, my mind beginning to focus. Was that what Penny Hart had been doing? Had she, too, made love on the beach, then gone for a swim. Who was her partner that August afternoon twenty-four years ago?

With difficulty, I shook off my thoughts as the product of too much sun and emotion, not enough sleep. Lancelot had discovered my empty yogurt container and was working hard to lick it clean, getting his nose sticky in the process. Zeke looked on anxiously, his explosive tail flicking sand and pine needles when I called to him. Walking up the fragrant path to the house, the cicadas still drumming in my ears, I noticed that it was nearly three o'clock. Ray's funeral was at 4:30.

I hurried to the house and fed the dogs an early supper. While they ate, I fished the yellow 1969 newspaper out of the rolltop desk and reread the account of Penny Hart's death. The police thought she had been in the water only hours when Ray Tilghman found her body. Again, I studied the grainy newspaper picture of a small-faced, dark-haired girl, her bangs fringing over her eyes.

"I can't bear this, too," Ray had said as he cradled Will's lifeless white dog. Had he been referring to finding Penny's body, the two deaths somehow equal in his mind, the years between them forgotten? I looked at Penny's picture once more before dropping the newspaper back on the desk. Had there been something between Penny and Ray?

*   *   *

Miller's Funeral Home was south of the Packer King office on Ritchie Highway, next to a vacant lot where a woman was selling crabs out of the back of her truck. Traffic hadn't been bad, but the parking lot was nearly full when I arrived. I was greeted at the door by a quiet young man in a blue suit who asked me to sign a guest book. The crowd of mourners were mostly the same people I'd seen yesterday at the AA meeting.

"Eve." Weller Church broke away from a small group and came up behind me. "Lillian's not here yet, but she called from her car phone to say she's on her way." He looked closely at me. "You okay? No more rats last night, were there?"

"No rats." I tried to smile.

"Good, maybe we're done with the dirty tricks." It was comforting to have this ruddy-cheeked, bow-tied lawyer around, I thought, glad even for the smell of his old man's aftershave.

He steered me to the small chapel prepared for the service, pointing to three reserved chairs in the back row. A plain closed coffin, flanked with vases of gladiolas, rested on a platform at the front of the room. We sat down and Weller took off his seersucker jacket and put it over the chair next to him, fussing with getting the sleeves folded just right.

Will appeared in the chapel doorway. His dark hair was wet and he was wearing a sport coat and tie. Hank Crouse was beside him. They were about the same height, but that was where the similarities ended. Not only was Hank completely gray; he had lost Will's easy slenderness, carrying instead the stubborn paunch of a middle-aged man trapped in an unforgiving uniform. He removed his hat and held it carefully in both hands. One was still partly bandaged from his accident with the handsaw. He and Will exchanged a few words, unsmiling, both looking straight at the casket. Behind them, Lillian hurried in, perfect in a crisp black dress, the same one she had worn a year ago to bury Max. She put her arms around both men, eliciting weak smiles. Then, spotting us, she made her way through the crowd, greeting those she knew.

"I made it on time. I wasn't sure I would." She reached over Weller and squeezed my knee. "Everything okay at the house last night?"

I nodded, watching as Will and Hank Crouse found seats in the front row. Marian Beall sat down beside them. A man in a badly tailored suit with heavy black-rimmed glasses went to the podium. He was the same man who had been in charge of coffee at the AA meeting the day before. He watched as many of the regulars from the Lido Beach Inn quietly took their seats, then he cleared his throat several times, waiting for the crowd to get settled.

"We are here," he began, "to mourn one of ours." The crowd rustled. "Ray Tilghman was a man many of us have known for a quarter of a century. Maybe more. We honor his passing." There was talk of Ray's higher power, of his concern for the Pines on Magothy community and the Chesapeake Bay, of his love for his dogs, of his courage to endure his pain. If I thought I was going to learn anything new about this man whose house I now lived in, I was wrong.

A slight rustling at the side entrance to the chapel got my attention. Shirley Bodine, dressed in a black suit, was quietly led by a young usher to a seat nearby. Valerie trailed after her, her long blond wavy hair fanning out over her shoulders. Their resemblance was striking, separated only by twenty-odd years. Gilbert came behind, dressed in his Sunday clothes. Russell Crouse, handsome and awkward in a neat dark suit, took a seat by Valerie, then leaned over and said something to her in a whisper. She turned to him and scowled, then shook her head. Gilbert gazed steadily at the coffin.

The man in black-rimmed glasses opened the floor to anybody who cared to speak about Ray. My mind wandered, half-listening to people stand up and praise him. I studied those seated around the chapel, thinking of my list of names. The only Pines on Magothy resident on my list who was not in this room was Penny Hart. A tiny shudder expanded and surged through me. Was someone in the room being protected by the community? Although I had no proof, my intuition said yes. And if it wasn't true, my intuition wasn't worth much. But I knew better. Tightfisted Joe Lister had paid me very nicely all these years for that intuition. I decided to trust it.

CHAPTER
SEVENTEEN

The funeral service for Ray Tilghman lasted much longer than I expected, taking on a life of its own and worrying the hushed young men in dark suits. They glanced at their watches as half a dozen people suddenly found something in their hearts to say about a man they most likely hadn't seen in years. Those—like Lillian or Will—who might actually have said something meaningful said nothing. Finally it was over.

"Well," said Lillian, standing up and stretching, "I, for one, thought that was much too long. Not that it wasn't lovely, of course." She looked past me and smiled. "Hello, Will."

Will St. Claire greeted my aunt and Weller Church, then turned to me, guarded and unsmiling. "Everything all right last night?"

"Fine," I said.

"No bruises from your fall?" His eyes were deep blue, serious, unreadable.

"Fall? Bruises?" Lillian turned to me. "I thought that things had been quiet. What are you two talking about?"

"Oh, Lancelot lunged into me while playing with Zeke,

knocked the wind out of me," I said. "Will picked me up. No bruises."

"Well, thank God. I thought it was something much worse."

Involuntarily, she looked in the direction of Ray Tilghman's coffin. The three of us followed her gaze. Valerie was standing in front of it. She hesitantly touched the coffin a last time, then walked toward the chapel door.

I glanced at Will. He was watching Valerie as she stopped to talk with Hank Crouse. Russell Crouse and Shirley joined them and the foursome stood chatting, the way people do after funerals or church services. Valerie kept glancing around. Will excused himself, then looked directly at me, his eyes seeking mine. Brushing my shoulder lightly, like an echo from last night, he made his way out, past Hank and Russell and, with a small wave, past Valerie. She turned to watch him leave. She was, I could see, not happy about it.

Weller Church cited a dinner engagement and, after a brief chat with Lillian, left. Marian Beall joined us.

"I'm glad that's over," she said. "It was too long." She fished around in her dress pocket for a cigarette. Finding one, she held it carefully in her fingers, then looked around the room for someone with a light. "Are you gettin' along okay?" she asked me. I nodded. She turned to my aunt. "And you, Lil? You put Mitch Gaylin in his place?"

"For now. His buyer offered almost full asking price for the Weller's Creek Road property. I'd be surprised if we didn't settle quickly." Lillian looked relieved. "The place on the other side of the Blackburns'," she explained for my benefit.

"What happens, Lil, to Shirl and Gilbert when the Weller's Creek Road property is sold?" asked Marian.

"They'll have to leave, of course, but I don't think Shirley will be too broken up. That house is in terrible shape and she'd love to get out." My aunt turned to me a second time. "Shirley's been living there to save money in order to pay for Gilbert's treatment."

"Well, he needs some bad," said Marian.

Lillian was shaking her head. "Someone has to get him professional help soon. Lately he seems more out of touch than ever, and I'm afraid he's pushed around by all those surging teenage hormones. I know Shirley doesn't want to believe he's responsible for that dead animal business, but she can't watch him every minute. And Russ has been spending time with him. You can decide for yourself if that's really a match made in heaven."

Marian sighed. "Well, I suppose it's as much as anybody else is doin'."

"Yesterday I called a couple of residential treatment programs," said Lillian, "but the state refuses to pay, and God knows, Shirley doesn't have the money."

"So what happens?" I asked. "They wait until he has committed some crime? Involving people, not animals?"

"Exactly," said Marian.

"Did Gilbert kill Will's dog?" I asked her.

Marian coughed. "Could be, Eve. But I really don't know. I think Gilbert likes dogs, even if he doesn't like Will."

"Doesn't like Will? Why not?"

This time Lillian answered. "Nobody knows really, maybe because Will took care of things for Ray. And Ray was forever chasing Gilbert off his property. It is," she finished, "very hard to know what's going on with that boy." I remembered that vacant look I had seen on his face as he gaped at Ray's casket. Did he understand what death meant?

Lillian had clearly had enough talk about Gilbert. "I would be happy to buy you both dinner," she said.

Marian's desire for a cigarette had reached critical mass and she all but pushed us outside. I turned and took one last look at Ray Tilghman's coffin. The need to find out the truth about his death surfaced again momentarily, then evaporated in the everyday talk around me. We were soon standing outside in the steamy heat, and I discovered Marian and Lillian were looking at me, waiting for something.

"Hello, Earth to Eve," said Marian. "Are you goin' with us to Godfrey's for crabs?"

"No, thanks. I'm having dinner in Annapolis," I said. Both women stared at me. "Okay, it's Mitch Gaylin, but it's not exactly like I'm giving aid and succor to the enemy."

Lillian laughed. "Well, just don't drag out any family skeletons."

"Do you, does anybody, have skeletons that are not public property in the Pines?"

"She's right, Lil." Marian was enjoying this. She inhaled deeply on the cigarette, then began to cough. It became much worse and she turned away from us to clear her lungs.

I couldn't watch. I left the two women arguing in the parking lot over the best way to give up cigarettes.

Annapolis, my uncle Max once told me, was a town full of contradictions. It, not the Mason-Dixon line, was where the North ended and the South began. Naval cadets, rigid and neat, their pride flaking like dandruff off a dark shirt, would, Max said, find themselves face-to-face across the cobblestones with the Johnnies, eggheads reading the great books at St. John's College.

He had told me about Annapolitans, their ancestors going back to Colonial times; they abided the tidal waves of tourists by fleeing their charming city, once the nation's capital, to seek peace in suburban malls. Local merchants vacated Main Street storefronts, which were then snapped up by chain stores. Now the only difference between Main Street and mall was that the mall had parking.

Traffic was hideous. It was almost 7:30 when I turned right off Church Circle onto narrow Duke of Gloucester Street. Following Mitch Gaylin's instructions, I drove past restored houses and magnolia trees, turning here and there. Some streets unexpectedly deadended in tiny inlets, with dozens of sailboat masts sticking into the air. Unlike Pines on Magothy, I noticed that the BMW wasn't out of place here. I parked it behind Mitch's green Jeep and sat for a moment, noting that he lived in a big old white house with a porch. I had expected something newer, showier.

Mitch greeted me in casually elegant clothes: black silk shirt and pleated slacks. He was thinner than I remembered. I accepted a glass of white wine, went out onto his deck, and sloughed off my shoes. The ubiquitous sailboat masts were visible in the creek half a block from his house. I assumed one of them was his.

"Make yourself at home," he said. "We can eat out here, if that's okay." He had set a table with tablecloth, candles, and real china and silver. I was surprised and touched by his trouble. From the messy kitchen came the smell of something Italian. "Are you hungry?"

"Starved." I stood in the sliding glass doorway, watching him open another bottle of wine and pull bread out of the oven. He carried pasta primavera and salad, the wine and bread to the table and we sat down.

"Did you cook this?"

"Yes. And now you're going tell me it's out of character. That you can't run a successful business and have time for fun like sailing and cooking? Right?" He pushed back his plate and refilled our wineglasses.

"Well, I don't know," I said, "but I bet somebody else does the dishes."

"You bet right." His tone was playful, with a slightly defensive undertone.

"How long have you lived here?" I asked.

"In Annapolis? Only a few months. I grew up north of Washington, but I've wanted to live here my whole life."

"And you have real estate offices in Virginia and Washington?" He nodded. "And in Annapolis?"

He waved in the direction of the large formal dining room, which was a clutter of papers and books surrounding several impressive-looking computer systems. "That's the office at the moment, but my real one will be ready by October." Beyond the computers in the living room was a baby grand piano and more boxes.

"And you plan to open an office in northern Anne Arundel County?" I was thinking of Weber Realty, with its green-and-pink decor, ideally situated on Mountain Road. He was studying me.

"You think," he said, "that I have some ulterior motive in inviting you to dinner? Like finding out about just how bad Lillian's finances really are? Or finding an inside track to getting my dirty hands on Ray Tilghman's property?"

"I didn't say that."

"No, of course you didn't." His voice became serious, the tone unexpectedly harsh. "Let's get something straight. I would love to have Lillian's waterfront business. She's got the best reputation in the county, with all kinds of ability to get listings from the local people who have owned there for years. Listings they just flat out won't give to me. I know. I've tried."

He stood up, stretched, and leaned over the far side of the deck, which overlooked a surprisingly large and hidden garden. The sailboat masts swayed in the distance.

"I also know," he said, turning around, "that since Max's death, she's had financial trouble. But buying Weber Realty may or may not be possible and it may not matter. There's a lot of money to be made in real estate here, enough for all of us. End of lecture."

"Okay. Why *did* you invite me here?"

"Because I don't like to eat by myself."

And that, I thought, was that. Maybe it was true. The sky was darkening now and the candles in front of us flickered. He sat back down at the table and looked across at me. He wasn't smiling. I could feel the wine softening the edges of my mind and body.

"Would you like to see Annapolis?" he asked suddenly. "I would suggest walking, but you're not wearing the right shoes, and it's farther than you think."

I wasn't prepared to like Annapolis much, but Mitch's enthusiasm rubbed off on me a little. The City Dock was jammed. People were in a party mood, eating ice cream cones, walking their dogs, and trying to keep their children from beneath the wheels of the pedicabs driven by strong-thighed young men and women.

Boat owners sat on their decks, drinking beer and showing off. The crowd was young and old and in love—with the hot night, with the fishy gasoline smell of the Severn River, and with one another. The old, I noticed, were doing a better job of keeping their hands to themselves. Across the water came the sounds of the Yacht Club's outdoor bar, the distant laughter punctuated by piano. A few couples danced.

"It's certainly not Pines on Magothy," I said. Mitch nodded, propelling the Jeep toward what looked like a parking spot, only to find a motorcycle already there.

"Looks like you'll have to come back if you want to see it on foot. Wear sneakers sometime and we'll have dinner at Middleton's." He pointed to a boxed-in outdoor café next to the central market. "For now, let me show you the rest of town."

We drove slowly past the Naval Academy, St. John's College, and the Maryland statehouse. On State Circle, at the top of Maryland Avenue, Mitch spotted a parking place, expertly maneuvered the Jeep into it, then steered me through a narrow alley. At the back was a garden restaurant and bar. A cheerful young waitress greeted us warmly, rolling her eyes when a distant peal of thunder rumbled.

"This is where all the legislators and lobbyists eat when the legislature is in session across the street," said Mitch.

The crowd was lively and mostly casual. The waitress took our order. I again studied this man in front of me. It appeared to amuse him a little, as if he was used to being looked at pretty closely. He had, I thought, what my mother used to call smiling eyes, benevolent and crinkly at the corners. Perhaps I should just take him at face value. The thunder came a bit closer, followed by a tiny burst of lightning.

"Excuse me a minute," he said.

As I watched, he walked toward another table to talk with a couple of older men. The waitress made her way back with drinks.

"Mitch is such a nice guy," she said. A few large drops hit the table, then stopped. "You know that really bad storm last week?

And how fast it came up? Well, he helped me get everything inside and got soaked doing it." She put our glasses of wine down, along with the check. Well, I thought, I now knew where Mitch Gaylin was the night Ray Tilghman drowned. Had he brought me here for that reason? That was ridiculous. Next I would believe that he'd paid the waitress to come over and tell me what a fine person he was. He sat back down.

"Couple of Aldermen on the City Council." He grinned. I found that I was secretly admiring his gift to charm just about everyone.

"How are the people in the Pines treating you?" he asked. "Are you finding dead animals on your stoop yet?"

I stared, then relaxed a little, remembering he had sold the Blackburns their house. "The short answer is yes," I said. "It's not easy to be a stranger there, although everyone has been polite because of Lillian." I took a sip of wine. "It may have something to do with my renting Ray Tilghman's house or the fact that I found his body."

Mitch wasn't smiling now, the crinkles by his eyes smoothed away. "Yes, it's hard to know what to think. I have heard all the talk, by the way, about the dogs being locked in the house, thus making Ray Tilghman's drowning suspect."

"They were in the house," I said. "Is everyone in Annapolis talking about that, too?"

Mitch shook his head, then leaned across the small table. "Not in Annapolis, but among Realtors and the police in northern Anne Arundel county there is speculation. I can only tell you to be careful. It's a very insular place."

I sighed. Mitch Gaylin didn't know anything more than I did; still, I liked him and was glad I'd accepted his invitation. We drank our wine and made small talk until I noticed the time and made my excuses. He drove me back to my car and stood waiting in the street as I unlocked the door. Surprisingly, an almost-adolescent awkwardness hovered between us. I turned the car around in the narrow street and waved good-bye.

CHAPTER

EIGHTEEN

Annapolis was still clogged with traffic, although it was almost eleven. Following signs, I managed to get myself on the highway. I hoped it was the right highway. The thunder and lightning had moved on, taking the rain but leaving the heat and humidity.

It had been a civilized evening in a civilized town. A real change, I thought, from the events of the week. Of course, beneath all of its southern civility, Annapolis was probably saturated with the usual sex, violence, greed, and fear that ran through most towns.

The Lido Beach Inn was going strong when I drove by, the only sign of life in the sleeping town, its parking lot filled with a dozen cars and trucks. I didn't recognize any of them. Turning onto Weller's Creek Road, I yawned. How on earth was I going to get up in time to study? Trees and bushes, overgrown from the August rain, scraped the BMW's paint.

Then something moved in front of the car. And for one extended moment, two savage eyes held me hostage. The animal's body struck the BMW's front-left fender. I absorbed the sickening thud along my spine, braking hard, the steering wheel jumping out of my hands as the car swerved onto the left side of the narrow road and smashed into a small tree, the front end tipped down into the embankment.

Oh shit. I was okay, but what had I killed? Unfastening the seat belt, I shoved the car door open halfway, twigs and bushes scratching my legs. Squeezing out, I lost my balance and stumbled a dozen yards down the embankment, my left foot finally finding a niche in the damp ground. By holding on to small branches and digging what was left of my shoes into the mud, I inched my way back up to the car and around the open door. The car's headlights gleamed in the silence, illuminating a narrow wedge of woods and a sharp curve ahead. I didn't see any animal.

From in front of me came the sound of a speeding car. Someone was driving very fast from the opposite direction. I jumped back and away from the BMW in time to see the headlights of a big-wheeled truck round the curve, then slam on its brakes when it saw my car in its path. The entire scene burst into motion as the truck hit the right back of the BMW, spinning it onto the pavement and back into the right lane. The truck skidded to a halt, its front end wedged in the bushes.

"Fuckin' stupid . . ." From the embankment, I saw Russell Crouse haul himself out of his car, a rifle in his hand. "Who the fuck is there?"

I climbed back up the muddy slope a second time, my left shoe gone, my heart pounding. "Russ, it's Eve Elliott."

"Who? Oh, yeah." He was standing on the other side of the road, making no effort to help me, waiting for me to appear, his rifle ready for something.

"An animal ran out in front of my car."

"You see it?" I shook my head. He half-pushed me out of his way, striding to the edge of the woods where my car had first stopped. Several yards from the pavement, hidden by brush, was a big-bodied, sweet-faced raccoon, still alive, its eyes demented with pain. There was no blood on its fur. Wordlessly, Russell Crouse raised his rifle and fired once. Its face erupted in blood and brains, its body jumping at the impact. There was silence. He walked to the bloody remains and, picking it up by its ringed tail, hurled it far into the brush. Revulsion ran down me like an orgasm, nausea instead of pleasure.

"Goddamn rabid 'coons," he said. "Out of control. Deer, too. Whole fuckin' animal kingdom." He was more relaxed now, the killing calming his nerves. A little of the raccoon's blood had splattered on his jeans. "Your car's pretty messed up. It run?" he asked.

"I don't know." The smell of too many beers came from him. Together we looked at my car. The left front and the back right were both badly damaged. I got in and turned the key. Nothing happened. The impact of his car must have knocked a wire loose. I sat in the driver's seat, trying to think, my mind busy instead with the way he had killed the raccoon, an act of hatred, not mercy.

In front of me, the truck's headlights suddenly burned through the windshield as he maneuvered his monster truck back onto the road. I sat there, not comprehending until he motioned for me to steer while he shoved my car off to the side. I put it in neutral and the BMW slipped obediently backward into the bushes. I got out. Locking the door seemed extraneous. I stood holding my keys and handbag.

Russell leaned over and opened the passenger-side door of his truck, motioning me to climb up. I had lost one shoe and my foot was already sore from the rough gravel. The truck smelled of beer and sweat and gunmetal. There was a small cooler in the hatch behind the seat, along with a gun rack. Fast-food wrappers, Styrofoam cups, a newspaper, and a couple of tools I didn't recognize lay strewn on the passenger's seat. He shoved most of it onto the floor with one movement and popped open another beer, offering it to me.

"No thanks. You think you could take me home?"

"Sure thing," he said. But he made no effort to put the truck into gear; instead, he sat staring at me, swallowing beer. "You're still dressed for the funeral."

I looked down at my linen dress. It was dirty and wrinkled

but not torn. All of a sudden I felt uncomfortable, and looking up, I found his eyes rolling down my body. "Can you take me home?" I asked a second time. This time he laughed. I could see traces of Hank Crouse around his mouth and eyes. I wondered how much he had had to drink. Crushing the beer can, he tossed it on the floor of the truck.

We drove in silence along Weller's Creek Road, then turned into the quarter-mile drive to Ray Tilghman's house. Will's pickup was parked by his bungalow and there were lights in the window. Russell slowed down, suddenly putting on his brakes. The truck crunched to a stop. Russell slammed out of the truck, pulling his rifle out of its rack as he went. I didn't know what he heard, but he disappeared into the woods around the back of Will's cabin.

I'd had enough. This guy was drunk and gun-crazy. There was no telling what he would do. I opened the truck door and half-slid, half-fell to the ground, my foot tangling in something. Pulling myself free, I saw that it was a spool of plastic yellow rope. A cold wave rolled over me. It was like the rope Will had gently removed from his dog's neck a week ago on the beach. Had Russell killed Will's dog?

"Let's go," he said, suddenly in front of me. Noticing the spool of rope, he picked it up and tossed it back on the floor of the cab. "You don't want a ride the rest of the way? It's a long way to go without a shoe." I shook my head and began to walk as fast as I could in the direction of Ray's house. The pine needles were softer than the gravel had been. He was striding heavily after me, not bearing down so much as keeping up. Without much effort, he came around in front of me, blocking my way. The night was deeper here, barely illuminating his face.

"Stay out of what you don't know," he said. "It's none of your concern. You people come from somewhere else and . . ." He came closer, barely a foot from my face. I could smell the beer. He grabbed my arm hard then, yanking me closer and staring straight at me. "Don't mess with what you don't know about."

There was a rustle in the bushes and he was alert again. In

the distance, something splashed in the creek. I pulled myself out of his grip and ran down the path, anger and fear all muddled together. The only thing was to get away. He killed Will's dog, said a voice in my head. He killed Will's dog. I was running flat out now, the house in view. He killed Will's dog. The outside light was on and Zeke and Lancelot were barking. He killed Will's dog. But there were no footsteps behind me.

Then I was inside the house, sliding down the inside of the front door, grateful beyond words when Zeke and Lancelot bounded to greet me. They stood impatiently, waiting to be let out, wondering why I didn't open the door. In the darkness, I found my way to the desk and dialed 911 on the old black phone. After several rings, a female voice answered. In the distance, I heard Russell's truck leave. With shaking hands, I hung up and collapsed in the swivel chair. The dogs whined at the door.

The danger was over for now. For how long, I didn't know, but I felt sure that Russell Crouse was through with me for the night. I looked down at myself, half-surprised at my muddy dress and scratched legs. My chin and jaw felt bruised. A scratch near my eye must have been bleeding. Was I same the person who only a short while ago had been sitting with Mitch Gaylin in an outdoor café? The same person who a week ago threw my Valium in the Magothy River in some silly ritual of new beginnings? Everything seemed so far away and unimportant.

I suddenly had a mental picture of Ben, with his heavy beard and graying curly hair. Where was he right now? What was he doing? It seemed unbelievable that less than an hour ago, basking in male attention, I had been congratulating myself about the emotional distance I had put between us. Now, unnerved from the encounter with Russell Crouse, I was again thinking about him. With an effort, I shook off my thoughts.

The dogs whined. Looking around the clearing and listening carefully, I snapped on their leashes and took them out. All was quiet. Back inside, I wearily stripped off the soiled linen dress and got into the footed tub to soak away my aches. It was becoming a ritual, day and night. Maybe I didn't need the outdoor shower. Ray's clock said close to 1 A.M.

Exhausted but too troubled for sleep, I wandered about the living room, wondering if I should call anyone. But what would I say? And what would they do except come get me and take me somewhere? I didn't want to go somewhere else. And I couldn't leave the dogs. Taking my list of names, my pad, and the yellowed newspaper from the desk, I went upstairs. Zeke and Lance padded along beside me.

Sitting up in bed, I drew a sort of grid on a fresh page on the pad. Across the top, I wrote headings: "Ray Tilghman's Death, Penny Hart's Death, Will's Dog, and Dead Animals. Then down the left-hand side of the page, I wrote: "Who?" and "Why?" Under the "Will's Dog" heading, I filled in "Russell Crouse" and "Because he is a nasty, vengeful drunk and jealous of Will and Valerie." Under "Dead Animals," I wrote: "Gilbert" and "Because he is a troubled kid." The other four squares in the grid I left empty.

I studied the sheet of paper for a while, then put it down, picking up the old newspaper to reread the account of Penny Hart's drowning for the third time. There was nothing new. Flipping through the pages, I read the rest of the Pines on Magothy news for that August week in 1969. Woodstock may have been attracting thousands in New York, but it had been a largely uneventful week in the Pines. The weather had been good. There were flea markets and bull and oyster roasts.

I studied ads for pools and decks and boats, sailboats and powerboats. This place was overrun by boats. I wondered if whomever Penny Hart had met on the beach had come by boat, tied up at Ray Tilghman's dock, and then quietly left by way of the creek? And if that had happened then, what about the night Ray died? I reminded myself that a hectic and storm-filled night is a little different from a quiet Sunday afternoon. And besides, I didn't even know that Penny had met someone on the beach.

Lying back against the pillows, I could hear the wind blowing a little. But there was going to be no rain tonight. The appalling image of the raccoon spun through my mind. What kind of terrible place was this, I thought, with such hideous ways to die? I thought again of Ray's funeral that afternoon, suddenly reliving the sensation I'd had in the chapel: Someone or maybe more than one person there knew more than he or she was saying. I looked one more time at my chart, then reread my list of names. It was like a puzzle. All I had to do was fill in the empty squares. I was good at puzzles, but sleep and exhaustion were catching up with me now. I'd just have to figure it out tomorrow.

CHAPTER
NINETEEN

I awoke to a beautiful morning, my mind refusing thoughts too awful to remember right away. Zeke's fragrant paw was lodged close to my face. The night before came rushing back. Shoving aside the covers, I looked over my arms and legs to see if the scratches and bruises were real. They were—not serious certainly, but real. My shoulders ached where I had fallen down the embankment and three oval blue blotches on my arm marked Russell Crouse's powerful fingers.

My watch said seven. I threw on jeans, made a cup of instant coffee, and called Will. He answered after several rings, his voice clogged and incoherent.

"Will, it's Eve. I know you were asleep, but please just listen. I had an accident last night. The car needs to be towed to a garage and I need to get a rental car so I can go to my class." I gulped the coffee, scalding my mouth. "Huh? Oh, no, I'm okay . . . sort of. You know a garage I can call?" I wrote down a name and hung up. He was coming over. I didn't argue.

I called the garage, a place named Chandler's. No one answered, so I went outside with the dogs. The air felt fresher than it had been in days, the sun burning off the early-morning dew. Zeke and Lancelot stayed close, nervous because I was nervous, coming quietly back onto the porch without being asked.

While they ate, I went into the bathroom and inspected my face. A wide bluish splotch ran around and underneath my jaw-bone, but compared with the long scrape from my left eyebrow to my mouth, it was nearly invisible. One eye looked a little puffy. I hadn't noticed anything last night, or maybe the puffiness and bruise hadn't been there. Now I tried to repair things with liquid makeup and pressed powder. It helped some, but I still looked pretty bad. The dogs barked as Will drove into the clearing and came into the house.

"My God, you look awful," he said, pulling me close to look at the marks on my face. He smelled of sleep. A dart of pleasure went down my body and I pulled abruptly away. He went into the kitchen and made himself coffee. I followed him in.

"I'm okay. What time does Chandler's open? I called and no one was there."

"It's just Jim Chandler, so he gets in whenever he wants. Try in a few minutes." He sat down at the kitchen table. I got another cup of coffee and sat with him. "What's the whole story, Eve? You look more like you were in a fight than an accident."

I explained what happened as succinctly as I could, the part about hitting the raccoon and losing control of the car, anyway.

"There's more. What is it?"

I studied him. He seemed to be expecting something. "Yes, there's more." I told him about Russell Crouse and the demon truck. "Do you know that Russell Crouse may well have killed your dog? With a length of yellow plastic rope from a spool in his truck?"

He looked down then at the checkered oilcloth, his shoulders barely moving as he breathed. Lancelot squeezed under the table and nuzzled his hands, whining a little. When he looked up, I was shocked at the emotion in his eyes, something more than the grief I had seen a week ago, something dark and expanding outward.

"I'm sorry," I said. There was silence except for the twittering of a cardinal outside the kitchen window and the metronomic thump of Lancelot's heavy tail on the floor under the table. Zeke lay in the doorway watching us.

"Is that why you look like you've been mugged?" he asked. "Because you somehow found that out and confronted Russell, who was drunk and acting crazy?"

"No, I really fell down an embankment—twice, actually—and scraped myself up. Some branches hit my face harder than I thought." I then took a deep breath and told him the whole story, all the details this time, except for the part about Russell killing the raccoon. I still couldn't fathom or describe the hatred. He listened without interrupting, then sat silent, thinking and watching me. I got up and called Jim Chandler. He'd meet me at the car with his tow truck in half an hour. I sat back down at the kitchen table. Will was absently stroking Lance, staring straight ahead.

"Will, you owe me an explanation." Actually I didn't know if he did or didn't, but I wanted one anyway. "You knew all along that Russell killed your dog?" He nodded. "Why?"

"He's a drunk. He's mostly unemployed. He flunked out of the community college. Everyone idolizes his father. He used to date Valerie, but she told him to get lost when she got into AA. He's angry and wants revenge. I've become his target. It's not rational, of course."

"Because you and Valerie are seeing each other," I said. It was a statement, not a question.

"It's nothing serious, really. She wants to go back to school, so we've talked about the community college and I've loaned her a couple of books," he said. "We don't have a lot in common, but it's been okay, friendly and convenient."

Convenient. The word hung there between us. I watched him closely.

"I'm sorry," he said, flushing. "That was . . ."

"Yes, it was . . . ," I said. I got up. "I have to meet Jim Chandler at the car in a few minutes. Can you take me?" He nodded and got to his feet.

Zeke wandered back into the kitchen and sat down at his side, asking to be stroked. Will leaned down to touch the dark muzzle. I wondered if he could see the spinning golden spot in Zeke's eye. The Lab moved slightly, at ease under his hands. The dogs trusted him. And I wanted to trust him, too.

The BMW looked more damaged in the morning light than it had the night before. Ben would have a fit when he saw it. I walked to the other side of the road, looking down the short embankment into the trees and heavy brush where I had fallen. I could see my muddy footprints, but my shoe must have slipped down farther. No traces of blood remained on the shoulder of the road, but the unmistakable smell of dead animal came from the woods. As the heat rose, it would become unbearable. Will stood watching me.

"Will," I said slowly. "I don't think I can live here unless I find out what really happened to Ray Tilghman. Even if he really did accidentally drown, maybe someone saw something or knows something. And there must be an explanation for the dogs being in the house. I also want to know about a woman named Penny Hart." There was a ripple of something in his eyes. "Have you heard of her?"

He was leaning against the side of his pickup, edgy and alert. "Yes, Ray told me about her. He found her body in the creek, in the same place where he found my dog." His voice tapered off. "In the same place where he drowned."

"What else did he tell you about her?" I asked.

"Not very much, but he let me read a newspaper article about her. He also said she was a recovering alcoholic, although she didn't go to AA. They used to talk a lot before she went to New York, and that's why he let her use his beach, I think."

"Did he feel guilty about her drowning off his dock?"

"I tried to ask once, but he wouldn't answer me," Will said. "Just said it was a long time ago."

"Twenty-four years." We both stood in the heat, saying nothing, involved in our own thoughts.

Jim Chandler arrived with the tow truck and made short work of pulling the car out of the brush. He promised an estimate that afternoon. After he left, Will drove me to Baltimore-Washington Airport nearby to pick up a rental car. It was almost 8:30. I had a class to go to and a quiz to flunk.

As I got out of the red pickup, Will leaned over to the passenger side and watched me through the window. His eyes were clear now but worried.

"People around here can be a little touchy about questions. They will protect their own," he said. "Maybe at your expense." So he, too, thought that someone in the community was being protected. "Be careful, Eve." I watched him drive away, wondering if this was the same nonchalant young man who had mocked my concern for the dogs. I was troubled but not surprised. I also wondered if Will knew more about Penny Hart than he had said.

Marge Henderson had already handed out the quizzes by the time I arrived a few minutes after nine. The class was deeply absorbed, but Dave looked up when I sat down. Then he stared.

"I'm fine," I whispered. "I was in a little accident last night."

The words on the page jumped and played tricks with me when I read them. Agreements and contracts. Titles and deeds. I remembered hearing once that *b* is the most likely answer on a multiple-choice quiz, so I methodically answered *b* to every question and was done before anyone else in the room. Marge eyed me with suspicion. I flunked with room to spare.

"What on earth happened to you?" Dave asked. We were on a break, standing in the hall. A few others were in the kitchen and most of the rest were outside smoking.

"Accident," I said. I stuffed the last of my doughnut into my mouth, swallowing with difficulty. Then I told him a very abbreviated version of my story, leaving out the business about Russell Crouse and Will's dog and the way the raccoon had died. He shook his head, then started to make protective male noises. I excused myself and found a telephone directory, copying down a couple of numbers and addresses into a little notebook I kept in my purse. Then I called Lillian and agreed to meet her at Weber Realty late that afternoon.

The next four hours were as they had been the day before, a numbing parade of legal terminology punctuated by Marge's occasional story. My head ached. I fidgeted in my chair. Dave appeared not to notice. Finally it was over.

"Eve, you should be very careful," he said. "I mean, driving here is different from driving in New York." Lord, he annoyed me. I didn't know why.

I left him collecting his books and papers. Getting into the rented car, I sat for a moment, thinking about the afternoon ahead of me. I found I was starving, so after cruising Ritchie Highway a few minutes, I found a Chinese place and ordered lunch.

Waiting for my food, I went back to my list of names and my incomplete chart. Everything seemed a hopeless muddle of interconnected events, people, and motives. The one thing that jumped out at me again was the age relationships. Russell, Valerie, and Will were born about the same time that Penny had died, around the time Ray had been in the crane accident that sobered him up, and about the time Hank Crouse became a cop. Marian must have been in college. I needed more facts.

My food came then. I thought about Joe Lister as I ate pea pods and chicken and cold sesame noodles. He used to say that when you were drained and exhausted from a project, the best way to tap into your spare energy was with food. More than once over the years, we ate slice after slice of pizza, trying to keep the creative juices hot for the next day's presentation. I felt a small pang, missing it, wondering if that part of my life was behind me. It was at least for this afternoon.

CHAPTER
TWENTY

Asbury Bay announced itself with the same style of rustic wooden sign used by Pines on Magothy. The village wasn't much, just a town hall, a gas station with one pump, and a quarter mile or so of scraggly beach preserved by high grasses and overlooking Baltimore's old smokestack industrial section across the water.

I checked Valerie Bodine's address. Since the streets were numbered beginning with one and ending with five, with Maple, Oak, Pine, and Beech streets running perpendicularly, it wasn't too hard to find. The house was an improved bungalow, built maybe forty years ago and as ugly as Ray Tilghman's yellow teapot from the same period was wonderful. There were no cars on the street or in the driveways, the only sign of life the barest hint of a curtain moving as its owner watched me.

Now, sitting in the car, I read over my list of names, thinking about alibis for the night Ray Tilghman had died. Shirley Bodine had called Lillian from Weber Realty, then got caught in the worst of the storm as she drove home. She found Gilbert bludgeoning the possum and called Bob Fletcher to come kill it. Afterward, she and the boy had spent the night with Valerie. Or if they hadn't, I would soon find out. Marian Beall and Hank Crouse were probably both working. I made a note to check. Russell Crouse was an unknown. Bow-tied Weller Church seemed a ludicrous suspect, but I decided to ask Lillian more about him.

I dismissed the Blackburns and Mitch Gaylin as unlikely suspects. Hal and Lindsay were over an hour away in Washington, and I knew Mitch was helping the waitress drag tables and chairs inside the restaurant in Annapolis. Like an attorney questioning a witness, I mentally reserved the right to recall them if something surfaced that led me to think any one of them had somehow set the wheels of Ray's death in motion.

That left Will. And I had to know. I'd seen him late that night sitting on Lillian's dock after the storm, watching the river. He must have dug a grave and buried his dog earlier, but what had he done in the intervening hours? And for all the events of the last couple of days, what did I really know about him?

I shook off my uneasiness as I knocked on the door of the bungalow. The name on the mailbox said T. Lynch. A woman around Lillian's age, maybe a little older and much more frail, answered the door.

"Mrs. Lynch, my name is Eve Elliott. I'm Lillian Weber's niece. I'd like to talk to you for a few minutes. May I come in?" She looked me up and down, noticing the scratch on my face. I hoped the puffiness around my eye was gone.

"Come in." Surprised at how swiftly the invitation was issued, I found myself in a narrow wood-paneled hallway. Straight ahead was a staircase. Mrs. Lynch pointed to a door on the right, which led to a low-ceilinged living room, heavy with furniture and knickknacks. A fat dachshund lay on the gold-colored velour couch. She pushed it off with difficulty and offered me its place.

"How's your aunt? I haven't seen her in ages." We made small talk, the elderly woman rocking in the chair opposite me and waiting for me to say my piece.

"Mrs. Lynch, I'm living at Ray Tilghman's place on Weller's Creek Road. I have a few questions I'd like to ask you about the night he died."

She appeared unruffled. "Go right ahead. Terrible tragedy. He was a good man, though, God knows, he suffered after his accident on the dock. I was glad when he got that nice young man to help him."

"You know Will St. Claire?"

"I surely do. He visits Valerie Bodine—upstairs. She lives in my rental apartment, you know." Her voice lowered and she rocked toward me. "Too good for that girl."

"Valerie? He's too good for her?" She nodded. I was at a loss, but it didn't matter since Mrs. Lynch wasn't.

"The Bodines are quite a family, if you know what I mean, though Shirley works hard, God knows, what with no help from Ed or anyone else. And that big Gilbert . . . Well, you know what I mean."

I nodded. "Mrs. Lynch, do you remember what happened the night of the storm? Last Wednesday."

"Of course I remember." She laughed a small chirp. "You want to ask me the same questions as the police already did? Like if Shirley and Gilbert came to spend the night?"

"Yes, actually. . . ."

"Well, they did and I'll tell you all about it, but first I'll get us a nice big cold drink." She got up. I wondered how long it had been since Mrs. Lynch had had a real visitor. The dachshund had taken a fancy to my sneakers.

"There." She handed me a tall glass filled with a brown liquid. I thanked her and sipped carefully. It was sweet, but I couldn't identify its origin or flavor. "Now, here's what I told the police. Valerie and Will were upstairs early that evening as the storm was coming up. I could hear them." She rocked forward again, her voice low. "They do it up there, which I don't care for, but what am I going to do? Tenants are hard to find in Asbury Bay. Valerie Bodine pays on time and doesn't drink liquor, so I'm not complaining. I don't say anything."

"What time did Shirley and Gilbert get here?"

"About ten. I know because I was just beginning to watch my

show on the television. Looked out the window and saw them, all muddy and wet." She sipped her drink and rocked. "Don't you want to hear what happened earlier?"

"Yes. Please."

"Well, as I was saying, Will and Valerie were upstairs during the storm. Then maybe half an hour later, Russ Crouse pulls up in front of the house in that truck with the big wheels. You know the one?" I nodded. All too well. "I hear him come in and he goes upstairs and there's all this shouting and arguing." She rocked in my direction again. I leaned forward to hear her. "Drunk, you know."

"What time was that?" I asked.

"Oh, maybe nine-thirty or so. I was a little thrown off my regular schedule, what with the electric off for a bit."

"What were they arguing about?"

Mrs. Lynch looked regretful. "To tell the truth, I couldn't make out. But pretty soon, they're all outside on the walk, yelling at one another some more, mostly swear words. Russell and Valerie, anyway. Just like her mother, she can give as good as she gets when she's a mind to. Then Will St. Claire leaves, looking none too happy, and pretty soon Russell goes, too, cursing some more. And I didn't hear anything else until around ten."

"How do you know Shirley and Gilbert stayed the night?"

"Saw them the next morning, didn't I?"

I put my drink down and removed my right foot from under the dachshund. "Mrs. Lynch, you've lived around here all your life?" I began.

"Taught school for forty-two years, English and drama, you know. At Magothy Shore High."

"Do you remember a girl named Penny Hart?"

Something in Mrs. Lynch's eyes sparked. She sat up a little in her chair.

"My, my, I wondered when someone would bring up her death. Terrible tragedy. Penny Hart was a beauty. She went to New York, and you know what?" I shook my head. "She made it to

Broadway. Or maybe it was Off-Broadway. I don't remember. Anyway, people around here never appreciated her gift. They just viewed her as promiscuous or drunk or both, which I suppose she was, but she was talented, too."

Mrs. Lynch had known Penny Hart. I fairly jumped up and down.

"Did you know her well?"

"I was her drama coach, wasn't I? And she had talent to spare, let me tell you."

"Who did she date?"

Mrs. Lynch squawked with laughter. "Date? If that's what you want to call it. She probably went all the way with every boy in the senior class that year. And quite a few others, too—in half the towns around here." She rocked closer to me. I leaned in. "I even heard she had an illegal abortion when she was in New York." She shook her head. "Oh, she was pretty wild, but she always had ambitions, too. Wanted to make something of herself. Maybe I'm an old fool, but I can't take that away from her."

"Are her parents still alive?" I asked.

"No. No. They died years ago. She was a late baby, an only child, you know."

Mrs. Lynch put down her drink, then disappeared into her cluttered dining room. She returned with an old yearbook. The date was 1968. I found myself staring at the same photo of Penny Hart I had seen in the newspaper, a classic sixties face with long, dark, straight hair and bangs framing haunted eyes. It was a strangely familiar face.

"Did you stay in touch with Penny?"

"She wrote a couple of times, but that was all." Mrs. Lynch was rocking toward me again as I bent to hear her words. We had gotten the rhythm down nicely. "It's very strange that she drowned just like that."

"Yes, it is." Mrs. Lynch shrugged and rocked back meaningfully.

I leafed through the yearbook pictures. The senior class in

1968 resembled the cast of *Hair*. A thinner Marian Beall was there and Hank Crouse, his hair dark, his face serious. And Bob Fletcher and George Mink, whom I wouldn't have recognized without his name beside his picture. I looked for Shirley Bodine and found Ed Bodine instead. Mrs. Lynch noticed.

"Ed Bodine. He was a charmer, a regular Romeo, and always in trouble with the law. It's a wonder that Shirley married him, but she did, and he's given her nothing but trouble since."

I turned back to the picture of Hank Crouse and showed it to the elderly woman, who was clearly enjoying this. "Hank Crouse. Always so serious. Right after graduation, he married the Barnes girl and became a policeman. I can't remember her name just this minute, but she was as serious as he was, died in childbirth with Russell, you know." I hadn't known. "Lois Barnes, that was her name. Never got over her death, I don't think Hank has."

I was thinking about Penny Hart again. "What kind of acting work did Penny Hart get?"

"Oh, quite a number of things, I should think, serious parts, more than dancing and singing," said Mrs. Lynch. "I can't recall the names of any plays just this minute."

I began to wonder again if Penny Hart hadn't done rather more waitressing on Broadway than acting.

"Mrs. Lynch, could I borrow this for a few days?" I was still flipping through the yearbook. Shirley Bodine, then named Shirley Healy, stared out at me, a 1960s version of Valerie.

"Well, I don't know. . . ."

"I promise to bring it back next week." The assurance of another visit clinched it.

I settled into the rented car, thinking hard about what I'd learned. Penny Hart had been wild and talented. She went to New York, had an illegal abortion, and may or may not have had success as an actress. Then she returned home and drowned in Weller's Creek. And all of this happened in just over a year's time. Her life appeared to have intersected with Ray Tilghman's because he was a recovering alcoholic and so was she.

I thought about Ray Tilghman. I now knew that Shirley and Gilbert had indeed spent the night of his death with Valerie. I knew Russell's whereabouts for part of the evening. And Will? Will was here in Asbury Bay during the storm, finding comfort, or at least escape, in Valerie's bed after the death of his dog. I was more relieved than I wanted to admit.

CHAPTER
TWENTY-ONE

The Lido Beach Inn was empty when I arrived, a late-afternoon lull before the after-work crowd showed up to relax with a few beers. I sat down at the bar and ordered coffee from Marian.

"I'll join you." She came around the bar and pulled up a stool beside me, not hiding her interest in my scratched and bruised face.

"Heard about your accident," she said. "You don't look as bad as you could. Jim Chandler was in here for lunch. Said your car was goin' to need a good bit of bodywork." She blew on her coffee. "Don't worry about Jim. He's good and he's reasonable. What he isn't is fast."

I had forgotten to call him. Probably, I thought, because I wasn't all that broken up about the BMW. "Marian, I have a couple of questions."

"Shoot." She lit a cigarette and inhaled with obvious enjoyment.

"Was Russell Crouse working here the entire evening on the night of the storm?"

The smile on her face disappeared. "That is just the kind of question that I don't want to hear."

"Was he?"

"He was workin' the bar with me. Then he left for an hour or two during the storm to see if Valerie was okay. The power went down and he couldn't get through by phone. I was relieved he got back okay."

"Was he drinking?"

"He's always drinkin'. He's not got anything else to do. Makes Hank crazy." She drank the remains of her coffee and went to fetch the pot, pouring refills from behind the bar.

"Is that why Valerie dumped him?"

Marian nodded. "By the way," she said. "Just so you don't have to ask, I was here the whole evening." There was a trace of coldness in her playful tone.

"And Hank Crouse and Weller Church?"

She snorted with contempt. "Forget it, Eve. Next you'll be askin' me about Lillian." She came around the bar again. "People around here aren't gonna take to your asking too many questions—even if you are Lil's niece. If you don't stop, I wouldn't be surprised if there's worse than dead squirrels and bloody rats on your front step. So consider yourself warned."

"I'm warned. I also have another question."

"Oh Lord." She snuffed out the cigarette. "Now what?"

"Who in Pines on Magothy owns a boat?"

She turned to stare at me. Her eyebrows were touching what her hairdresser had left of her bangs. "You must have bumped your head worse than I thought last night," she said. "Just why do you want to know that?"

I shrugged.

"Just about everybody around here has a boat."

"What kind?"

"Mostly power. Still, the Magothy and even Weller's Creek are deep enough for a pretty good-size sailboat." She got up to wait on Bob Fletcher and George Mink when they sat down at the other end of the bar. I reached over the bar to touch her arm.

"Marian, you think a boat could have made it through that storm the other night?"

She inhaled deeply, then crushed out the cigarette in an overflowing ashtray behind the bar. "On Weller's Creek? Pretty damn unlikely." She was busy with the beer tap. Then she reached for a second mug. "I know what you're thinkin', and you can just forget it. Nobody tied up at Ray's dock durin' the storm and drowned him and then left." Her tone was curt.

Business picked up rapidly. I called Jim Chandler. The BMW was running, he said, only a wire shaken loose, as I expected, but the bodywork was extensive. He'd need a week and a signature to begin work. I agreed to stop by before meeting Lillian.

Returning to the bar to pay Marian, I found everybody staring at my collection of scratches and bruises. They were full of questions, so in as few words as possible I described my adventures.

"Russ was probably drunk," said Bob Fletcher. "But he's right about one thing. Too many goddamn wild animals around here. Hell, cars aren't just hittin' them; they're runnin' out and attackin' the cars."

"They makin' you earn your salary this summer?" asked George. He laughed.

Bob laughed, too, then looked furtively around him. "Deer kill's on for Saturday afternoon on Arundel Island. They're keepin' it quiet this year, but it's gonna happen."

"Give old Russ an outlet for all them spare bullets," said George Mink.

"Nah, I don't think so. Don't tell him, but I think he ain't been asked to shoot this year."

Marian was listening. She shook her head.

I left my money on the bar. The image of the raccoon's destroyed face floated to the surface of my mind again.

Jim Chandler was getting ready to close up when I pulled into the parking area in front of his garage. Next door at Weber Realty,

Lillian's Cadillac was parked near Shirley's Chevy and another car I didn't recognize. Walking through the overhead doors of the garage, I studied the BMW. It would have made Ben cry.

"It runs fine," Jim said. "But it's gonna take me a bit to pound out those dents, replace a few pieces of plastic, a headlight, and then repaint it. The insurance guy was here and said okay. He knows me." Jim showed me what he planned to do and I signed the work order. "Russ Crouse must have been going a bit over the speed limit when he hit you. That boy's livin' dangerously these days." He took a drink out of a can of orange soda. His fingernails looked permanently dirty.

"When do you think the car will be ready?"

"Week maybe."

Something that had been nagging, tilting around in the back of my mind, now thrust itself forward. I remembered Gilbert silently trying the doors of my car last Wednesday.

"Jim, does Shirley bring Gilbert to the office often?"

"Don't even talk to me about it. I feel sorry for Shirl, but it kinda makes me the baby-sitter, don't it?" He finished his soda. "He just stands here like a big oaf and watches me work. Gilbert's definitely got some faulty wiring."

"He just stays all day, hanging around?"

"Well, not every day. Sometimes Russ will take him crabbin' or someone will give him a ride home."

Another thought jumped into my mind. "Jim, do you remember the day of the storm?" He nodded. "Did Russell give Gilbert a ride home that afternoon?"

"Nah, it was probably Mitch Gaylin, that Annapolis Realtor who's after Lillian to sell Weber Realty. I remember comin' out late afternoon to see how the sky looked and his Jeep was there. Gilbert saw it, too, and went over. I didn't see the kid no more that day."

We talked for a few minutes more and I left with his promise to call me as soon as my car was finished. I walked over to Lillian's office.

Shirley was on the phone when I entered, the receiver wedged between her ear and her shoulder, both hands on the keyboard of the multiple-listing computer. She nodded and smiled and kept talking. Lillian was escorting her clients out. She motioned me to the glass-enclosed conference room in the back. I sat down heavily. An impressive number of legal papers were spread out over the conference table. Would I ever be able to sell real estate? I wondered. Advertising, with its storyboards, seemed so simple by comparison. At least there were pictures instead of these long, dense forms initialed until they were unreadable. I idly looked over a sales contract with its changes and negotiated clauses. Lillian had told me that the challenge was helping the buyer and the seller overcome their differences so that the sale could proceed. The goal was to let everybody win, she said, whatever rocky and convoluted path that took. The most successful agents, she had continued, getting warmed up, were really psychologists, supporting their clients, calming fears, and clarifying the facts in the heat of emotion. I was quite sure my aunt was magnificent.

Lillian came into the conference room and sat down. "Hi, want some coffee?" I shook my head. "That was another sale. It's amazing. Business has picked up noticeably this past week. After months and months, almost a year actually, of nothing much. I may survive after all. Mitch Gaylin can just forget buying me out. You can tell him that the next time you have dinner with him." Lillian grinned at me wickedly, gathering papers as she talked, expertly sorting them. She lowered her voice. "One other thing. I've heard of a nonprofit place, a sort of group home, which might take Gilbert. I don't know for sure, so don't tell Shirl. She's had her hopes up so many times."

I was happy to see Lillian so cheerful. It was the first time since I had arrived that she seemed like herself.

"So did you live through the first week of classes?" she asked.

"Are you avoiding commenting on my face?" I asked.

"Actually, yes, I was," my aunt said. "I know all about your adventure from Jim, of course. Knew you were all right. Saw the car. Not a pretty sight. Nor are you. I'm just glad you're in one piece." She slouched in her chair, kicking her shoes off. It was about as informal as Lillian got. "Want dinner later?" she asked. "I suppose I could microwave something and we could talk real estate."

After four hours of class that morning, I couldn't think of anything that sounded more unappealing. The cheerful glimmer in Lillian's eyes prevented me from saying so. "I can't. But I promise I will. I'm anxious to learn more." If Lillian noticed the patent lack of sincerity of this comment, she ignored it. "I just stopped by to tell you I need to go to New York for a couple of days—to get my finances in order and pick up a few more clothes and talk to Joe Lister. My attorney says there are also papers for Ben and me to sign, so it's going to be a fun trip. I'll be back Friday or Saturday afternoon."

"Can Will take care of the dogs?"

"I haven't asked him." There was a pause. I wondered if I should tell her that Russell Crouse killed his dog and Will knew and did nothing. I decided against it.

"I'm sure he'll do it," said Lillian. "I expect he misses his old dog and having the others around would probably be good for him." My aunt wiggled her toes back into her shoes.

"Lillian, Mitch Gaylin was here the afternoon before the storm. Jim just told me he saw his Jeep that afternoon. Shirley was still here at the office." I leaned forward across the table. "Remember, she called you at home to say Mitch wanted to see you the next day? Well, he didn't call. He was here."

"So?"

"Gilbert somehow got a ride home early. I bet Mitch drove him." Lillian's mouth was already open in protest. I held up my hand.

"Hear me out," I said. "Maybe it's just possible Gilbert is involved with Ray Tilghman's death in some way or maybe he knows or saw something. I don't know how exactly, but I was just thinking that if Gilbert went over to Ray's place . . ."

"You don't know that." My aunt sighed. "So none of your theories, please. Besides, Gilbert was at home when Shirley got there."

"But he may not have been earlier. And where was Shirley from the time she left the office until Bob Fletcher arrived at her house around nine?"

Lillian's expression became very stern. "That's really enough, Eve. Shirley would never lie if she knew something. You are just making this up out of whole cloth."

I shrugged. "I'm just trying to think of all the possibilities. You have to admit that life is very eventful on Weller's Creek Road."

"Next, you'll be implying that someone hired that raccoon to run in front of your car last night. Listen to yourself."

I had and it made me more nervous than ever. Nothing made sense. My mind just couldn't wrap itself around the facts in any reasonable fashion. And Lillian and Marian were simply unwilling to talk about the possibilities. I stood up. Lillian wished me a good trip and I went out into the late-afternoon sun. Through the window, I could see her standing in the reception area watching Shirley. Did my own aunt know something she wasn't telling me? I turned on the car radio, hoping to blast away the little twinge of anger that swept through me. I immediately felt regrets. How could I be so distrustful of Lillian? She had been living under a terrible strain since Max died.

CHAPTER
TWENTY-TWO

The dogs and I went for a swim when I got home. Then I lay face-down on the dock and looked out at the hazy water. Locusts shrieked, but otherwise there were no sounds except the occasional splashes made by Zeke and Lancelot as they chased each other in and out of the water and around the cove. The late-afternoon sun was warm on my back. I could feel it soaking into my sore muscles.

Leaving this place, even for a couple of days, was going to be harder than I expected. Or maybe I just didn't relish what I had to do in New York. When I returned, I would be well on my way to divorce. And then there was work. Even now, I wasn't sure what I would say to Joe Lister. It probably didn't matter, I thought. I just had to get through it. My easy solitude of a few minutes ago had turned to loneliness.

The dogs suddenly ran in the direction of the wide path that led to the house, reappearing almost immediately and dancing along beside Will. He was carrying a heavy stick, which he threw into the water. The retriever plunged in, treading water as he seized the stick and returned to shore, pleased with himself. Zeke watched, wagging his black brush of a tail and barking.

I struggled to sit up. "Hi. The water is terrific. Are you going in?"

"Maybe." He flopped down on the dock not far from me. I could see his eyes on the three darkening spots where Russell Crouse's fingers had dug hard into my upper arm the night before.

"Will, I have to go to New York tomorrow. Just for a couple of days. I'll be back Friday or Saturday latest."

"And you want me to take care of the dogs?" I nodded. "Sure," he said. There was a long silence. He pulled off his T-shirt and lay back on the dock. The dogs slumped between us, dripping and content. Suddenly Will sat up.

"I have something to tell you," he said, turning deep blue eyes on me. "Penny Hart was my mother. I thought you should know that."

I sat breathing quietly, stunned and not stunned.

"Everything I told you the other night is true," he said. "I did grow up in upstate New York, go to a local college, and later work for a landscaping company. My parents—the people who adopted me—are both dead. They were good people and I miss them, but I've always wanted to know who my real parents were."

"Did they know her?"

"No, they adopted me just days after I was born. The agency kept the information a secret from them. And my mother didn't want me to find out. She thought it somehow made her less my mother."

"How did you find out?" I asked.

"After my mother died around Thanksgiving last year, I decided to try to find them. To make a long story short, after months of searching, cajoling, chasing false leads, and flat out lying, I found out that I was born in a New York hospital in 1968. My birth certificate reads Penny Hart and an unknown father."

"Why are you telling me this?"

He stared at the three blue marks on my forearm, then shook his head. "I don't really know, except now you are sort of mixed up in it."

"In what?"

"In whatever is going on around here," he said. "You want to know how Ray really died and why. You found out that Russell killed my dog. And because of the other night. Between us." He shrugged, as if there were other reasons, ones I knew.

The silence between us lengthened. A slight breeze blew across the water and into the cove. From the distance came the buzzing sound of an outboard motor, followed by the faintest smell of gasoline. I didn't begin to understand it, but there was some mute understanding between Will and me, something I hadn't had with Ben for a very long time, and never quite like this.

"How did you trace Penny to Pines on Magothy?" I asked.

"I read a book about how to find people—mostly standard stuff like reverse phone directories. I simply did a lot of what it said. My plan at the time was merely to find my parents and confront them. You know, find out who they were and why my mother gave me away. Then I planned to get on with my life." He stood up and walked to the edge of the dock. "It didn't exactly work out that way."

"What did you find out other than Penny Hart drowned the year after you were born?"

"Not much." His voice became detached. "I know she was pretty wild in high school, dating a lot guys, not just in the Pines but in other towns, as well. I know she was pregnant with me when she went to New York and that just over a year later she came back and drowned in the creek during Woodstock weekend. That's about it," he said. "I read the newspaper account, which Ray showed me, but that didn't really tell me much, nor did any of the official records."

A shiver slid down my spine. "And your father?"

"I don't know."

"Does anyone here know who you are?" I asked.

"Ray did," he said. "He was the only one. I told him about a month ago, maybe a little more. I can't really tell you why, just that I was tired of being alone with it, and since he found her body . . ."

"Did you know that when you first came to work for him?" I asked.

"No. I just happened to be at the right place at the right time when I stopped in the Lido Beach Inn six months ago. I needed a place to stay and he had the bungalow and needed help. So Marian matched us up."

"When I found Ray holding your dog, Will, he said two things to me: 'She's dead. . . . I can't bear this, too.' "

The words drifted across to Will, who grimaced. Ray had uttered them in despair not yards from where we were. "I don't really know what that means," he said, "except for the obvious connection with my mother." Neither did I.

"What happened after you found out Ray was the one who found Penny?" I asked. For the first time that day, he smiled.

"You're really good at questions. Maybe if I was half as good, I'd know a lot more."

I stroked Zeke's long black fur, hot and dry and clean from the water and late-afternoon sun. Will sat down, his legs hanging over the dock and feet almost touching the water.

"Ray told me that there were rumors around here that Penny was pregnant when she went to New York but that people thought she had an illegal abortion." He stopped for a second. "And if she told my father that, then he would have no idea that I exist." Another pause. "Whoever he is."

Something was going around and around in my mind. "Will, forgive me for saying this, but you've been here for six months. It's very hard for me to believe that you haven't found out more than this in all that time. I found out everything you told me in just a few days. And I found someone who knew her well. I mean . . ." I stared at his back.

He turned halfway around, propping one foot on the dock while the other hung over the water. "You mean that maybe I didn't try too hard, that I found I didn't want to know who my father is after all or why my mother gave me away and then died less than a year later. Is that it? That I was just content to live in Ray's cottage, do a little landscaping, and have a woman occasionally to keep me in touch with the human race? Is that what you think?" His breathing was rapid, his eyes saturated with emotion.

I waited. The dogs were silent. He turned away again for a few seconds, then got to his feet. When he turned back, his face was full of the same pain that had shocked and repelled me that first day.

"Yeah, well you're right, of course," he said. "But you have to believe that everything has changed. Ray's death changed it. Now I have to know what really happened."

"And you think Ray's death is related to Penny's death?" Suddenly, I knew the answer. "And you also think that you are somehow indirectly responsible for Ray's death because you told him who you are?"

"Yes," he said. "Eve, help me find out what really happened. I can't live with this anymore. It's not just a matter of finding my birth parents. That seems all pretty self-centered now. It's much bigger than that. Things have happened and I'm somehow central to them."

The invisible net was pulling tighter around me. I hardly knew Will, I reminded myself, but in my heart I knew he was right: He was the key to whatever had happened on a Sunday afternoon in August twenty-four years ago and in a driving storm last week. I got to my feet. "Let's talk some more when I get back," I said. He nodded. Zeke's cold nose lightly touched the back of my leg as I walked up to the house.

Mitch Gaylin was waiting for me when I returned to the house, leaning nonchalantly against the side of his Jeep, talking on the car phone. Will had stayed at the cove to swim. Mitch hung up.

"Hi. Thought since I was in the neighborhood, I'd stop in

and say hello. What happened to your face?" I could also see him staring, as Will had done an hour earlier, at the blue marks on my arm.

"I hit a raccoon and ran off the road last night. Got a little scratched when I got out of the car and slipped down the ravine."

"You okay?" I nodded. He apparently decided not to press me for details. The dogs were sitting protectively one on either side of me in the pine needles. "I came to tell you that I've invited a couple of friends to go sailing Saturday night." I didn't say anything. "That's an invitation."

"Thanks, but I'm going to be in New York for a couple of days, and I may not be home until late afternoon on Saturday."

"That's fine. I could pick you up about five or a little later," he offered.

"Mitch, I can't. I'm still getting settled and I'm also in the middle of that licensing course. I need to study."

"Oh, yes, the licensing course. It's a bitch," he said, "but everybody gets through it sooner or later. In my case it was later. I must have taken the course and the exam three times before I passed."

"Well, then I'm off to a good start," I said. "So far I've flunked half the quizzes."

That made him laugh. "You'll probably make a great agent." Was he now recruiting me? I studied his Jeep, with its forest of antennas piercing the air. In addition to the phone, he had a laptop computer and a fax machine, a living example of how the real estate agent of the future would do business. I wondered how the Lillians of the business would adjust.

"Mitch, did you take Gilbert Bodine home from Weber Realty the afternoon of the storm?"

"Sure, the kid was just hanging around waiting, so since Shirley was going to be at the office awhile and I needed to see the property anyway, I offered to drive him. He got a kick out of calling his mother on the car phone."

"What time was that?" There was a trace of something in his eyes, I thought, but his voice remained even and smooth.

"Must have been about six-thirty or even seven. Why all the questions?"

"You didn't see any cars, did you?"

"I didn't really notice anyone special, but there's always some traffic going to and from Arundel Island that time of day during the week. Why?" he asked again.

"No reason."

"You're going to try to find out how Ray Tilghman died, aren't you?" I didn't say anything. "Well, that's okay, I guess, but I think you should be very careful." His voice and his dark eyes had turned serious, as when he'd explained last night about his offer to buy Weber Realty. "The people who live here protect their own. They don't like or want outsiders in their community. That means us. And don't think that Lillian can protect you. She can't. Am I repeating myself?"

I stared at him. He smiled suddenly, eyes crinkling. "End of today's lecture. I seem to do a lot of that when I'm around you. Just be careful, will you?"

His car phone rang.

"I'll pick you up around five—make that five-thirty, on Saturday. Bring a sweater," he said. With that, he was in the car, backing out of the clearing and talking on the phone and waving at the same time. I sighed. I guessed I was going sailing. If he sold houses the way he got dates, no wonder he did so well.

The sun was setting and I had to pack a few things for the next couple of days. I called Joe Lister in New York and made a lunch date for the next day, then called Peter Fox to confirm our meeting in the afternoon.

Finally, I called my old friend Martha Frizzell to see if I could sleep on her couch. To my regret she was leaving town for the long Labor Day weekend, but agreed to leave the key with the doorman. I asked a few questions, thanked her, and put the phone down, sorry that she wouldn't be there. I had been looking forward to Martha's common sense and humor. Anybody who had survived the New York theater scene for forty years, and actually made a living as an actress, took the long view. I could have used a long view right now.

I heard Will pass the house on his way back to his bungalow. I was grateful he hadn't come in and a little disappointed at the same time. I had an idea, but it would have to wait. I'd tell him when I got back from New York.

In the meantime, there were dogs to feed and a footed tub filled with soapy water. I was hardly missing the shower anymore. I settled in the tub, thinking about what Will had revealed. Simple solutions are best, I reminded myself, another Joe Lister truism that had worked well for twenty years. Maybe I should remember it more often.

CHAPTER
TWENTY-THREE

New York was hot. And everybody who could leave town had already gone. That left the tourists, the criminals, the poor, and, with luck, a parking spot. Or so I hoped as I eased the rental car slowly up and down the double-parked streets between West End Avenue and Riverside Drive. It was nearly eleven. A van pulled away and I parked, relieved and a little surprised how foreign New York felt to me after just a week in Maryland.

The morning had been rushed. I'd made sure that the house was locked and settled the dogs with Will, then drove away quickly, not looking back as Zeke and Lance stood in the clearing and gazed at me with liquid eyes. My uneasiness about them persisted even in New York.

Martha's apartment was the usual jumbled mess, but I found her welcome note among the dirty breakfast dishes. She had left me the phone number of a friend at Actors Equity. I called and found that Penny Hart had been a member in 1968. They had no record of her since then. Listed on her file was the name of her roommate at the time and the address where they had lived. It was on Riverside Drive, just across the street and around the corner. Was it possible she still lived there? I picked up the phone. Two minutes later, I had an appointment. Sometimes, I thought, things actually go smoothly.

Ellen Ruehl must have been forty-five or fifty, but she looked ten years younger, trim and brown-haired. Her apartment was surprisingly like Martha's, cluttered with books and papers, comfortable and welcoming. A yellow cat sat in the living room window along with a tangle of plants. The floor was littered with dried leaves.

She offered me a seat and some coffee, her face pleasant and unreadable. I got down to my reason for being there. Her face changed a little then, some sadness and puzzlement creeping in.

"Penny Hart. I never knew what happened to her really, except she drowned in a swimming accident. Why do you want to know about her?"

In as few words as possible I told her the story of my adventures in Maryland, about the hidden cove on Weller's Creek, leaving out the details of Ray's death. I could see her swallow a couple of times. When I was done, she sat staring at me, silent at first. When she spoke, her voice was low.

"What happened to Penny has always been something of a mystery to me," she said. "She was talented and beautiful and she was beginning to get decent parts in Off-Broadway shows. Then she went back to Maryland to see her father, who was not well. I never saw her again. She drowned during Woodstock weekend. I've always felt that there were unanswered questions."

"She couldn't have been here in New York more than about fifteen months," I said. "What happened during that time?"

"Penny was about four months pregnant when she got here—although you wouldn't have known it by looking at her. Did you know that?" I nodded. "We were both staying at a hotel for women over on the East Side, so we decided to get an apartment together. She got a waitress job in a café and worked up until the time the baby was due. And she was taking acting classes and auditions at the same time, mind you."

"Had she decided in advance to put up the baby for adoption?" I asked.

"Yes. Abortions were illegal then, which made things far more difficult. She was getting some money from someone in Maryland. I always thought it was the father of the baby, but later I realized that it must have been someone else, maybe her parents." She picked up a stray leaf that had fallen on the back of the couch. "Penny was very single-minded. She had the baby, which was healthy, and put it up for adoption. And she returned to work at the café and carried on with her acting classes. Within six months, she had landed a rather satisfactory part at Circle in the Square. I was very jealous at the time." She smiled.

"What was her mood during all of this?"

"I wish I could tell you. Penny always baffled me. Strangely enough, we weren't particularly close, even though I was the one who took her to the hospital and saw her through labor and the birth." Ellen leaned back on the couch. "One thing might explain it. Penny told me she was an alcoholic, although I never saw her take a drink. She didn't go to AA meetings, I don't think. I've always wondered if that wasn't the reason that she was so controlled, so unemotional about things."

"On the stage, too?"

"No, she changed on the stage, let her emotions run." Ellen Ruehl sat quietly. "There's only one other thing I can tell you. About seven, or maybe eight months after she had the baby, I was visited by a young man who claimed he knew her. From what he said, I thought he was the baby's father. He asked me all kinds of questions about her and I'm afraid I rather naïvely answered them. I was from a small southern town and more trusting than I should have been. I do remember at the time being puzzled at how little he seemed to know about her. I told him that she had snapped back from putting the baby up for adoption and that her career was taking off."

The yellow cat jumped into her lap and, making several turns, settled in.

"Can you describe him?"

"My memory is a bit dim and remember I saw him only once, twenty-four years ago. What I recall is a dark-haired young man, quiet and reserved, a little stiff maybe, almost as if he was in the military."

"Nothing else that would distinguish him?"

"Only that his nose was a little crooked, perhaps, as if it might have been broken." Her face changed a little. "Penny came home from rehearsal while he was still here. There was a bad scene. I found out that the young man was indeed the baby's father, but Penny had apparently told him that she had an illegal abortion."

"How did she know it was his baby?" I asked. "Even her high school drama teacher says she slept with half the boys in the county."

"Penny told me she forgot her birth control once," Ellen Ruehl said. "She blamed herself."

"But she blamed you for talking to the young man that day."

"She was furious with me but I had absolutely no idea I was giving her secret away."

"What was their fight about?"

"Once he found out there was a baby, he immediately wanted to adopt it. He cajoled and begged and then when he found out she wasn't about to tell him anything or agree to name him as the father, he got abusive, almost violent. I thought at one point I'd have to call the police."

"Why was she so opposed to his having custody?"

"She said that it would mess up the child's life and the lives of the people who had adopted the baby." Ellen Ruehl abruptly stopped talking.

"But you didn't believe that," I prompted.

"No, I really didn't. Penny had never shown much concern for other people's lives before. I think she didn't want to be bothered, didn't want her career interrupted. I also got the strong feeling that the young man was much more enamored of her than she ever was of him."

"Why?"

"Well, he made the trip up from Maryland apparently just to see her." She carefully deposited the yellow cat on the floor. "Actually, I am just sort of guessing that he was more in love with her than she was with him. She never said that."

"What happened then?"

"A few days later she got a call from her mother saying her father was sick. She went to Maryland and drowned."

"Did you go to the funeral?"

She shook her head. "I had a small part in a play and couldn't get away. I sent her clothes and things back to her parents. I believe her mother wrote me a thank-you note. But that was that until . . ."

"Until what?"

"Until about a month ago." She got to her feet and rummaged around in a small, crowded desk.

"I got this." She handed me a letter. It was from Ray Tilghman. I read it slowly; the handwriting was difficult. Ray had pretty much done what I had done that morning, called Actors Equity, then written to Ellen Ruehl asking the same questions that I had just asked her. I looked up. She was staring out the window.

"Did you answer it?"

"Yes, I told him exactly what I just told you. I never heard from him again."

"I guess I should have told you, but he drowned a week ago in the same cove where he found Penny's body," I said. "I found his body." Ellen Ruehl looked dazed.

"One other thing," I said. "The young man who visited you, do you know his name?"

"I don't remember, although I'm sure he told me."

I pulled out the yearbook that Mrs. Lynch had loaned me yesterday and handed it to her. The cat rubbed around my legs as

Ellen Ruehl slowly flipped through the pages. I saw her stop at Penny's picture, study it, and then move on, back and forth for untold minutes. All of a sudden, she stopped, then wordlessly handed the yearbook back to me. I studied the picture in front of me. I was looking at Will St. Claire's father. How, I wondered, would Will take the news that Russell Crouse was his half brother?

I sat through lunch with Joe Lister, not tasting the food and only half-hearing what he said.

"Eve, are you listening to me?"

"No, actually, no, I wasn't," I said. "I've had a bit of surprising news and I'm still trying to take it in."

His face softened at that. "Good news?"

"I don't know." I forced myself to put Penny Hart out of my mind. "Joe, I'd like a leave of absence from the agency. My aunt needs my help in Maryland. And I need to rest and renew my spirits."

The chopsticks loaded with sushi stopped halfway to his lips, then returned to the lacquered tray. He studied the fading scratch on my face.

"How long?"

"Two or three months, maybe more." He said nothing. "Look, I know you'll have to hire someone temporarily, so make it an unpaid leave. The time is more important to me than the money. And I'll try to be back by Christmas."

"Christmas? That's four months!" His voice had risen a notch. Two Japanese businessmen sitting nearby looked over at us.

"Come on, Joe. We've known each other for almost twenty years. Besides, I'll be fresher when I get back. You said it yourself . . . that I was sort of getting stale." Actually, he hadn't said it. But he knew it and I knew it.

There was another long silence. I was watching him. He didn't want to do it. If it had been anyone else, he would have immediately said no. Then he shrugged it off, not understanding maybe, but putting it behind him. "Well, if that's what you really need, Eve, I'll try to keep your job for you. But I can't absolutely promise. Though I think there is a copywriter at . . ."

His voice trailed off. It didn't matter, since I was no longer listening. The free-floating anxiety of a week ago was completely gone now. I had some time. A few minutes later, after getting the details worked out, I stood on the sidewalk in front of the restaurant and watched Joe Lister walk up Madison Avenue, showing his sixty years a little.

An hour later, I was sitting in Peter Fox's elegant wood-paneled office. Ben paced in front of me, his curly hair longer than I remembered it. He wasn't taking the news about the car very well.

"You crashed the car to save a raccoon?"

And I hadn't even saved it, I thought. The animal had died an excruciating and lingering death. The moment of the bullet's impact exploded again in my mind's eye, the sweet face ruined. Shaking a little, I turned to Peter for help.

"She'll get the car back to you, Ben, as soon as it's been repaired," he said. "Can we get a few other things out of the way now, please?"

Ben sat down at the far end of the couch, his head in his hands. I looked at him. Sadness and disbelief settled over me. I suddenly wanted to cry for our twenty-one years of married life. How had it come this far? Had we both changed so much? Did a young man searching for his father and mother mean more to me than Ben did? The thought surprised me. No, I thought, not more to me. Will was just part of my life right now, a catalyst forcing me to make the transition between my old life and my new one. And I probably served a similar purpose for him. That was not to say that there wasn't a growing bond between us, I thought. There clearly was, and if it was sexual, well then it was. Let people think whatever they wanted about the fifteen-year difference in our ages. It was a relief not to care.

'A picture of Will, his chambray work shirt open against

tanned skin, surfaced. He'd told me he would build my shower while I was gone. The scene opened in front of me: Will unloading lumber as the dogs chased each other in circles around the clearing. The air would then fill with the smell of sawdust and the sound of hammering. I wanted to be there rather than sitting in Peter's airtight, temperature-controlled office.

"Eve, are you listening?" Peter asked. I nodded and tried to pay attention.

Pete was going over financial details, all the legal and necessary things needed to separate two people's lives. Ben barely responded when Peter asked questions. Money had never been an issue with us. It wasn't now. Peter stood up, papers in hand, then left the room.

I studied Ben again. He turned to look at me and in his face was more sorrow than I thought was possible.

"It's amazing, isn't it?" he asked. "We sign a few papers and it's over. Just like that." I nodded. "On the whole, it was a pretty good twenty-one years, wasn't it?" He laughed hoarsely. "Well, twenty years of it, anyway."

That made me laugh a little. "Sure," I said. "I have many, many good memories."

"And now what?"

I told him about my leave of absence, about getting a real estate license to help Lillian. He listened carefully.

"Have you fallen in love, as well?"

"Only with a couple of dogs and with the creek and the smell of the pines and the little house where I live." I sat quietly. No, I thought, I haven't fallen in love. That would take awhile.

"Cheryl and I are going to get married when the divorce is complete," he said. "I wanted you to know that first. We haven't told anyone else yet."

"Congratulations." I felt no surprise, just the desire to be gone.

"Thanks. When do you want to get your things?"

"First thing tomorrow," I said. I wanted to be back in Maryland. This didn't feel like my life anymore. "I'll go to the apartment right now and pack as much stuff as I need, then stop by tomorrow morning early to pick it up. Peter has the details worked out about our accounts." I reached over and touched Ben's shoulder, then stood up.

I had done what I had come for. I was ready to be back at the cove with the dogs, with Lillian and Will. Ben stood up to kiss me good-bye. I smiled and quietly shut the door to Peter's office, my heart sad at the closing of a long chapter.

CHAPTER
TWENTY-FOUR

There were no glad dogs to greet me at Weller's Creek Road, no bright eyes and soft red tongues to insist that I forget everything and go swimming. Will's truck wasn't in the clearing, and when I banged on the door of his bungalow, there was silence. I climbed back into the rental car, hating the irrational fear in my stomach.

The drive from New York had been an uncomfortable and obsessed four hours, my thoughts alternating between what I had found out about Penny Hart and what it meant to snap apart a twenty-one-year marriage.

The scene this morning at the Central Park West apartment replayed in my head. The affection that had surfaced in Peter's office yesterday between Ben and me had fled. He sat silently at the kitchen table, pretending to read the newspaper as I carried boxes and shopping bags to the elevator. He'd made no offer to help me and I hadn't asked. When I was finished, I stood in the living room and looked around at what was left of our marriage: framed vacation pictures, pieces of pottery and silver from Mexico, some Indian hangings, and the matched set of tiny red glasses from an island near Venice. Most of my books would be packed later, but

I'd grabbed up a few favorites. The holes where they used to be on the bookshelves showed like missing teeth.

"I'd like to take the crane."

Ben looked up from his paper. "Today?"

"Yes, today."

I had struggled to hoist a giant brass crane, its pointed beak tilting high into the air, making it four and a half feet tall and a couple of feet wide. I had found it in the dump at Southhampton one summer. For fifteen years, it stood not far from a spiteful stone angel Ben had rescued as the wrecker's ball demolished a neighborhood church. Yesterday afternoon, at Peter's insistence, Ben and I had flipped a coin for them. I won the crane. Ben won the angel. Neither of us had been happy.

Now the crane shifted in the backseat of the car as I turned into the pine-needled clearing in front of Ray's house. The heat here was different from New York, more penetrating and savage. It took me an hour to unload the car and I was soaked with sweat when I finished. After inspecting my half-built new shower, I sat down on the screened porch with a beer, my feet on the table, Lillian's fan moving hot air around me.

What had prompted Ray Tilghman a month ago to contact the actors' union to find out about Penny Hart? And then to write to Ellen Ruehl? Since Will had confided his identity to Ray at that time, maybe the old man had been suspicious and merely wanted to confirm Will's identity. Somehow, it didn't ring true for me.

The other possibility was more troubling. Had Ray Tilghman had doubts that something was wrong about the way Penny Hart drowned so mysteriously twenty-four years ago? Had something happened recently that made him remember or question? It was anybody's guess. I'd probably never know why he'd made inquiries or how he'd planned to make use of anything he learned. Maybe, I thought, when you find someone dead, you need to settle things, not for the dead person as much as for yourself. The horrifying scene at the cove, with the dog frantically trying to lick life back into Ray's hands and face, washed through my mind again. Isn't that what I was doing? Resolving something about Ray's death so I could live here?

I got up to get myself another beer, wishing the dogs were with me, wishing I knew whether or not to tell Will what I'd found out in New York. Was I the person to tell him his father was Hank Crouse? It had troubled me since Ellen Ruehl handed back the yearbook yesterday.

My apprehension grew as Will pulled his pickup into the clearing and parked next to my rental car. Lancelot and Zeke jumped out of the cab, all happy with life and unconcerned about the human dilemmas that swirled around them. I tried not to make too much of the tiny sigh of relief that went through me at the sight of them. Will put on his shirt and retrieved a paper bag from the back of the truck. Suddenly, Ben's question from yesterday echoed in my mind. Had I fallen in love? It was a disturbing thought, but no, I didn't think so. Pushing it from my mind, I went to greet them.

"Hi, you have a good trip?" I nodded, my head down and my arms full of dogs. After an initial greeting, Zeke ran in ecstatic circles around the clearing, kicking up the pine needles into a fragrant spray. He then came to rest at my feet in an exhausted and happy heap, brown eyes welcoming me home, pink tongue dragging from the side of his mouth. Lancelot kept calm, accepting my return with more dignity, the greasy auburn curls on his back still damp from a recent swim.

"It is very strange," I said. "This place has grown on me in a very short time. I'm happy to be back." I stood back to look at Will. Something about him was different. He held the screen door for me. The dogs raced by, practically knocking each other over on the way to the water dish in the kitchen. "Want a beer?"

He nodded, looking around, taking the bottle from me and handing me the paper bag in return. It was filled with flowers, asters in brilliant late-summer colors this time. I found a tall glass.

"Great crane," he said. The tall brass sculpture now stood next to Ray's rolltop desk, its sharp beak pointed away from the late-afternoon light streaming in the window. It looked oddly ill at ease, too tall. Maybe I'd find a better spot. "I didn't expect you back today. You take care of everything in New York?"

Then I knew what was different about him. Something in him was lighter, easier, as if the act of telling me his story two days ago had transformed him. Or more likely, I thought, he had deposited some of the responsibility and guilt he felt about Ray onto my shoulders. A little twitch of indignation went through me. Then I looked at the flowers and his face and felt sorry.

"I saw the shower. Thanks. It looks good."

"Won't take me long to finish it."

I glanced over at him. He was watching me, unsmiling now, waiting for something. I motioned to the porch and we sat down.

"Everything okay here?" I asked.

"Just heat and humidity. No dead animals." He drank deeply, finishing the bottle and getting up to get himself another. "Valerie and I have reached a sort of agreement," he said. He was standing in the doorway to the porch. "As friends. I thought you should know that."

"Why?" I asked.

"Because you thought I was using her. For reasons I don't understand, I don't want you to think that I use people," he said.

I didn't react, thinking instead how complicated things were getting. Or maybe how simple. Sex is always simple and complicated. Love even more so.

"The locals are revving up for the deer kill tomorrow," Will said.

I shivered involuntarily. "Weller says they bring in marksmen and it's done humanely and all over in a couple of hours."

"You feel okay about it, then?"

"No, of course not. I am what the guys down at the Lido Beach Inn call a Bambi lover. There must be other choices."

◆

He nodded, apparently resigned, not angry. The Chesapeake Bay retriever nuzzled his hand. He leaned down to scratch the dog's cinnamon fur.

I knew then I wasn't going to tell him what I'd learned about his father and mother from Ellen Ruehl. Not now. And why would he think I'd learned anything in New York, anyway? He was watching me across the porch, his eyes steady and dark blue. He knew I knew something. It hovered between us, this unspoken something I wasn't telling him. He was going to trust me to tell him when I could. But not yet. Not now, I couldn't. Tomorrow maybe, when I was less tired and had time to figure out how to say it.

"Will, I had a lot of time to think during the drive up and back." He still said nothing, just stroked the dog. "About our conversation two days ago . . ."

"And you want nothing to do with the whole mess?" The heaviness seemed to take hold of him again.

"I didn't say that. I just think we need to think carefully about what we know about Ray's death and Penny Hart's death and about what we don't know. We are both outsiders here. . . ."

"You're right," he said. "And my guilt is my guilt, not yours."

"Wait a minute. It's not about innocence or guilt. It's about taking our time to think clearly and act reasonably. About not jumping to conclusions or making any accusations."

He shifted in the doorway, leaning against the doorjamb, his eyes studying first a far place on the porch, then my face. A dark musk scent, like damp pine needles and the smell of an oncoming storm, seeped through the air. Why had he, as he said, reached an agreement with Valerie? I tried to push away the thought and found I couldn't. Was whatever was between us the real reason I wasn't telling him about Hank Crouse? I stood up. He made a strange awkward movement toward me, then, changing his mind, patted Zeke and left. I felt relieved and I felt sorry.

It was just after four. I fed the dogs an early dinner, then wandered aimlessly around Ray's house, wishing that I could have ten minutes to talk with the old man who two weeks ago had lived here. Just ten minutes to ask a few questions, get a few answers.

I sat down at his desk and methodically began to go through the cubbyholes full of papers. Lillian had been right. There was nothing much of value here, just old Christmas cards and all the financial junk that builds up over the years. And Ray never threw anything away. I began loading it into an empty carton to take to Weller Church: decades-old paycheck stubs and more recent checkbooks, itemized medical bills, and union newsletters. And near the bottom of one pigeonhole, hidden among bank statements, was the letter from Ellen Ruehl. If the police had searched Ray's desk, they hadn't done it very carefully.

Her handwriting was neat and careful, but the story, written out, was long and involved. She had told Ray exactly what she had told me, but seeing it on paper made it more real. Had I been Ray Tilghman, I would have recognized a young Hank Crouse from her description. I felt a little sick. I was toying with Will's life and I had no right. Tomorrow I would tell him, show him this letter, for sure. The decision made, I felt a little better.

Putting the letter down, I found the old newspaper account of Penny Hart's death and reread it for what felt like the millionth time. Maybe the reporter was still in the area and would remember something. Flipping the phone book open, I looked under Justice and found one W. Justice listed in a nearby community. Like Ellen Ruehl, it was as if he had been waiting for my call. In five minutes I had an appointment for eight that evening.

As soon as I put the phone down, it rang. Lillian wanted to know how New York was holding up without me. We made a date for an early dinner and I went to bathe and nap and read for an hour, the dogs nearby. It felt good to be home.

CHAPTER
TWENTY-FIVE

Ward Justice and his wife lived in a new condominium town-house, or townhome, as Lillian said real estate agents liked to call them, the emphasis on the *home*. It was just one of the many communities that littered the Maryland landscape. Acre after acre of woodlands had been razed to make room for roads and construction equipment. The houses were attached in blocks of eight or ten, many with a tall fence in the back, in a last ditch effort to carve out some privacy from the vacant fields and the neighbors.

Fair Waters was a little different, however. It edged the Chesapeake Bay and boasted not only the usual swimming pool, tennis courts, and community center but also a large marina. There were bay views and docking privileges for those willing to pay a few tens of thousands more. An identical string of pastel houses was under construction several football fields away. There were no trees. Not one. Parking spaces were neatly numbered on the concrete cul-de-sacs behind the houses.

It was almost 8:15 when I reached the townhouse community. Even in the near dark, I could see enough to make me shudder to think what a developer could do to Ray Tilghman's property and the parcels of land next to it. A hundred townhomes with names like the Somerset or the Ashburton could ruin a village like Pines on Magothy forever. It was surely understandable why Ray and the others fought so hard to keep things as they were. Better a few run-down rental properties than roads and schools overburdened from too much traffic and too many young families with children or from the dreaded government lawyers with their foreign cars.

Mr. Justice had told me on the phone to park in space number 102. I couldn't see the numbers, so maybe I did and maybe I didn't. I dumped Mrs. Lynch's yearbook, the old *Magothy Leader,* Ellen Ruehl's letter, and my list and chart into my briefcase, then sat in the car for a couple of minutes to gather my thoughts.

I had just come from dinner with Lillian. My aunt continued to be cheerful and relaxed. She had been delirious to hear that I'd secured a four-month leave from the ad agency. I'd be able to get my license and plunge right in, she said. The thought of the real estate class didn't make me exactly ecstatic, but if that's what it took, I'd just do it. We made plans to spend Saturday and Sunday together, showing properties and doing paperwork. I found I was looking forward to it.

The Justices were waiting for me at the door of their townhouse, opening it before I rang the bell. They were in their early or mid-seventies, I guessed, and he was about twice her size, like a giant, slovenly Goofy compared with her tiny, delicate, and aging Snow White. They had tea ready for me in their living room overlooking the water. I admired the view—substantially lovely, I was forced to admit—and then explained in greater detail my reasons for being there.

"Miss Elliott," Ward Justice began, "I can't say that I was surprised to hear from you. Oh, I didn't know who would call me exactly, but I've had a feeling about Penny Hart's death since I read about Ray Tilghman drowning in the same place. I knew that sooner or later someone would look into it. And," he said darkly, "I didn't think it would be the police."

"Premonition," murmured Mrs. Justice, looking up from pouring tea into fancy china cups.

"What kind of feeling?" I asked him.

"Don't know if I can say," he said, settling at the table with his teacup. It was much too small in his hands. "I'm an old reporter, you know. Worked for all the local papers around here one time or another but ended up at the *Leader*. We reporters deal with facts, not feelings, so this is a little embarrassing."

"Everyone I talk to about this," I said, "has owned up to feelings about it."

He appeared to take comfort from my statement, swallowing his tea in one gulp and handing his cup back to his tiny wife.

"Okay, then I'll go and make an old fool out of myself and tell you what you want to know."

"I've read your story about Penny Hart's death a dozen times," I said, "but I would like to hear what the people you interviewed actually told you—all you left out of your story and what you thought it meant."

He nodded, accepting another cup of tea and a thin slice of cinnamon toast and finishing both in a bite and a swallow before speaking.

"I interviewed Ray Tilghman first. He felt terrible about Penny. She was one of the few young people he liked, I gathered. He told me he had let her use his beach since she was a senior in high school, rather than having her swim at Lido Beach."

"What's wrong with Lido Beach?" I made a mental note to go see it for myself.

"It's not really a beach, more of a pile of dirt at the edge of the water, with a public dock for resident's boats. Nobody but renters use it." He said *renters* the way he might have said *white trash*.

"She was a fast girl," murmured Mrs. Justice. Her husband glanced at her.

"Yes, she had that reputation. Who knows," he said suddenly, "maybe Ray was watching her from the bushes. I've always thought we might find out something like that."

Ray Tilghman as a Peeping Tom? It was a new thought. I decided not to tell them what I had heard about Penny's alcoholism and Ray's apparent support of her decision to give up drinking.

Mrs. Justice looked unembarrassed. "Mark my words," she was saying, "this will have to do with sex. These things always do."

And an unwanted pregnancy and the birth of a child. I wondered if Mrs. Justice knew how right she was.

"Anyway," Ward Justice said, "Ray let Penny use his beach. He said she stopped at his house to say hello before going down to the cove. Then he went to an AA meeting. Her car—rather her parent's car—was still there when he got back a few hours later, so he went down to the cove himself. That's when he found the body."

"What else did he tell you?"

"Nothing. That was it. He appeared to be shocked and saddened by her death, but he said nothing else to me. No details except the obvious ones."

"Who else did you interview?" I asked.

"The police, of course, but if they knew anything, I couldn't get it out of them. Hank Crouse was a new recruit at the time— had even gone out with Penny in high school, I think—but he didn't know anything. He told me that there was no evidence of foul play and that it was considered an accidental-drowning death."

"You think the police knew more? That they covered something up?"

"I didn't mean to imply that. But, like always, the police can do only so much and spend just so much time on each case, and since this time there was no evidence of anything other than accidental drowning, they let it go."

"Did you talk with Penny's parents?" I asked.

"They were broken up, of course." Mr. Justice ran his hand through his heavy white hair. "It's the hardest part of being a reporter, you know, asking grieving family members about their tragedy. I never got used to it. But I did the best I could and the Harts cooperated." He stopped, remembering. Minutes dragged by.

"Her parents," prompted his wife in a low voice.

"Her parents—you know her father was bedridden?" I nodded. "They told me how she had arrived late the night before, then had gone with her mother to church that Sunday morning. When they came home, Mrs. Hart made a big Sunday dinner and the three of them ate and talked about Penny's role in some play."

Mr. Justice stopped to drink a third miniature cup of tea.

"Word had gotten around by that time that Penny was home for a visit," he said. "Her mother said Penny got a phone call and a few minutes later she took their car and went to Ray Tilghman's cove. She told her parents where she was going and that she had to memorize a script. Her parents didn't want her to go. Her mother said they hadn't seen her in nearly seven months and they were greedy to keep her with them."

"But she went anyway," said Mrs. Justice. "Didn't even see the friends who stopped by."

"Friends stopped by where?"

"At her parents," said the reporter. "Several of those who graduated with her from Magothy Shore High stopped by during the afternoon. Shirley Bodine, I remember her mother said, and Marian Beall. The three were great friends."

"And no one ever saw her alive again," said Mrs. Justice.

Her husband nodded. "Ray found her script and her clothes and towel all neat on the beach. Even the car keys were found in her shorts pocket. She drowned in shallow water."

"Your article said she was a good swimmer . . ." I began.

"She was on the high school swim team for a year. That's what makes this all so puzzling. The official cause of death was drowning. End of story."

"What do you think happened?" I asked.

"I think there's something that we don't know about."

"Or somebody," said Mrs. Justice.

Mr. Justice agreed and turned to me. "I know you found Ray Tilghman's dogs in his house. They wouldn't have been there if nothing unusual had happened to Ray. Everybody in the Pines knows he always took them with him when he went to the cove. You believe that?" He was looking at me closely. I nodded. "Well, it is sort of the same thing with Penny Hart's drowning. She was a good swimmer. It's unlikely she would have drowned on a calm afternoon at low tide. It just doesn't go down right. Didn't then, doesn't now."

"So you are saying that in both cases, little details are wrong or just don't add up?"

"Yes. In fact, I've noticed when I hear people talking about Ray Tilghman's death in Lyle's, their comments are very similar to what I heard twenty-four years ago about Penny Hart's death."

"How so?" I asked.

"I was just thinking again of that sense of something being off, of things not quite adding up," he said.

"An intuitive thing?"

"Well, though it embarrasses the reporter in me to say it, yes," he said.

"Well, what about the factual similarities?" I asked.

This was safer ground, I could see. Mr. Justice took his time. "Yes, of course. But you already know them, I think: the unexpectedness of both deaths, both bodies found in the hidden cove, neither dying from something like a heart attack, neither with any marks on their bodies to show there had been a struggle, no signs of a struggle on the beach. . . ." He was thinking again. "I still can't help but wonder if either death was accidental."

"Then what happened to Penny Hart?"

"Probably the obvious." He looked at me for encouragement.

"A very smart man I used to work for always said that the simple and the obvious are the best choices."

Mr. Justice nodded. "Someone docked a boat at Ray Tilghman's dock that Sunday afternoon and no one saw or heard. A small motor might have been quiet enough, and that cove is completely hidden. I remember that there were rumors about something like this at the time."

"How about a sailboat?" I asked.

"Maybe, but I don't think so. The Pines is more a powerboat kind of place," he said. "Though it's changing now. But in 1969 . . . no, a small powerboat, maybe for fishing, would have been about right."

I sat back in my chair and looked from one Justice to the other. Between them and Ellen Ruehl, I had a pretty good idea of not only why Penny had drowned but how and at whose hands. Now I only needed to prove that Hank Crouse came ashore in a small boat and docked in Ray Tilghman's hidden cove that August afternoon in 1969.

CHAPTER
TWENTY-SIX

I slid into the seat of the rental car and sat in the hot darkness, not turning the key in the ignition. Something Mr. Justice had said not ten minutes ago suddenly vibrated deep in my mind, setting off an unknown process below the surface. The more I tried to focus on it, the more evasive it became. I knew what Joe Lister's advice would be: Give it up and let the unconscious work on it. Your mind would tell you in its own time, he used to say. But suppose there wasn't enough time? A vague uneasiness settled over me.

I looked over my map of Anne Arundel County and headed back to the Pines. There was something I could do while my unconscious was doing its work, I thought. It probably wasn't wise, but I knew I was going to do it anyway. The car's clock said 9:15. I'd been at Fair Waters only just over an hour. I stopped at a convenience store and bought the only flashlight they had, a small red plastic model that fit in my pocket.

The Lido Beach Inn was doing a good business, but then it was a Friday night. There were maybe a dozen cars parked in the lot and the whine of country music came from the jukebox when the door opened. I had heard the song before. Something about lost love, fried eggs for breakfast, and driving all night to Alabama.

I drove slowly past. Then, turning around in an empty street at the end of town, I circled back to the inn and parked at the far end of the parking lot, near the street. After stashing my handbag and briefcase under the seat, I left the car and walked away from Marian's tavern and in the direction of the rows of small houses that lined the streets in the center of Pines on Magothy.

Hank Crouse's house was dark and neither the police cruiser nor Russell's big-wheeled truck were parked out front. The house itself was a 1940s bungalow with its characteristic front porch and jalousie windows. Easy-care aluminum siding had replaced the original wood. The house stood back some from the sidewalk, sheltered by silver maples and good-sized oaks. Fifty feet away and also set back was a small one-car garage. A chain-link fence ran from the garage to the house, enclosing the backyard. I walked by, searching for signs of life. There weren't any. A dog barked in the distance. Two cars drove past.

Turning right into a small gravel street wide enough only for a small car, I walked for a couple of hundred feet, then made another right turn into the alley behind the house and yard. Sure enough, the chain-link fence had a gate. I wondered if I could be seen by people in nearby houses. The two small ranch houses with backyards across the alley were dark. I'd have to take the chance. I opened the gate and slipped in, latching the mechanism as quietly as I could.

Even in the darkness, I could see that the yard was the kind every child should grow up in: deep grass and green shrubs, a picnic table and grill, and trees for climbing and shade. An old swing set creaked when the breeze came up a little. On my right was the tree that the storm had taken, a mature silver maple split in half, its light interior visible in the night. The raw smell of living wood filled my nose. The Crouses had been lucky. The storm's damage could have been much worse.

If Hank Crouse owned a boat, I thought, it was probably going to be in the garage. I could see only one small, high window in the back. I needed something to stand on. Looking around, I saw a plastic milk carrier near the house, the kind used to carry half-gallon jugs or decorate college apartments. I crept to the concrete patio near the back door. Suddenly, there was a sound from the front yard, a sound that I knew too well. Russell's truck turned onto the parking pad in front of the garage.

I sprinted past the split tree, the milk carrier in my hand, and wedged myself into the small space between the far side of the garage and the chain-link fence. I was glad I had. Within seconds, a floodlight illuminated the yard as if it were midday.

Russell Crouse came out with a small chain saw and went to work on the silver maple, methodically cutting off branches and throwing them to one side, then getting to the heavier parts of the trunk. The saw whined loudly in the humid night. I wondered what the neighbors thought. As if in answer, a nearby window went up and an elderly and irate female voice shouted, "Knock it off, Russell Crouse. Some folks are trying to have some peace and quiet around here." Close by, a car with too many amps of stereo pounded awful music through the night, a clattering accompaniment to the chain saw. In a few minutes, Russell was done, the tree dismembered and lying about the lawn like pieces of a carcass. He went back into the house. Not once had he glanced in my direction. The floodlight went off. I breathed deeply and explored my surroundings, careful to shield the beam of the flashlight.

Grabbing the milk carrier, I hefted myself up to look through the little garage window. A dim slat of yellow from a streetlight shone under the front door, not enough to penetrate the darkness. With some difficulty, I shone the flashlight's beam through the small window and got a glimpse of cobwebby windowpane for my trouble.

This had been a truly stupid plan, I thought. And what would it prove if I did find that Hank Crouse owned a boat? A lot of people owned boats, a point Marian had made most clearly the other day. I got down and stood wondering what do to next. Then suddenly, the window above me was illuminated at the same time that a grating noise told me Russell had thrown up the garage door. Quickly stepping back up on the crate, I watched him deposit the chain saw on the floor near the front door. He gave it a final shove, poked around a bench for a few seconds, found what he wanted, and then slammed the garage door shut.

The cluttered garage was in darkness again. But it didn't matter. On the right side, hauled halfway up and attached to the wall, I had seen a small fishing boat with an outboard motor that couldn't have been more than just a few horsepower. On its side was a name, Lois, and a Maryland license number I couldn't read. In white letters was the date: 1968. I stepped down off the milk crate and told myself that it proved nothing.

After a glance around the Crouse's yard, I stood wondering how to get out without being seen. Pushing the milk crate out of sight, I edged along the fence on the far side of the now-amputated silver maple. The kitchen light filtered through a low window and onto the patio in a wide yellow strip. I could see Russell sitting at the table, apparently watching some sports event on television. Occasionally, he got up and opened the refrigerator, going through a case of beer like a brass band on a hot summer day.

I sat wondering whether to run for it when a Volkswagen Beetle chugged up the alley and parked directly behind the house. I shuffled quickly to safety behind the large stump, my left ankle slipping sideways on a fresh pile of sawdust. Sinking to the ground, I yelped at the pain, then held my breath and watched the alley.

Valerie, her hair bewitching in the dim light, let herself in through the gate and walked determinedly to the Crouse's back door. Russell had heard the car stop and come out of the house to meet her. He had taken off his shirt, looking handsome in an overblown and sweaty way, a kind of young blond Elvis. In his hand was a beer. The television played dimly in the background. This time he left the floodlight off. They sat down at the picnic table at the edge of the patio.

"Well, you should be happy, Russ," Valerie began. She lit a

cigarette and threw the match onto the grass. "Will and I broke up yesterday. So you got what you wanted."

"He dump you?"

"No, he didn't dump me. We just decided that our relationship wasn't going anywhere. We're just friends. He's going to help me with my courses at the college."

"He's got another woman. Bet on it."

"You fool," said Valerie. "You're mad at him for dating me and you're mad at him for breaking up with me." She took a deep drag on the cigarette. I could see her eyes on his beer can. "You drink too much, Russ."

At that, he finished the beer and, in a gesture I found familiar, crushed the can and tossed it on the far side of the patio. It banged and rattled to a stop. Then he went inside and with a slam of the refrigerator door carried out a couple more. Valerie smoked passively. If she was tempted or even concerned, it didn't show. He popped both tops and offered her one.

"Nope. My life is on track now. And it's time you got yours together. You got any soda?" Without waiting for an answer, she went inside and returned with a bottle of something. "People are talking about you, Russ, that you can't get a job because you drink too much. There're even some construction jobs coming up over at that new development in Millersville, but I heard nobody would hire you."

"That's bullshit. Who told you that?"

"Doesn't matter. Everybody knows you were drunk when you hit Lillian Weber's niece's car the other night."

"What of it? Who told you they won't hire me for a construction job? Somebody from your precious AA meeting? Yeah, I knew it." He crumbled another can and tossed it after the first. The clanking made a sharp sound in the still night.

"Why don't you come with me to a meeting, Russ." Valerie's voice had turned pleading. "It's a good thing, and everybody helps you to stay sober."

"Like Will St. Claire. He help you stay sober? Not anymore, I guess he don't. Lost interest because now he's got bigger fish to fry. Miss Hotshot New York."

I could hardly believe what I was hearing. He thought I was the bigger fish. Then I flushed in the dark. Was this just a good guess, or had he been wandering in the woods the other night?

"Oh shit, Russ, there's no talking to you. Forget I ever came." She stood up. He grabbed her arm. I could almost feel the oval blue marks rising on her arm. She struggled free in a movement that came of long practice.

"Ever occur to you that Will St. Claire probably knows what happened to old man Tilghman?" he asked. "Maybe even had somethin' to do with it? And then that woman turns up from New York and rents the house a few days later? All ready to take care of Ray Tilghman's dogs and everythin'. How very convenient."

"She's Lillian Weber's niece, you jerk," she said.

"Don't matter," he said, sweating freely in the eerie kitchen light. Behind him, the television flickered and droned. "But it's a true coincidence, ain't it? Ask your mother if it ain't?"

"Will had nothing to do with Ray's death. You should know that. You were at my apartment when Will was there the night of the storm. Or were you in a blackout?" He shrugged. "I wouldn't go around making stupid statements like that, Russ. Your father can't protect you forever." With that, she picked up her handbag from the picnic table and walked across the lawn to the gate.

"It'll be more than a dog next time, you hear?" he yelled at her back. "Remember that."

The window went up across the alley again. "Shut up, Russell Crouse," said the same female voice. "Or I'm callin' your father."

The gears of the Volkswagen slipped into place and with a jolt the car bumped its way down the alley and turned right at the street. It needed a muffler, I thought. Along with Russell. He waited a couple of seconds and went back into the kitchen, slamming the door hard.

I sat where I had fallen, rubbing my ankle and praying it

wasn't broken or sprained. Cautiously, I stood up, testing it with my full weight. It throbbed, but it held me. I'd have to hope that I didn't need to run anywhere very fast anytime soon. I brushed off what I could see of the sawdust on my pants and limped through the gate and down the alley. Across the way, a woman stood outside in her backyard, openly watching me. I waved and she waved back. Just another Friday night at the Crouse place.

The Lido Beach Inn was more crowded than it had been two hours before, but the cars on both sides of my rental car were gone, leaving it by itself at the edge of the parking lot. I shuffled slowly up to it, putting the little flashlight in one pants pocket and patting the other for my car keys. They weren't there. For the first time that night, I could feel my resolve failing me. This was too much. The keys must have fallen out when I slipped behind the tree stump. My ankle throbbed a little, reminding me I needed some ice, and I needed it now, before my ankle was swollen to the size of my thigh. I stood holding on to the car door, fumbling one more time in my pockets, when Russell Crouse's truck pulled up beside me.

CHAPTER

TWENTY-SEVEN

Russell Crouse got out of his truck with less difficulty than the quantity of beer I had just watched him drink should have allowed. The gun rack was fastened to the hatch behind the seat. I could almost see the spool of yellow plastic rope on the floor on the passenger side. He walked around his truck and stood next to me.

"Look who's here."

"Hi. I think I dropped my keys . . ." I began. My left ankle throbbed then, making it easy to pretend to stumble and fall in the dark. I yelped convincingly and grabbed his arm and held on hard, probably hard enough to bring up blue marks like my own, I thought with satisfaction. He was surprised but remarkably solid, holding me up, even steadying me with his beery bulk.

"Oh God, I've twisted my ankle," I gasped. "Can you please help me inside?" A fresh attack of pain helped my acting and together we stumbled inside. Heads turned.

"Lord, now what's happened to you?" Marian came around the bar in a rush, as fast as the crowd allowed her. She all but shoved a young man I'd never seen before out of the booth he was occupying with his girlfriend so that I could sit down. "Russ, get ice and that first-aid kit under the bar." If she noticed that he had been drinking, she didn't show it.

"She's lost her car keys," he said to no one in particular.

The young man had joined his girlfriend on the other bench across from me, honored probably to have front-row seats to the drama. His girlfriend, all peroxide and dark roots, asked me if my ankle hurt. It did, but maybe less than it could have. Maybe because I was more concerned about how was I going to get back to the Crouse yard and find the keys.

George Mink spoke to the middle-aged woman next to him, getting off his stool and giving her a tiny shove in my direction at the same time. Together, they came over to the booth where I was sitting.

"This is my wife, Myrna. She used to be a practical nurse at North Magothy Hospital." Myrna smiled and patted my hand, then took charge, demanding a chair for me to prop my leg on. Bob Fletcher produced it. Someone appeared with ice and the first-aid kit. Myrna asked for a towel. A small crowd gathered around to observe the action.

"How'd it happen?" asked Marian.

"I think I dropped my keys when I got out of the car and then just sort of twisted my ankle as I was looking around for them in the gravel."

"Pines on Magothy is damn near killin' you, isn't it?" said Bob Fletcher. "First, Russ runs you nearly off the road and now this." He turned back to the bar, where Russell was standing sullen and quiet. "You tryin' to kill this young lady?" Laughs arose from the rest of the crowd. "Better stay away from her, Russ."

"Shut up, Bob, and go look outside in the lot for her keys," said Marian, then turning to Russell, her voice low and stern. "Get yourself some coffee and sober up—before your father knows you were drinkin' and drivin' again." He slunk off.

The makeshift icepack that Myrna held on my elevated ankle

187

was beginning to do its work. Bob Fletcher returned to report that he couldn't find the keys. I turned to Marian, who stood silently watching Myrna work.

"Marian, can I use your phone to call the rental-car company and get them to bring me another set of keys." I made a big deal about looking around the booth, then looked up at her. "I must be really tired. I also seem to have left my handbag in the car."

George Mink laughed. "You want me to break into your car and get your handbag?"

"Could you?" He nodded. "I'll go with you."

Myrna shook her head. "No, you'll stay here. George will get your bag. You got to keep that ankle elevated. You should go to the emergency room for an X ray."

"No. No. It feels much better," I said. "The ice is helping. A bandage would help, too." She clucked her dissatisfaction but didn't press the issue, for which I was grateful. George returned with my handbag and briefcase.

"Thought you might want this, too, since I can't lock the car back up. It looks like a nice one, and you never know these days who might come by and take it."

"Yes," said Myrna, looking at George. "You never do."

Everybody laughed at that, happy to have some real entertainment this Friday night. I searched my handbag for the rental-car agreement and started to get up to phone. Marian took it out of my hand and headed behind the bar, where Russell stood drinking coffee and watching me.

In a couple of minutes Marian was back. "Someone will be here in a few minutes, but I had to promise them a big tip," she said. "Really big."

Myrna was now expertly winding a bandage tightly around my ankle. It felt almost all right, but then I was still sitting down, with my leg propped on a chair.

The door to the bar opened and Hank Crouse came in. I had a flash of Ellen Ruehl picking out his yearbook picture and handing it over to me wordlessly. Russell moved furtively behind the bar. Hank glanced at my bandaged ankle, then at the first-aid kit. His hand where he had cut it on the dull saw last week was still covered, but with a smaller bandage.

In a flash I knew. My unconscious mind, given its freedom, had produced the missing piece. When Ward Justice had mentioned that there had been no marks on Ray Tilghman's body and Penny Hart's body, my mind had taken it in to play with. I knew with the certainty that intuition brings that there were marks on Hank Crouse's hand and they weren't from any tree-cutting accident. I needed to see under his bandage, to see the wound. Looking up from his hand, I found myself staring directly into his eyes. They were a cold and penetrating blue, more so against his gray hair and austere face with its crooked nose.

"Thought you were in New York," he said. I explained in as few words as possible that I'd returned early and now I'd lost my car keys and twisted my ankle. "You stay mighty busy, don't you?" he said. I didn't bother to answer.

We were interrupted when an athletic and middle-aged black woman wearing a rental-car uniform appeared at the door. She instinctively hurried in my direction, knowing that the Lido Beach Inn wasn't a place she wanted to linger. I thanked her for the keys and handed her a couple of ten-dollar bills, then stood up to see if my ankle would hold my weight. It did. And rather well, I thought. Myrna looked at it disapprovingly. I followed her glance, and seeing that the back of my pant leg was still covered with sawdust, I nonchalantly brushed it away. It was too late. Hank Crouse had seen it, too.

"I'll be fine," I told Myrna. "And I promise to have someone look at my ankle tomorrow." I suddenly needed to be out of the bar, to be by myself to think about what I had found out tonight and to figure out what it meant. I limped to the door, taking care not to put too much weight on my ankle. Thanking everyone, I looked one last time at Hank Crouse. He was openly watching me, unsmiling. From the bar, both Marian and Russell were both watching him, with something like fear on their faces.

*   *   *

The drive home was uneventful, although I was grateful that the rental car had no clutch to challenge my left ankle. Once wrapped in a snug compression bandage, it felt fine. I was quite certain that it would be fully okay in a few days. I wasn't sure about anything else. I'd had the sense for days that people here were covering up something about Ray Tilghman's death. The uneasiness that swam over me earlier in the parking lot at Fair Waters increased. Tiny Mrs. Justice had used the word: *premonition.*

Everything at the Weller's Creek Road house seemed peaceful. The dogs were pleased to see me and I stood in the pine needles watching them chase each other around the yard, glad to be away from the music and lights and chatter of Marian's tavern. Then a twig snapped in the distance and I felt my heart jump. The dogs, I could see, hadn't even heard it. My imagination was out of control. I needed to do something that would bring it down to earth. This unrest, I knew, would send me fleeing back to New York the way no dead animals could. And for Lillian's sake, I couldn't leave. Or for my sake, I thought. I'd have to face these unseen and unknown fears.

I hadn't been down to the water since before New York. It might help me figure something out. And if there were ghosts there, I would see they were benevolent. After all, I was on their side. Oh Lord, I thought, I was acting as if I believed in ghosts. Well, did I? Finding the old stick that Will told me Ray Tilghman used for walking, I headed to the water. Myrna would have had my head examined, but God knows, it wasn't the most stupid thing I'd already done this night.

The heat and humidity had retreated some and the moon rose high and almost full in the sky over the creek. The water lapped softly. Admonishing the dogs that I wanted no swimming, I sat down with them at the end of the dock to think about the evening.

The meeting with the Justices seemed days ago. They confirmed that the circumstances of Penny's death and Ray's death each had a peculiarity that made people uneasy. In Ray's death, it was the dogs left in the house; in Penny's case, the fact that she was an experienced swimmer.

I already knew that Ray had been in the habit of letting Penny swim from his dock. With everybody else, he protected his privacy fiercely. Was it only because she had admitted her alcoholism to him, maybe even as early as high school? Maybe he had felt guilty about Penny's death all these years, thinking that if he hadn't let her swim in his cove, she wouldn't have died. I stored the thought away to consider later.

I also knew what Penny's parents had told Mr. Justice: that she went to Ray's cove to study her lines and sun herself. This despite the fact that her parents would have preferred her to stay home. I hadn't known, however, that Marian and Shirley had dropped by later that afternoon. Had Penny's parents told them where she went? And then there was the matter of the phone call. The reporter had seemed to imply that Penny had left right after it—almost as if she'd planned to meet someone. Had Hank Crouse been the caller?

Mr. Justice and his wife both thought that someone came ashore that Sunday afternoon, tying up a small boat on Ray's dock. There had been a fight and Penny fell or was pushed into the water, perhaps being held under until her breathing stopped. The person then left by boat, leaving no evidence. Is that what had happened? Could have, I thought.

My mind skipped back to my brief glimpse of Hank Crouse's fishing boat. Lido Beach, Mr. Justice had said, had a public dock for residents of the Pines who didn't own waterfront property. Maybe Hank used to keep his boat there during the summer, perhaps for fishing. But then his wife died. Did he stop using the boat named for her? I'd have to find out. Still, just because he owned a boat, it didn't make him a killer. Maybe someone else had used the boat, or another boat. How would I ever know?

Okay, I told myself. Settle down. This is all conjecture, like my list of people in Pines on Magothy and their motives for this and that. Penny Hart's drowning had happened over twenty-four years ago. That made it highly unlikely that I'd ever know for sure, to say nothing of finding any proof. It was Ray's death that I needed to focus on now.

My heart did an unnerving little dance. I admitted to myself the terrible knowledge I'd kept tightly wound inside of me for the last hour. I had absolutely no doubt that under Hank Crouse's bandages were a dog's deep teeth marks. I looked from Zeke to Lancelot, wishing they could tell their story. I'd put money on Zeke, my fierce protector, to have been the biter. There was no hate in his heart, I knew, but with Hank Crouse yanking him away from the cove and back to the house without the old man, he must have been pushed to the limit. The black dog stirred restlessly.

I stretched my leg and sprained ankle out straight, grateful once again that it wasn't worse than it was. All at once, I wholeheartedly wished that there was no mystery, that I could let my mind drift pleasantly in the moonlight, with no thoughts except for the peace and beauty of the place. Zeke groaned a little in his sleep, his tail whooshing against the dock once or twice. It had been a long, long day, I thought.

Suddenly, both dogs were standing on full alert. Then Lancelot ran hell-bent for the wide path that led up to the house, stopping all at once at the edge of the woods. Zeke stayed behind, his throat rattling with the same low warning I'd heard from him that first day he had held me off.

Close by, a car engine cut off. The door slammed and I could hear steps as someone walked over some loose brush on the path. Involuntarily, I got to my feet, glad for Ray's walking stick. It was sturdy, though it certainly wouldn't be of any use to me against Russell's rifle. Zeke backed up against my legs, as if to tell me he'd handle it. Lancelot barked loudly and steadily. I held my breath. In the widening of the path as it opened onto the cove stood Hank Crouse.

CHAPTER
TWENTY-EIGHT

"Lance. Come." The dog, bronze-colored coat glowing gold in the moonlight, stopped barking and looked at me from the wooded path, then back at the cop, puzzled. Then he bounded in my direction, glad for someone else to make the decision for him. Zeke growled again, too low for Hank Crouse to hear. I touched his black head and felt him relax a little.

"Hello. I've got hold of them."

"Thought I might find you here," he said. "I'm not surprised. You have a thing for this cove, don't you?" Without waiting for my reply, he said, "It's a lovely spot. But so many terrible things have happened here. Scares a lot of people off. I expect Lillian will have some trouble selling."

He didn't seem to be waiting for an answer. Instead, he came closer to the dock, stopping short when Zeke shifted his weight and growled. Lance moved nearer to my side, his ears up, alert again for a signal from me to act. I couldn't think of anything to say. Maybe I should just run for it. Will's truck had not been at the bungalow but maybe I could make it back to the house and call 911. But what good would that do? Hank Crouse would get the call and radio back that he would take care of things. No, I had to stand my ground here. I had ghosts to avenge, I thought wildly, and dogs to protect. His gun was strapped to his tightly controlled waistline. I wondered if he had trouble passing the police physical.

"I found your car keys," he said. "For your rental car."

Although his voice was neutral, my heart surged. He'd guessed about the sawdust and after I left the Lido Beach Inn, he'd gone to his house and looked around. And bingo, there were the keys by the stump of the silver maple. They might as well have had my name on them.

"You'll never guess where I found them," he said.

I shook my head and waited. There was another long silence, the dogs quiet, the wind lapping the creek water into tiny wavelets that broke under the dock where I was standing. The moonlight grabbed hold of something metal on Hank Crouse's uniform shirt and spun the ray of light it produced in my direction.

"Mind if I sit down?" he asked, coming closer. He half-leaned, half-sat on the elbow of the sycamore tree, just yards from where Lancelot had towed Ray's body out of low water and ashore. He looked out to the water, not in any hurry to get this conversation over with. It was as if he were actually enjoying himself. "It is peaceful here. You are lucky to have it. I don't feel any ghosts, do you?" He laughed a little.

"No, but then I don't believe in ghosts." What I did believe in was that I was in deep trouble. There was a good possibility that Hank Crouse had twice killed people at this cove. Why wouldn't he do so again? I reminded myself that I had no proof that he was responsible for either Penny or Ray's deaths. And probably never would. The boat named *Lois* proved nothing. My imagination had taken off skyward again.

"You don't believe in ghosts? I thought you did." He smiled then and I was reminded of another smile. He had passed that smile along to Will, I thought, on whom it became face-changing and radiant. But maybe Penny was also responsible for Will's smile. Is that what everyone had seen in her? Had she used her smile to get what she wanted? Is that why her acting career had blossomed so quickly in New York?

These thoughts were crazy. Pay attention, I told myself. Your life may depend on it. Hank Crouse moved a little, tipping his head in my direction and causing the dogs to adjust their positions to keep an eye on him. I had to get away from here and from him, no matter how tired I was. But with everything in me, I suddenly wanted to sleep, to have this nightmare go away. Instead, I shook my exhaustion off and tried to take charge.

"Officer Crouse, I appreciate your bringing me the keys. Now I better just say thank you and head up to the house. It's been a long day."

"I found your keys," he said slowly, "in the gravel at the far end of Marian's parking lot. Whoever looked for them didn't look too good. Could have saved you a few dollars."

"Oh yes?" He was lying. I was sure of it. No way had the keys fallen out of my pants pocket in the parking lot. "Bob Fletcher looked. I guess, like you say, he didn't look hard enough. It happens," I finished weakly.

"Well, Bob may have had a few beers in him, too. And he's always been a little absentminded. I've known him since high school, and let me tell you, he wasn't a rocket scientist then any more than he is now. Most of us didn't even think he'd graduate." He paused meaningfully. "I think Mrs. Lynch, our old high school English teacher, gave him a passing grade so he'd get his diploma."

Mrs. Lynch. He knew I had been to see Mrs. Lynch, I thought wildly. That's where he was going with this inane conversation. That must mean he knew that I had the 1968 Magothy High yearbook. He also knew I just had come from New York. I couldn't see his eyes in the moonlight, but I felt the slivers of blue ice penetrate my body. How long could Hank Crouse and I tango like this?

The radio pinned to Hank Crouse's shirt buzzed suddenly, breaking into my thoughts and carving a slice of static through the dark night. He spoke back, then, heaving himself off the tree trunk, he walked out onto the dock. Both dogs stiffened. I grabbed Zeke's collar. All I needed was to have him attack. Hank wouldn't hesitate to use his gun. If he'd passed his smile to Will, Russell got his twitchy fingers from somewhere. A brief glimpse of the massacred raccoon passed in front of my eyes. I took the keys, shivering.

"You cold?" he asked.

"No, just tired."

"Then you're right. You should get some rest. I'll walk you up to the house."

He stood aside for me to pass. I still held tightly to Zeke's collar. Lance heeled beside me. The four of us walked across the beach toward the wooded path, the dogs twisting around to keep an eye on him.

"If you're going to live here, you gotta get a boat," he said conversationally. "I've got one myself I could sell you. I haven't used it in years. Named for my dead wife."

"I'm afraid I don't sail," I said. Two could play this game.

"Oh, it's not a sailboat, just a small fishing craft. Just for dilly-dallying around the creek, really. Not like the Cigarette boats you see now. It used to be fun, but without a private place like your dock to berth it, there're always problems. Even for ten horses on a rowboat." He laughed. "Just impossible to keep people from using it if you dock it at Lido Beach. Kids, I think, take it when no one's around. When my wife died in 1968, I took it out of the water."

Well, not exactly, I thought. I stumbled and then stood frozen, willing my bad ankle forward up the path to the house.

"You need help?" he asked.

"Thanks, but I'm fine. Myrna did such a good job of wrapping my ankle that I forgot for a moment that I'd hurt it."

"Yes," he said. "It's easy to forget when nothin' hurts. And then somethin' happens and you're reminded of the hurt all over again."

My head swam. What was he talking about? Had something hurt him? And if so, what was it and why was he telling me? We reached the clearing. The white police cruiser was parked next to the rental car. Pine needles crunched under foot. I still held Zeke's collar.

Hank Crouse walked to his car and opened the door, then he walked back to me. There was a kind of controlled emotion about him now, sadness maybe or resignation. Whatever had happened at Ray Tilghman's cove twenty-four years ago, it had forever changed his life. I knew now he'd survived all these years in a web of half-truths and loneliness, forced to live with the guilt of Penny's death, however it happened, accident *or* murder.

Then with Will's arrival six months ago in the Pines, the whole thing had been unleashed all over again, I thought. Will had told Ray who he was. Ray went further and wrote to Ellen Ruehl. And although she had not remembered Hank Crouse's name, her description of him in her letter to Ray must have been enough for the old man to have guessed what Will instinctively didn't want to know: who his father was and that his father had probably been responsible—directly or indirectly—for his mother's death.

I guessed now that when Ray received the letter from Ellen Ruehl, he must have called Hank Crouse. The policeman had come by Weller's Creek Road the night of the storm and the old man must have accused him of murdering Penny or otherwise being implicated in her death. And Ray had probably been right, I thought, even if he couldn't prove it. But the damage was done. Hank Crouse had been forced to kill again, to keep his secret a secret. Or maybe Ray Tilghman had fallen in the water during their argument. For the moment at least, the details of the night of the storm didn't matter.

I stood in the silent clearing and looked at the cop, understanding for the first time that Hank Crouse was filled more with despair than anger or hatred. I knew it as strongly as I ever had known anything. I could feel the emotion coming off him. It was almost physical, harrowing and real. He must, I thought, despise the streak of brutality in Russell's character.

We had been standing in the clearing for long, silent minutes. Even the dogs hadn't moved.

"Thank you for bringing my keys," I said. He nodded. "You didn't have to." I glanced at his hand and wished that I had imagined everything, that there was a reasonable explanation for the puncture wounds under the white bandage. He followed my glance. We both knew that there wasn't.

"Miss Elliott," he said, "let things stay between us."

I didn't have time to answer. The dogs turned all at once to the path that led to Weller's Creek Road, then barked joyfully. Will's red pickup pulled into the clearing.

"I thought I heard voices when I got home. Anything wrong?" Will asked me.

"Uh, no, just Officer Crouse returning my car keys." Will looked with interest at the bandage wound round my ankle. I laughed a little. "Twisted it just a bit, but it's fine. It's a long story about the keys. I promise to tell you tomorrow." He said nothing. "Everything, Will," I said.

Will looked first at me, then at Hank Crouse. The dogs wiggled for attention at Will's side, forgotten for the moment. I stood transfixed. Did either of them know who the other was? Will edged backward to his truck, his face more unreadable than I'd ever seen it. He guessed, I thought. Like I knew things, he knew them, too. It was what was between us, the complex and deep connection we didn't understand and couldn't say aloud. We both knew who Hank Crouse was.

"I'm okay, Will. I'll talk to you tomorrow," I repeated.

"Okay, then," he said. His face was a mask. "Good night." Turning the truck around, he headed back to his bungalow, leaving me to my fate. The dogs looked bereft, not understanding.

I turned back to Hank Crouse. He was watching me. He knew, too, I thought. He knew that he'd just come face-to-face with his past, the past he could never quite get rid of. But Will was not the threat. I was. Why had I ever let Will go home? Here I was with a man who may have killed twice. Apprehension filled me all over again. How stupid could I have been? Then Hank Crouse got into the cruiser.

"Let it lie," he said. The car turned around and was gone. It was no longer a threat, more of a plea. I stood in the clearing, wondering why. Had the knowledge that Will was his son saved my life? Had he decided that I would be his judge and jury? I felt sick. Motioning to the dogs, I ran for the house.

CHAPTER
TWENTY-NINE

I woke early, before first light. In my dream, tiny Mrs. Justice had been saying something about a premonition over and over, a sort of musical backbeat to an adventure concerning car keys and raccoons and running away from someone who might have been Ben. When he caught me, I had turned his face to mine and found it was Will, his eyes wild and demanding. Now I shivered in the gloom and pulled the sheet closer.

Zeke and Lancelot stirred, then jumped on the bed, happy that I was awake. I was glad for their solid bodies and warm sleepy-dog smell. Maybe I could go back to sleep. Turning over, my ankle throbbed a little and the events of the night before came rushing back. There would be no more sleep.

I made coffee, walked the dogs and fed them, then sat down at the rolltop desk. The tall brass crane, its sculpted feathers bluish green, stood nearby, its beak upturned to the rising sun. It looked more at home this morning than it had yesterday afternoon. Outside the window, birds sang a little in the early light, before the day's heat sent them exhausted and quiet to the trees.

I had to face Will, to tell him the details of what he had already guessed. How had it fallen to me to be the one to confirm who his father was? Here I was, a perfect stranger who dropped into his life less than two weeks ago, and now I held the knowledge he had wanted for so long. And it wasn't happy knowledge. Finding out about your parents rarely was, I thought. Even acknowledging my father's alcoholism had taken something from me. And Will would have the far larger task of coming to terms with the awful truth that his father may well have killed his mother. Still, people are resilient. And the St. Claires had probably given him more strength than either Penny or Hank alone ever could have. But that wouldn't make it easier for him, maybe even harder by comparison.

Hank Crouse. I didn't want to think about him, either. Something had happened last night in the clearing. He had made a decision when Will showed up. Had Ray told him who Will was? Probably he had guessed that Will was the son that he had wanted all those years ago, the son Penny Hart wouldn't let him be a father to.

Zeke slumped against my leg, drowsy from his breakfast. He yawned when I stroked his sleek head, his eyes holding mine in a burst of adoration that would have been indecent from another human. Something else was rattling around in my mind. Then, my heart sinking a little, I remembered. The deer kill on Arundel Island was scheduled for this afternoon.

Finishing the coffee, I felt wearier than I ever had. I searched my mind for someone wise and old and unshakable to talk to, someone who didn't have an emotional investment in what was happening around me. Weller Church. The clock said 7:30. I picked up the phone and called him. He would come over.

A half hour later, Weller's old Lincoln pulled up beside the rental car parked under the pine trees. I had made more coffee and was watching from the enclosed porch as the lawyer made his way to the house. He looked weary, too, in the morning's dappling sun. I thought about the deer kill. What was it like to sit in your living room and listen to the shots, knowing that each represented the death of yet another soft brown and sweet-faced creature? Was

I being sentimental? Did the animal-rights people or the Arundel Island residents have it right? Surely there was a better way to get rid of the deer than this.

"Morning," he said, heavily climbing the few steps to the porch. He was dressed as always in baggy suit and bow tie. I poured him coffee and he settled into a wicker chair, carefully blowing across the cup to cool his coffee. Dog tails thumped on the floorboards. "Does this have to do with Lil?" he asked.

"No. Strangely enough, it doesn't."

As he settled back with his cup, I asked him to represent me, and when he agreed, I told him the whole story—everything I knew, felt, and still wondered. His face remained expressionless until I got to the part about snooping outside Hank Crouse's garage last night. That made him mutter a little, then he waved his hand slightly to get me back into the narrative. When I was done, he put his cup on the table and leaned over to scratch Lance's curly coat.

"What you've just told is not unexpected to me," he said slowly. "Like Mr. Justice, all these years I've wondered about Penny Hart's death. And now it's coming out. Though I don't think that Ray was any kind of pervert. There's no evidence and I can't think Ward Justice really believes it either. It's more likely that Ray felt guilt that she died on his property." He looked at my ankle and then at my face. The scratch was nearly gone. "I'm just sorry you had to fall into the middle of it. I had no idea, of course, when Lil and I drew up the rental contract for Ray's house."

"I know that."

"Because I imagine if I look hard and creatively, I can still find some way for you to break the lease."

"No. I want to rent the house and stay with the dogs. Will is building me an outdoor shower." I heard my voice. It sounded strong and sure.

"Okay, then."

"Must I tell the police what I know about Hank Crouse and Penny Hart and Ray Tilghman?" I studied Weller. He was staring into the clearing. "I have no proof of anything, you understand. Not one shred. In fact, I don't even know what really happened, either last week or in 1969. Every last bit of it is conjecture, but I don't want to carry it around anymore."

"I suggest," he said slowly, "that perhaps you could make a confidential statement to the homicide people. Legally, you cannot then be considered an accessory. You will have done your civic duty." He sighed. "Then the pieces will have to fall where they may. It will no longer be your problem."

"What about Will? I owe him an explanation."

"Yes, I guess you do." Weller appeared to be thinking. "Why don't you talk with him this morning? I'll make a few phone calls and set up an appointment with the police for later."

A thought occurred to me. "Weller, I'd prefer not to run into Hank Crouse if I can help it."

"Not to worry. Homicide is located in a different office. You can call me to find out where and when we'll meet."

In the distance, from across the water, came one lone rifle shot. I looked at the old lawyer. He knew what I was thinking.

"Not yet. It's not until about four or five this afternoon. The residents of Arundel Island are all given plenty of chance to leave the island if they like. It will all be over in a couple of hours."

That lone shot must mean that Russell Crouse was out early with his rifle, shooting everything that came his way. He may never have gone to bed, I thought, just stayed up drinking and angry and vengeful after his talk with Valerie last night. I didn't say anything.

Weller Church got up, leaned over, and pressed my hand. "Call me in a couple of hours, at the house. And don't worry more than you have to. I'll go with you to the police. And it will all be over soon."

I took a bath and dressed carefully in a narrow black skirt, vest, and a crisp white shirt, glad to have fresh clothes. Carefully applied makeup covered what was left of the long, thin scratch. I began to look better, I thought as I pushed silver earrings through my ears, just a little tired around the eyes. Finally, I rewrapped my ankle in the compression bandage. It was only slightly swollen this morning, although it still hurt a little. I didn't think I wanted to run a race just yet. In a couple of days, maybe.

The coffee had done its work, giving me a wide-awake mind in a body that throbbed with fatigue. I made myself go in the kitchen and find some breakfast, hoping it would take the edge off the coffee. Pulling a package of corn muffins out of the freezer, I suddenly remembered that I had agreed to go sailing that evening with Mitch Gaylin and his friends. I dropped my frozen muffin back on the plate and headed for the phone.

Sitting down at the desk, I dialed, listening as the phone rang once, twice, three times. I hung up. Maybe it would be better just to go. Lillian had already told me she was going to an AA meeting. The worst thing I could do was to sit here by myself, listening to the shots being fired across the water, visualizing the slaughter. Weller said that it was done humanely, one shot to the head if possible, sudden death with no suffering and pain. I didn't care. I wanted out of here until it was over.

It was almost ten when I gathered my courage and drove up the long driveway to Will's bungalow. I had stuffed Ellen Ruehl's letter in my pocket. The pickup wasn't there. Where was he? Had something happened? After about six seconds I flew out of the car and ran to the front door. Attached with tape was an old envelope. *Eve. Back this afternoon. Will.*

Instead of relief, I felt worse. Maybe it was a job. He often worked seven days a week during the summer, I knew, driving to local nurseries to pick up fall shrubs as they became ready for transplanting. I pulled out my pen to write a note back, then changed my mind and left for Weber Realty.

Lillian and Shirley were both in the middle of phone calls when I arrived. I called Weller from the phone in the conference room and was told to meet him at the police station as soon as possible. He gave me directions and I left after telling Shirley I'd be back in an hour or two.

The Anne Arundel County homicide detective was outrageously polite, one step from being openly patronizing. Weller's solid bow-tied bulk prevented it, for which I was grateful. We were ushered into a small office, where I told him what I knew as the tape recorder recorded what in the light of day sounded like feverish hallucinations. Death at Ray's cove seemed so trite and impossible in this institutional office. I was told to come back on Monday to read and sign my statement. Feeling dispirited, I thanked Weller and left. I'd done what I needed to do. Finding a pay phone, I called Will. There was no answer. It was about noon.

I returned to the real estate office and spent the afternoon going through the paperwork with Lillian and Shirley. Ginger Clancy showed up briefly, as did a few clients. My head pounded and my body and soul ached for the peace of sleep. I'd never, I thought, get all the damn forms straight, dozens of legal-sized documents of fine print. Offers and counteroffers, all initialed until they were nearly illegible. Contracts and appraisals and termite and well and sewer reports. Fortunately, Shirley knew almost as much as Lillian. During a spare moment, I wondered what Gilbert was up to that afternoon. By three, Lillian noticed my increasing inability to pay attention and insisted that I go home. Tomorrow would be more fun, she promised, with several appointments to show properties and an open house.

I got into the rental car and looked at my face in the rearview mirror. It was haggard. I wasn't much looking forward to seeing Will. I drove home, rehearsing what I would say. Turning off Weller's Creek Road, I started to turn into his parking area when I saw Valerie's car parked behind the red truck. My talk with him would have to wait. I was relieved and then annoyed. I drove the last quarter mile to Ray's house, thinking about what Russell had told Valerie last night. Next time, he said, it wouldn't be a dead dog.

CHAPTER

THIRTY

The clearing in front of Ray Tilghman's house was oddly quiet as I parked the car. No birdsong or locusts broke through the early fall afternoon, only the faint sound of trees brushing against each other and an occasional and distant powerboat engine. I crawled out of the car, drained from the long day. My head ached a little.

I locked the car door, then stood, not moving. The scent of the pines permeated the air, swirling around me, holding me hostage to what seemed a lethal, sun-dappled radiance. I shook myself free of my foreboding, putting the deer kill from my mind.

The sliver of creek was visible from the clearing. Land and trees and water were just property, I thought. They had no soul or heart. They didn't cause what had happened here or care that it had. There was a lone bark from the house, Zeke reminding me that the dogs needed to be let out. Then from behind me, pine needles crunched.

I turned and saw Gilbert appear out of the woods along the path. Not far from him was an old posted sign. I realized I'd never heard him speak.

"Hello, Gilbert."

He stared steadily at me, then strolled calmly into the clearing by the car. He must have been nearly six feet tall. And up close, he looked like any other teenager having a terrible time with acne. His skin was mean and irritated from an onslaught of adolescent hormones. They had caused abscessed pimples, white and deep red around the edges, to play over his face and neck. They would go away, I thought, unlike the vacant look that filtered from his eyes. That would stay forever. I wondered if he knew the effect he had on people.

"Gilbert?" I tried again. There was a faint response in the unresponsive eyes. "Do you want a soda?"

He came toward me, looking around, as if not wanting anyone else to see that he had been seduced by my offer. In his hand was a toy rifle, suitable for a six-year-old. I hadn't noticed it and now it shocked me. If he was strange now, three years from now he'd probably be armed and dangerous.

"Gilbert," I said firmly, "you sit here and wait for me. I'm going to get you a soda." He sat obediently on the steps of the house. I went inside, closing the door behind me, a little shaken. He was just a badly retarded kid, I told myself. I patted the dogs and quickly moved to the refrigerator.

"Here's your soda, Gilbert." He accepted the cold, wet can, watching me as he popped it open. He could talk just fine, I thought. He just wasn't going to. A small shiver went down my back. Was I going to be frightened by a toy gun–toting and retarded adolescent? To my relief, he then turned and walked into the heavily wooded stretch on the far side of the house, apparently forgetting that I existed.

I let the dogs out and then went back inside, unsettled and mad at myself. My imagination was running free. Too free. How much longer was I going to let it control me? How could I live here if every time a twig broke, some unnamed fear unleashed itself over me? I hoped it was just the knowledge of the deer shoot later this afternoon that made me so jumpy.

I got myself a glass of milk and two aspirin and went upstairs to unpack my clothes and find something suitable for sailing. An old NYU sweatshirt, its black-torch emblem indistinct against the faded purple background, was the best I could do. In the yard, the dogs began to bark. I ran back downstairs, the fear welling up inside me all over again, refusing to be sweet-talked away by reason and common sense.

"Lance. Zeke." I could hear running in the woods as they plowed through the heavy brush. There was no answer. Then Russell Crouse slogged into view, from the same place that Gilbert had appeared a few minutes ago, the dogs a distance on either side of him and barking furiously. Zeke, in particular, was riled, his growls low in his throat and dangerous. Russell didn't appear to notice. He was dressed in hunting gear, red long-sleeved shirt and visored hat, and sweating freely in the late-day heat and too-heavy clothes. There was a cartridge belt at his waist. Had he been invited to kill deer after all?

"Russell, what . . ."

"Call your dogs off," he said.

I called and they came to me, Lancelot more composed than Zeke, who only sat when I seized his collar and pushed his hindquarters to the ground.

"They won't hurt you now," I said. I didn't for a moment believe it. Zeke would tear into him at the slightest request from me. Russell would end up with a bandage worse than the one that still covered his father's hand. The thought gave me the creeps.

I looked at him closely. If he was drunk, it didn't show yet, but he certainly sounded like he had the night he plowed into my car. I could almost feel the marks on my arm where his strong fingers had dug in a few days ago. Above me, a cicada began its long, piercing crescendo, then abruptly stopped.

Russell stood there staring at me, then shifted position and glanced toward Will's cottage. In a rush, I knew why he was here. He had seen Valerie's car parked next to the red pickup. I remembered his threat to her last night.

"What do you want, Russell?" He didn't answer, just turned at the sound of something in the bushes and, hefting the rifle, fired. The sound reverberated through the woods, deafening and deadly. Zeke shuddered under my hand and Lancelot moved closer. I tried to remember everything I'd ever heard about self-defense, but mostly it had addressed random urban violence—car jackers and muggers and people who wanted your money. This was different, more primitive and personal.

Russell Crouse smiled a little in my direction, glad, I guessed, that he had frightened me. I thought back to the first day I'd met him in the Lido Beach Inn. He'd been calmly tapping kegs and carrying cases of beer for Marian, easygoing and cocky, almost benign. But this brute, dressed for killing, was the one I had seen the other night on the road. Perhaps even more frightening, certainly more angry. The difference, I knew, was alcohol. He was a caricature of a mean drunk. I had to get into the house somehow.

"Russell, you have to leave."

"Why?"

"Because someone is going to get hurt," I said.

"And it's not gonna be me." He laughed, shifting the weight of the rifle to the other forearm. In the distance, from Arundel Island, came one lone shot. A pang of something passed over his face.

This really had to stop, I thought. Taking both dog collars and holding my breath, I turned my back and walked to the house. I couldn't let him see my fear. My ankle hurt again and my mouth trembled.

"Oh, no, you don't just walk away from me."

I sent the dogs up the steps to the porch, when suddenly he was beside me, pushing me the last few steps into the house. Both dogs lunged at him, Lancelot's strong body knocking him down and Zeke all over him. I watched as the rifle fell clattering to the porch floor and lay a few feet away. I ran for it, kicking the screen door open and pushing the dogs outside again at the same time. I dove for the rifle, but it scuttled out of reach, his and mine.

There was no going back now, I knew. He stood enraged and foul with sweat and drink. Suddenly he moved forward, knocking me backward with his arm and picking up the rifle. Behind me in the yard, I could hear the dogs barking furiously. He turned and through the porch window fired three shots. I heard an unearthly noise, then a crashing in the bushes and the lone sound of Lancelot's frantic barking. He'd killed Zeke, I thought, Zeke of the loyal brown eyes with their spinning fleck of gold. I could feel my heart burst with pain and rage, the adrenaline rush through my muscles. I had to get help for the dog. On my feet and running to the rolltop desk, I picked up the phone. He followed me, grabbing it out of my hands and ripping it from the wall.

In the confusion, I clearly saw the huge metal crane, its beak pointing away from the afternoon sun. I pirouetted and lunged toward it, turning the beak in his direction. And with everything I had, I shoved it. I could hear Russell's scream as the metal beak made contact with skin. Without turning back to see the damage on his face, I ran as fast as I could out of the house and through the clearing, then up the wide path a quarter mile to Will's bungalow. My ankle throbbed, but it held me up. I heard my skirt tear as I ran, the kick pleat in the back giving way. Behind me came the sounds of Russell running, his breathing heavy but the sounds of his feet muffled in the pine needles. From Arundel Island came two more shots and I saw again the raccoon's exploding face as clearly as if it was happening in front of me.

"Will," I screamed. "Call 911. Will. Will!" Behind me, Russell was getting closer. And then we were running strangely side by side. I looked across and saw a thin trail of blood on the left side of his face where the crane's sharp beak had caught him. The rifle was in his left hand. "Will. Get help."

With his left hand, Russell reached over and hit me in the face. The blow was glancing, but I stumbled and fell. Will's bungalow was a hundred yards away. When I tried to get up, he pushed me down again, waving the rifle in my direction.

"Shut up," he said. Then he pushed me again. I fell back, my ears alive with the sound of Zeke's awful cry. Where was Lance? I prayed he'd stay in the woods, where he had a chance. Here there was no chance. I moved slightly, turning to see what Russell was doing. His back was toward me. He stood looking at the bungalow. Didn't they see him? Had they called for help? I made a tiny noise in my throat, but nothing came out. He looked around at me, and seeing no movement, he walked closer to the two-room cottage.

I lay crumbled in Will's yard, my mouth full of dirt and rage. Zeke's yelp went through me again. And now Will and Valerie were in danger. I knew it wasn't me Russell wanted. I was just in his way. He wanted Will, I thought.

"Russell," I screamed. "He's your brother, your half brother."

He turned in my direction for a minute, blue eyes doubting. "Shut up, you don't know nothin'." Did he know? The way his father had known last night? As I watched, he moved closer to the bungalow, saying nothing. In the distance, the shots from Arundel Island were coming regularly now. I wondered wildly if Weller Church and his wife had stayed to listen or whether they had fled the sounds of slaughter. There was momentary quiet. Another cicada began its song, changed its mind, and quit. Russell moved toward the house, forgetting me, waiting. He said nothing.

From around the corner came Mitch's Jeep. I'd forgotten all about sailing. Fear swam through me again. Russell was out of control and probably wouldn't hesitate to shoot at Mitch. But strangely enough, he apparently hadn't heard the Jeep, focusing only on his victims in the little house. I pulled myself to my feet as he disappeared inside.

"Mitch, call the cops. He's going to kill Will." My voice came to me from a distance, calmer than my words. I saw him pick up the car phone, then, leaving the door ajar, run in my direction.

"No, no. Stay there. I'm okay."

He half-pulled, half-carried me to the car. My ankle twanged with pain. I fell into the front seat and waited, trying to get my breath. From Weller's Creek Road came the sound of sirens.

CHAPTER
THIRTY-ONE

A police cruiser thundered down the long drive off Weller's Creek Road, its tires throwing pine needles and dirt as it braked. The young cop with the blond crew cut jumped out, his gun ready. After taking one look, he radioed for help. I stumbled out of the Jeep and pointed to the house. Mitch tried to pull me back.

"In there. Russell Crouse. He's got a deer rifle." As if to prove my point, a volley of shots came from Arundel Island, then another.

A second police car, its lights flashing, pulled into the clearing. Hank Crouse, his face tight and eyes nervous, looked directly at me.

"Hank," I screamed, "it's Russell. Will and Valerie are inside. Russell's very drunk and he's got his rifle."

"Get back in the Jeep and get down," he said.

My skirt, I noticed, was shredded, the white blouse that had been fresh this morning covered with dirt and pine needles. My head was hurting, the bump beginning to grow where Russell Crouse had slugged me.

In the distance, Lance's forlorn and uneven barking threaded its way into my consciousness. Mitch pulled me toward cover again and once again I fought my way free. I couldn't help Will, I thought wildly, but I had to get to Zeke before it was too late. Maybe it already was and he was dead. Tears fell silently down my face, but I stood rooted to the ground behind the Jeep, watching the door of the bungalow.

Then from inside the bungalow came one shot, a short silence, then a heart-stopping female scream. I looked at Hank Crouse. His masklike features hardened as Valerie appeared in the doorway, Russell behind her, holding her around the shoulders with one arm, waving his rifle with the other. She suddenly emitted another unearthly shriek. Panicked and angry, Russell pushed her into the clearing and began shooting randomly, almost casually. I saw the blond cop hit the ground as something zinged beside him. Mitch jerked me down beside him on the ground in back of the left-front fender of the Jeep.

In the next second, as the scent of the pines floated over us and the sun dappled across the clearing, Hank Crouse lifted his gun and shot once. In one movement, Russell Crouse dropped his rifle, clutched his leg, and dropped into the pine needles ten yards from Will's front door. Valerie turned and ran screaming into the woods behind the bungalow.

For a split second everyone stood paralyzed, not understanding what had happened. Then the young cop ran to kick away the rifle. Hank Crouse stood back, his gun in his hand, watching his son's distorted face as he struggled to sit up. Blood oozed from his leg. In the distance, the ambulance siren wailed.

Then my head cleared and a terrible fear surfaced. I pulled myself up and staggered to the center of the clearing. "Will." I broke into a run, charging past the scene in the clearing and into the bungalow. "Will. Please be all right. Will . . ."

I ran through the small, grubby kitchen, with its boxes of seedlings and bags of peat moss, and into the combined living room and bedroom. Will was sitting on the floor, holding his upper arm, the blood leaking through his fingers. He turned to me, his eyes queer. My heart filled with relief.

"Will. You're bleeding. The ambulance is coming."

He looked at me, not comprehending, as if he'd never seen me before.

"What happened?" he asked pleasantly. He struggled to his feet, still holding his arm.

"I don't know." I went to help him, but he shook me off, pushing hard on his wound to stem the flow of red. Between us on the floor where he had been sitting was a small rag rug with an irregular and darkening stain. Faltering a little, he walked out of the house into what was left of the afternoon sun. Then he stopped dead.

In the clearing, Hank Crouse, his gun forgotten on the ground beside him, was kneeling beside Russell. The young cop gently pulled him up to let the medics through. Hank Crouse looked over at Will, his face consumed with an emotion I hoped I'd never feel. Across the water came one last lone shot.

Will sat in Ray Tilghman's comfortable chair, his arm in a sling and his face quiet as he stroked Lance's copper fur and sipped beer. I lay back on the couch, my head throbbing a little, my body comforted from a warm bath. On the rug by my feet, Zeke lay quietly sleeping, his leg encased in a white bandage. No one said anything for long minutes. We had been here for what must have been hours, first talking, now just sitting with each other, each pondering alone the horror of what had happened. Neither of us had any words left.

The scene in front of Will's bungalow was still vivid. After Russell Crouse had been carried to the ambulance, a score of policemen and reporters had appeared in the clearing, a replay of the scene at Weller's Creek Cove the day I found Ray Tilghman's body. Will, silent, had been led to a second ambulance, turning back to look at me. I ran over to him.

"Will, I'll come by the hospital in a little while," I said. "I need to see about Zeke." For the first time, something normal reg-

istered in his eyes. He nodded. I touched his shoulder, then he was
gone.

Hank Crouse, forgotten in the commotion of the ambulances
and medics, had turned in my direction and walked unsteadily to
where I stood with Mitch Gaylin.

"I didn't kill Ray Tilghman," he said to me. "I want you to
know that. We had an argument and he lost his balance and fell
into the creek. The storm came up fast and I tried to help him, but
it was too late. He was too far out and I couldn't reach him. I guess
his body washed back to shore later. I was afraid to tell what happened because people might associate his death with Penny's
death and with me. Ray said he had a letter from a woman in New
York. I was afraid then. Now it no longer matters."

His voice was unemotional, almost indifferent. His arms
were at his sides. In the distance, I saw a plainclothes cop take
charge of his gun. He had left it lying on the ground, a sign perhaps that things were already different.

"I put Ray's dogs in his house afterward." He held up his
hand and then removed the white bandage. Underneath was a
cluster of puncture wounds, reddened and not healing very well.
"The black dog bit me pretty bad. I was lucky to get away."

"Did you kill Penny Hart?" I asked. Mitch's face registered
astonishment.

Hank Crouse nodded. "She wouldn't tell me where my baby
was or even admit I was the father. I was angry and drunk. It
wasn't planned, you know. . . ."

"You should be telling it to someone else." A uniformed cop
I had never seen before came up behind Hank and led him to a
cluster of police cars.

"Come on," I said to Mitch. "We have to find my dog." Forgetting Russell lying in a puddle of late-afternoon sun, his face
contorted with pain as he clutched his thigh, and Hank Crouse's
wounded hand and wretched confession, I ran down the path and
into the woods where Russell had fired his rifle. Pushing aside the

brush, I could see Lancelot sitting in a small hollow, waiting by the black dog. Zeke looked up, his brown eyes vacant with pain, his feathery black tail thumping once as I came near. A wound in his right front leg was bleeding.

"He's alive, but he needs a vet right away," I said. "Can we lift him?"

"Okay," said Mitch, "but I hope he won't do to me what he did to Hank Crouse."

"He won't, not while I'm here."

Together we struggled to get the dog into the clearing in front of Ray's house. His eyes were open and oddly calm. Mitch ran back up the path and returned in minutes with the Jeep.

"The police," he said, "are going to want to talk to both of us, but I explained about the dog and that we would be back."

I nodded. I sat with Zeke in the backseat. His leg was bloody, but the flow had almost stopped. At my whistle, the Chesapeake Bay retriever jumped into the cargo area in the rear of the Jeep. Mitch drove to the main road, one hand on the wheel, dialing information with the other. Within minutes, we were on Mountain Road and heading toward an emergency animal clinic.

The next couple of hours were a blur. I found I couldn't focus clearly on what I'd seen that afternoon in front of Will's bungalow. And after the speed at which it had happened, the waiting now was a torture of anticlimax. My head still ached. The sun had long since gone down and with it some of the heat. The humidity stayed.

What can it feel like to shoot your own son? I asked myself. Even to prevent another death? And how would Will come to grips with what happened? It was incomprehensible. I sat quietly in the waiting room with Mitch, accepting the juice and aspirin he brought me, grateful when the front-desk attendant produced a bowl of water for Lance, who lay at my feet.

After half an hour, I helped Mitch carry a half-conscious Zeke to the car, the dog exhausted and drugged after his ordeal. The back door of the Jeep closed with a bang.

"Thank you. Could you do one more thing for me?"

"Sure. Name it."

"I'd like to go to the hospital to find out how Will is. I won't stay long, but if you could keep the dogs company in the car . . ." There was one more thing. "I also need to call Weller Church and tell him what has happened and have him set up an appointment for me to talk to the police tomorrow. I don't think I can do it tonight."

He nodded.

"Thank you." He had no idea how grateful I was. I'd have to tell him, later.

The hospital emergency room was buzzing with rumors and half-truths. Will came out to the waiting room at the nurse's request, his arm bandaged, not seeing or commenting on my disheveled appearance.

"Are you okay?" I asked.

"Fine. Bullet just grazed my arm. I lost a little blood. They want me to stay overnight or at least for a few more hours, but I'm not going to." He hesitated. "What about Zeke?" There was anxiety in his voice.

"He's fine. Dopey from drugs. He was hit in the leg the way you were hit in the arm. He's in the car with Lance and Mitch Gaylin."

"Can I get a ride home?"

"Will, are you sure you're okay?"

"I'm okay."

"I don't think you can go back to the bungalow. You can stay at the house with me tonight, so if you need something . . ." My voice trailed off.

"Okay."

I looked at him more closely. He was more undone by this than he was letting on, tightly wound and not letting the full impact of what had happened settle in. It was probably too dangerous to confront all at once.

He went to get discharged. I stood waiting, noticing for the first time that people were staring at me with my uncombed and matted hair, my dirty and torn clothes, the bandage around my ankle coming off. I was surprised to find that it barely hurt, even when I walked.

Mitch looked concerned when we reached the Jeep, then he opened the door and Will arranged himself gingerly on the passenger side. Zeke lay sleeping on the backseat. I got in beside him, petting Lance, who sat in the cargo area, watching the black dog with worried eyes.

"Will's going to stay with me tonight."

Mitch said nothing, just nodded. We drove the long miles back through Pines on Magothy in silence, Will staring straight ahead. The Lido Beach Inn parking lot was jammed. I could almost hear the conversation, feverish with rumors and speculation.

Soon, I thought, they would find out that Hank Crouse had confessed to killing Penny Hart, that he had carried within him the awful truth for all these years, unaware that the gods weren't done with him yet. He would helplessly watch an old man die in the creek, then wound his own son to save another cop. It seemed to complete some relentless cycle of events.

As we turned off Weller's Creek Road and drew near his cottage, Will turned his face away from the media trucks and police cars and looked into the dark woods on the other side of the road. I was too tired, too headachy, to do much more than notice when Mitch stopped the Jeep and got out. I saw him talk to a plainclothes detective, who nodded, then took down something in a small notebook.

"We can all talk to the police tomorrow," Mitch said, putting the Jeep in gear. "I'm only beginning to find out just how persuasive a man Weller Church is."

Reaching the house, Mitch and I helped the wounded dog into the house. Lance followed at our heels, glad to be home. Will settled immediately into the wing chair by the stone fireplace, staring at nothing in particular. Mitch stood awkwardly in the living room, not knowing how to stay or how to leave. He watched me closely.

"We'll be fine, Mitch. Thank you."

He nodded, unconvinced. Finally, he pulled out a business card and handed it me.

"Put this by the phone and call me if you need something," he said. "I can be here quickly." He patted the beeper in his pocket. I didn't have the energy to tell him that Russell had pulled the phone from its moorings.

"Thanks. But I'll be fine," I repeated. "We'll all be fine." We walked to the porch door. "Mitch, thank you again. I can't say it enough."

"Call me. Tomorrow," he said. I nodded.

I watched the Jeep turn around in the clearing and drive up the path, its taillights fading in the night. I could still hear the faint sounds of cars and voices from Will's cottage. Arundel Island was silent, the bloodshed ended.

CHAPTER

THIRTY-TWO

Sunday dawned fresher, the heavy air that had dampened the sheets over me all last night now burned off by a bright sun and a slight breeze. Seven hours of restless sleep on the couch had helped. My ankle felt better than it had any right to. Even the slight bump on my head wasn't too painful. But it would, I knew, take more than a few hours of sleep before I would shake the truth of what had happened last night.

Zeke was much improved, accepting food and limping with difficulty down the porch steps to the clearing. Lance raced around him joyfully, not understanding why his playmate wouldn't play. Will was another story. He had come downstairs, his clothes rumpled and his face haggard, like a man who had been refused sleep.

We had talked until I could talk no more last night, then when we were done, we sat in silence, thinking our thoughts. I told him of my visit to Ellen Ruehl in New York and showed him her letter to Ray Tilghman just weeks ago. We talked about Ray and Mrs. Lynch and Russell and Hank Crouse, about the storm, and about an old fishing boat named *Lois*. Slowly and with difficulty, we had patched together a confused collage based on facts and intuition about what had happened at Weller's Creek cove twenty-four years ago—and just days ago. It was probably true and not true, and it didn't matter. We were talking to settle things for ourselves, not for a judge and jury.

I now helped Zeke back into the house and made coffee. Will took the mug I handed him and collapsed on the wicker couch on the porch. Lance rushed over to greet him, with Zeke limping slowly on his injured leg, his tail swishing.

"I hope your arm is okay," I said.

"I think it is. Throbbing but not bleeding. It made sleeping just about impossible." I was sure it wasn't the only thing. He awkwardly drank his coffee, unbalanced by the sling. "How does a person accept that his father killed his mother?" he asked.

I didn't know and said so.

"Maybe he didn't actually kill her," said Will, "maybe, like with Ray, it was an accident."

"Maybe," I said, knowing better, thinking about what Hank Crouse had said to me last night. He'd been angry and drunk at the time and when he wanted to know where his baby was, Penny wouldn't tell him. Will looked up at me, his eyes cloudy, knowing the truth but not wanting to know it.

I thought about the statement I'd made to the police. Yesterday's events had confirmed much of it. Will and I sat in silence, not finding enough emotional strength to talk about it all over again this morning.

A car pulled into the clearing. It was Weller Church's old Lincoln, with Lillian in the front seat. She jumped out and ran up the steps and onto the porch.

"Oh my Lord," said Lillian. "Are you okay?" I nodded and then she looked at Will, who nodded. "Weller called me this morning and told me what had happened. I was just so tired yesterday, I went to bed about seven o'clock. Or maybe it was six-thirty. I didn't know a thing until this morning. Will, how's your arm?"

"Fine, Lillian," he said. "It's just a little scratch." He shook

Weller's offered hand. Lillian hung back, then decided to hug us both.

"You were very lucky," she said to him. "You could have been killed."

"Russell was blind drunk," Will said. "I don't believe he could even see what he was shooting at."

Involuntarily, I shivered, remembering Valerie's awful scream. Will was kidding himself, I thought. Russell had been blind not just from drinking but also from anger. Had the gods not smiled, Will might have had no more chance than the raccoon on the side of the road.

Lillian sat down, then caught sight of Zeke, her eyes widening when she saw his bandage. "He got hit, too?"

"Yes, but he's fine. Mitch Gaylin found this emergency animal hospital that patched him up. He feels better than any of us, I think." The black feathery tail flapped on the floor.

We settled on the porch after I poured coffee for Lillian and Weller.

"I suppose you want to hear what happened," I said. Both nodded, and Will and I went over the whole awful scene all over again. It seemed unreal now, sitting on the porch, smelling the pines, a made-for-television movie. When we were through, Lillian sighed and sat back. Will stared blindly into the pine clearing, his thoughts somewhere else, I knew. The lawyer mopped his face with his handkerchief, then wordlessly got up and found the portable fan and set it going.

"What happened to Valerie?" Will asked.

"She went to her mother's house," said Weller.

"Gilbert was in the woods, too, looking for Russell. Fortunately, he did not see the whole awful scene. So they are both safe," said Lillian. She turned to me directly. "You know that home for handicapped teenagers I thought might take Gilbert?" I nodded. "It's looking pretty good. They will probably have an opening next month. Then Shirl can get herself a nice apartment."

I suddenly wanted to put my head down and cry until I couldn't any longer. For my aunt, impeccably dressed in a new fall suit and matching shoes, was quietly doing what she always did: taking care of everybody. I swallowed hard, still choking on emotion. Lillian was watching me. Then she leaned over and patted my knee.

"You must hate this place," she said.

I shook my head. "No, I don't." I glanced first at Will and then at the dogs and at Weller Church and then back at Lillian. They had all become more dear than I ever could have expected. My aunt saw my glance and said nothing, just nodded a little to herself.

"What happened to Hank Crouse?" Will's voice was tightly controlled. He looked at Weller.

"He confessed to Penny Hart's murder but denies that he killed Ray Tilghman," said the lawyer. "I expect both cases will be reopened." There was a long silence.

"And Russell?"

"He'll recover, though the wound is deep." The lawyer unconsciously glanced at Will's arm in its sling. "I don't know what he'll be charged with. It will be attempted murder, I suppose. I don't know what else." Will breathed quietly, not reacting.

"Have the police finished with Will's bungalow?" I asked, breaking the silence.

"Yes, I think so," said Weller. "At least nobody was there when we drove by, and there was no yellow tape around the house."

I looked around the side of the living room that Russell had wrecked and began to think of the safe, practical tasks that would fill the day ahead: clean up the mess, call to get my phone fixed, talk to the police.

Lillian stood up. Sunday was an important day in real estate. People fell in love with houses on Sundays. I wondered all of a sudden if Mitch was hosting an open house somewhere or, having scraped Zeke's blood and dog hair off the Jeep's backseat, was showing clients million-dollar Annapolis waterfront properties. More likely, he was telling what he saw to the police.

"I made an appointment for both of you to talk with the police at three this afternoon," said Weller, echoing my thoughts.

"Thank you," I said. Will barely responded.

"I have to go," my aunt said. "I have an appointment at ten-thirty. Will you two be all right? You both can come and stay with me for a few days. The dogs, too. Just until things settle down and you get your phone back and all."

Will was shaking his head. "Thanks, but I will be fine here. And I think Eve will be, too." I looked at him. It was true. I would be.

"Well, suit yourselves, but I'll come back later," she said. Weller held the screen door for my aunt, then turned back to me.

"I forgot to tell you something," he said. "It wasn't Gilbert who threw that dead rat on your porch. Valerie told the police that Russell Crouse had bragged to her that he did it. She doesn't know why."

I did. The full significance of it hadn't dawned on me until now. I had no proof, but I was as I sure of it as it was possible to be. Russell must have seen his father's excessively wet and muddy uniform from the night Ray Tilghman drowned in the creek. And maybe he had also seen the puncture marks on Hank's hand, marks that could only have been made by an angry dog. Putting it together, Russell must have been terrified that his father knew something about Ray's death. Flinging a bloody rat to scare me away so I wouldn't ask questions about how Ray died had been one way to protect his father.

Last night's scene in the clearing replayed quickly in my mind. I felt a chill seep through me, made worse by the heat. Will was staring at me.

"Eve." He was standing in the doorway to the house.

"What?"

"Thanks for letting me stay here last night. And for sticking by me through this." I felt self-conscious and awkward. He was still staring at me, his gaze frozen on my face.

I nodded. "You're welcome to use the room upstairs," I said, "for as long as you wish."

He nodded. "Thanks, but I think I'll go up to the bungalow now. Clean up the mess."

"I'd be happy to help you," I said. "It won't take long to clean up here." I picked up the brass crane and set it on its feet. Sunlight glinted in bands across the sculpted feathers.

"I think I need to be there alone, think things out and make sense of what happened, if that's possible." He came over toward me, touched my shoulder for a few seconds. "You understand?"

"Yes."

"I'm going down to the cove for a little while," I said. "I can pick you up to go to the police station this afternoon." It was Will's turn to nod. I opened the door and Lance bolted out and danced in the yard. Zeke insisted on coming, limping down the steps. For a few seconds, we watched as Will walked slowly up the driveway to his bungalow. He turned around once.

"Maybe I can finish your shower tomorrow," he said.

"There's no hurry. I have time."

I turned to face the wedge of blue creek in the distance, Zeke walking with difficulty beside me as Lance ran ahead. Where the path opened onto the little cove, the water sparkled, lapping at the dock. Lance looked at me for permission to swim, then shot into the water with a splash. Zeke sank down beside me with a groan. I threw a big stick for Lance and watched the red dog swim far out into the creek to retrieve it.

I had time, I thought, four whole months. Then I would decide what to do. In the meantime, I'd help Lillian and learn to sell real estate. A picture of my aunt came to me, the pencil threaded through her blond bouffant hair as she read legal documents or talked on the phone or punched at the multiple-listing computer with two manicured fingers.

I had time, I thought, to make peace with the end of my

marriage. Had it only been a couple of days ago that I had been in New York to see Ben and Joe Lister?

Maybe I would fix Ray's house up a little. Refinish the floors, replace some of the furniture, paint the rest of the walls and ceilings. I would have time to read and begin running again. Zeke flapped his tail when I looked at him. Well, maybe the running could wait for a few weeks. Maybe I could learn to cook a little. Then I laughed out loud. No use getting crazy about all this domestic stuff.

Lance charged out of the creek, dropped the stick at my feet, and shook himself violently, splashing Zeke and me with big drops. Beyond him, the sunlight scattered over the water. The cicadas embarked on their first song of the day, the notes climbing rapidly skyward. Then the song ended as abruptly as it had begun.